PHOEBE'S
HEART OF STONE

By

James J Hill III

This is a work of historical fiction. While most of the characters and events are true, some of the characters and events were created to fill in the blanks that were long lost with time and unknown to anyone alive today. The author's imagination was used where he felt it was needed.

Phoebe's Heart of Stone, Copyright © 2021 by James J Hill III. All rights reserved.

ISBN paperback-978-1-7367105-2-4

ISBN hardback-978-1-7367105-3-1

Copyright James J Hill III

Also available on ebook

Contact the author at:

Jamesjhill3rd@mail.com

JamesHillAuthor.com

Facebook.com/JamesHillWriter/

Instagram @girldadof5

Dedicated to those that have come before me,
that have provided a path so that I may have the
stories in which to write.

Special thanks to Charolet, Mary Ellen, and Jara, for sharing
a piece of their family with me.

CONTENTS

The Bradway children.
Back, left to right, Emil, Aletha, and Russell.
Front, left to right, Mary Elizabeth and Kenneth.
Photo Courtesy of Mary Ellen Henderson.

"Rusty, come here boy."

The air had an eerie silence about it, and nothing could be heard but that old brown dog, Rusty, as they called him, barking with such despair out over the thinly frozen ice-covered Mahoning River. The same stretch of river that Carl fished in with his boys when the thinning ice was a distant reminder of the cold that had once come and would return in a few months' time. The very same untamed river that they watched dumb ducks waddle aimlessly back and forth with no apparent reason, dropping out of sight for a quick dip to cool themselves from a blazing hot sun, and then emerging once again shaking off the droplets of water.

The children would be back in the family home, just a short distance from the frozen river's edge, so Carl wanted to just quickly grab old Rusty, pull him by hand and drag him back towards home. It was supper time, and he had just worked an extremely long hard day as a Teamster, driving a delivery truck for Standard Oil and Company. All he wanted to do was get home, sit down in his chair with his family and eat.

It was January the eighteenth in the year 1919. The country was still in the midst of the deadly Spanish Flu pandemic, that would eventually kill an estimated 675,000 Americans in just two short years. Carl had lost so much already and wasn't willing to let this new pandemic take more from him. He was now only concerned with protecting those of his family who had somehow averted its horrible, deadly wrath.

Alliance, Ohio, was just like any other small town of its

time, trying simply to survive a pandemic that took mercy on no class, nor man, woman, or child. During the Fall of 1918, the townspeople decided to shut down everything they could to try to control the impending spread of the virus that would grow like wildfire throughout the rest of the world. Eventually, it would claim some fifty million souls worldwide. The people sprayed down streets, closed the doors to the local YMCA, and ordered all children not to take anything home with them from their schools. Those same schools were disinfected nightly after the last class of the day, and people did what they could to control the spread throughout their humble blue-collar town.

Yet, life still went on as time dictated it would. Folks still had to work to survive. Farms needed to be tended to, and children still needed to be educated on the ways of the world, so that they could take over the reins of what their parents would one day leave behind. It was a continuous life cycle that could not be broken, although for the time being, sadly it was being interrupted in a way that was disastrous to people and businesses. There seemed to be no reason or explanation for any of it, and people looked to the heavens for answers and understanding. They looked to their parents, and to their clergy. They looked to their politicians and begged for information and relief. No one seemed to be able to soothe their fears or answer their questions adequately, and it became obvious that the people of Alliance would simply need to ride out the virus' deadly destructive path through their little town with simple hope and prayer. The people of the town quietly prayed, "Not me God. Dear God, please, not my family."

Chapter 1

The Storm

Maybe John Emmer was right. That August sky in 1892 did appear as if there were a strange brilliance to it, and the wind had suddenly whipped up a sound of frustration desperate to be heard. John felt a storm was heading their way and perhaps it was time to gather the loose hens roaming just outside the gate and bring them on in. He removed his soft felt hat and using a white cotton handkerchief that he had in his rear pocket, gently wiped his brow. The sun had been beating down upon his now scarlet face for the better part of the day. His wife, Mary, had stepped outside to see what the noise was.

"John, I hear the animals rustling all the way from the kitchen. What do you suppose is going on?" she said as she looked around at the leaves being sprayed off their tree limbs, floating higher into the air in a nearly perfect circular motion.

"A storm's coming, Mary. Wicked one. Better get the

kids inside and I'll see to the animals," he replied.

The farm was a modest one. They had more crops than livestock, but still John would need to hurry along to ensure all the animals were under cover and safely tucked away from the looming storm. John needed to be quick but smart. Grab the animals that were slower and a little dumber first, then help those that struggled in the confusion to get past gates, and ensure they were all locked in tight and secure. It was normally a mundane task, but the sky grew dark with anger, and the air grew crisp and bold within minutes. He knew that at any moment, the sky would open up and unleash the rain that would cascade down onto where he now stood, bringing with it only God knew what.

Carl came dashing out of the home just as the rain started to pelt the warm earth below his feet and asked his pa how he could help.

"There! Grab the goats and get them in! They are nervous and stuck in their place. I'll get the horses. Hurry!" his pa screamed.

Carl sprang to his right and ran with all he had towards the goats as he tried to dodge as much of the rain as the now closing sky would allow. When he finally reached the goats, the rain was growing fierce. It came down heavy and slammed hard onto the pen he was forcing the goats into. He could feel the sting of each hard drop on the top of his head and shoulders and begged for the animals to just comply, so that he could get to cover himself. Two wayward billies had been stubborn, or perhaps scared out of their minds and tried to push through the fence that lined the area that they were in. Carl ran over, slipping through the mud created by the puddling rain on top of the hard earth below, and came to rest right near the stunned billies. As he grabbed one under his arms, it began to cry an awful noise, but he paid it no mind. He knew it did not understand what he was doing and would be thankful later. He tried to simultaneously drag the other one along with him but could not get a solid grip. He made the only choice he could and ran with the one, with the intent to go back to get the other; hoping he could lock them both down before returning to the safety of the farmhouse where his parents were surely waiting with his siblings.

John finished securing the horses in their stable and nervously looked around to make sure there were no rogue animals milling about the farm. It was getting harder to see through the dense rain under the thick black sky. He called out for Carl, as he could no longer see through the deluge. The wind and rain were creating such an awful commotion that he could barely hear himself think, let alone see more than a few feet in front of him. Not knowing how Carl had faired getting the goats away, he rushed blindly over to where he instinctually knew the pen was, even though it was impossible to see.

When he was maybe 12 feet away, he was able to make out an outline of sorts, and knew it had to be Carl.

"Carl, get them in! We need to get inside now!"

As he finished his demands, through the barreling rain and crying winds, came a loud racket just north of where he saw Carl's outline a second prior. Cries through the air came towards John, as he realized what happened. The large wind turbine had collapsed and toppled over onto the pen area where Carl had been chasing the billies trying to get them to safety. For a second, he heard nothing, and then, there it was: a cry for help coming from just over the fence. John pushed forward, with no regard for his own safety, and reached out to feel for the fence with his hands. As his fingers grazed the tip of the fence, he grabbed ahold and using all his strength, pulled his body over the top, dropping hard on the other side onto the soaked ground below.

"Carl?" He cried out.

"Pa? Pa, I'm hurt. Somethings got my leg pinned and I can't get it unstuck," Carl cried out in sheer pain and panic.

John felt his way over to where he heard his son's pleas and grabbed onto whatever he could. As he moved his body along the wet surface, he could feel long pieces of warm metal alongside his hands and legs. He dragged his body closer to where Carl was laying, and eventually, he was able to reach his boy.

"Carl, son, I'm here. What hurts, son?"

"Pa, my leg. It's stuck under something, and it's a God-awful pain."

Without another word, John went to work. He quickly assessed the situation, felt around to see what exactly Carl's leg was pinned down by, and rapidly devised a plan to move it off him. The old wooden fence was destroyed from the fall, so John was able to grab a split post and placed it underneath the twisted metal from the broken turbine. He told Carl that he would need to act fast and use all his might to pull himself to safety just as soon as he gave the go ahead. Carl did not respond, but John knew that his boy understood.

Carl was an extraordinarily hardworking young boy and always understood the task before him. Whenever he worked alongside his pa on the farm, he knew instinctively what was needed two steps ahead. His brain was remarkable like that. It was almost like he knew what the future would bring and so he met it halfway as if to say "gotcha!", before it could surprise him. His pa knew this and so whenever they worked side by side, he did not question his son much. There was a level of trust that simply existed between the two of them, and it was without doubt clear now.

As the rain picked up and the wind roared louder than before, John knew it was now or never. He forced the bottom end of the post as deep as he could under the turbine, and with one swift motion, he placed all his weight, using his armpit as an anchor, onto that post. When his full body mass was leveraged against the pry he was using, he screamed to Carl,

"Now boy!"

In a matter of just a second or two, the weight from the turbine was lifted a few inches into the air, and swiftly fell back down, slamming on the ground with an intense force and making a terrible sound. John's arm took the brunt of the impact, and his shoulder was torn from its socket. He cried out in deep pain and grabbed onto his shoulder, realizing in that instant that he still did not know whether he had freed his son from under that heavy frame. If Carl were indeed still pinned down, John did not know if he had it in him to give it another go with the same brute force he had just exerted. Lifting the turbine took all his strength, and here he was, injured and wondering if he, in fact, had managed to help his son as he had so desperately set out to do.

He was exhausted, in agonizing pain, and numb from the torrential rain that poured mercilessly against his body. It was still difficult to hear anything other than the howling wind circling them, but he knew at least he was by his boy. His hope was that Carl had been able to muster up just enough strength to pull free, and they would simply wait out the storm, however long that may take.

Mary, still inside, had no idea what was taking her husband and son so long and she grew increasingly concerned for the two of them. Maybe they had decided to sit it out in the barn with the horses. Or perhaps they decided that the pen was a safe place until the storm settled. Either way, she was terribly worried, but knew she needed to be as patient as she could be and hope that Mother Nature had a little mercy on them all. So far, she had not. The powerful storm that came out of nowhere and had not even given them a few minutes to gather themselves together before she unleashed her raw power and intense, unforgiving fury down on all of Alliance, was not yet ready to relent.

Over by the downed turbine and shattered fence, lay two silhouettes bathed in the downpour and hidden by the sheer force of the storm. Mother Nature would not let up, so John and Carl were forced to stay where they were to face her wrath, endure their pain, and pray that she would give them a small break. Carl prayed she would let up, just enough to give them a chance. All John wanted was a fighting chance, and he felt he had earned it. He knew he needed to gather his strength, so he rested in agony on the ground waiting for whatever came next and readying himself to continue the fight. John had given all he had to save his son, and he lay there wondering if it had been enough.

Suddenly, just as it had rifled in from the west, the storm began to quickly clear out, as if to say, "That was what I had to serve to you, and now I am rather bored and moving on to another town." She was finished with her destruction, and her incredible fury had calmed. Her tears departed one by one, until only a trickle of her cry remained in the air around them. The wind she howled with such intensity died down as well, and now simply whispered through the trees in her passing, allowing what few leaves she took mercy on to bow in her absence. Finally, John was able to stretch out and look over to his boy, Carl, to see if he had indeed freed him from the weight and agony that the storm had cast on him for reasons only she knew.

Carl sat up, using his lean arms to hold his weight, and in an astonished state of confusion, looked around at the destruction left in the storm's wake. The frightened billie he had run out to retrieve in that final moment, was laying silent and motionless just a foot from his arms. He had not been able to save her from the terrible storm, as hard as he tried. That hurt Carl enough that he still was unaware of the shape of his legs that only moment prior had been pinned to the earth by a manmade wind generator.

John crawled over with his one good arm, dragging his bad one behind, and placed it onto Carl's shoulder. He looked up at his boy and forced a smile through his intense pain.

"She tried, didn't she? She tried like hell to whip us, but she failed. She didn't know who she was messing with huh?" John said through tears of relief and laughter.

"No, Pa, she did not. We showed her who's boss around these parts, that's for sure," Carl replied, with less of a smile, because he knew that at any moment, he was going to feel the effects of what had happened to his legs.

Mary, along with the other children that John Emmer and Mary had raised together, dashed outside as soon as they could see beyond the air in front of them. They carefully maneuvered to where both John and Carl were laying and asked how they were. Mary could see that her husband, John, was trying to hide his pain as he always did, but he was in severe agony. She knew he would need tended to medically more than she could provide, so she quickly told one of the boys to go and fetch the doc, who lived about two miles down the road. John was a man full of pride, and merely proud that he had reached his son and had been able to somehow pry his legs free of the metal that tried to take his boy away, all without being able to see a thing. That was unequivocally all he cared about in that moment. So the pain would need to just be patient with him and wait its turn.

"Carl, your legs boy. They hurt bad?" John asked at last.

Carl knew he was hurt something terrible, but in trying to emulate his old man, he used all the pride he could muster up to push the pain aside and just mumbled,

"I'll be all right, Pa. Thank you. I'll be just fine."

He was not entirely fine. Neither of them were. Both needed plenty of rest, and John would sadly lose the use of his right arm because of the tear sustained to his muscles. It would forever have a purple-colored tint to the skin, and as time went by, as it always does, he began to lose the muscle almost entirely. Oh, he worked still on that farm, but not as he once had. Being limited on such a profound scale when you operate a farm can be devastating. But Carl and the other children did the best they could to pick up for their pa and fill those big boots of his, knowing all along they would never fill them entirely.

Carl lost most of the feeling in both his legs for a short time, but eventually he would heal almost completely, barring for a slightly noticeable limp that he carried with him as a reminder of how Mother Nature, and life in general, could give to you and take away just the same. You could put up the fight of fights and throw your back into a wedge, pushing with all God had given you, and maybe, finding even a bit more hidden deep within. But in the end, if time and fate had something in store, they would prevail. It was that simple. You may kick and scream, but you only have so much control of how it will be, and on that day, they both understood that reality more than ever.

Chapter 2

His Beloved Phoebe

* * *

The year was 1903, significant to Carl for an awfully special reason. It was his time to build a family, and it would all begin with him marrying the woman he had fallen in love with not long before, his beloved Phoebe. Phoebe was excited to begin a life with Carl and had an intriguing idea. She wanted to remember their wedding day as the important occasion it was, and so, being a woman of faith as she had been raised to be, she approached Carl with the idea of a Christmas Wedding. Carl, well, his greatest desire was for Phoebe to be pleased. He saw their wedding as her day, not his. As far as he was concerned, he had what he wanted. He had the love of a beautiful woman by his side, who decided she needed to spend her life with him faithfully, making their dreams a reality, making plans and putting the work in together to ensure those plans came to fruition. For Carl, he was already married in his mind, but he knew that Phoebe wanted that special day, and so he would see to it that she would have it. Christmas Day,

1903, would be her day. It was meant to be.

Phoebe was born one of six daughters to William and Mary Whinnery in Smith Township, Mahoning, Ohio in the year 1885, just one township to the east of Alliance, Ohio. Alliance was the same town where Carl was born and raised by his family. Her father, William, also owned and operated a farm for most of his adult life, before retiring from that line of work to work for the same Teamsters Union as Carl. Many Farmers took to driving for the Teamsters later in their lives to rest their worn-out bones and exhausted muscles that had spent decades tirelessly working day and night to survive the daily life of a farm. Plus, driving turned out to be much more reliable work, as the country was booming, and the need was so great.

William had also been a Civil War infantryman fighting for the 143rd National Guard in Company D for the US Army back in May of 1864 under Colonel William H Vodrey, and was honorably discharged in September of 1864 when the unit was officially deactivated. So, he was a true hero in the eyes of his daughters, but also for many people in the state of Ohio and beyond who believed in the Union's cause.

Phoebe and Carl wanted children and tried to get pregnant soon after they were wed, but she was unable to conceive for some reason. At first, it brought a tear to her beautiful sad eyes each time they spoke of it, so Carl for his part tried to assure his young impatient wife that things would happen when God was ready for them. They were both devout Quakers and prayed nightly for a child to be given to them when it was their time. He truly believed that they just needed to learn patience and continue to try. Their time would come, he assured her. And as it turned out, he was correct.

In the Summer of 1907, Carl and Phoebe were blessed with a son, and they named him Russell Carl Bradway. Russell was the second love of Phoebe's still young life and because she begged so hard for a child of her own to nurture, she found herself overwhelmed with love each time she held him in her arms. She would hold him for hours, stare into his beautiful baby face, and promise him with all her heart, that she would love him and raise him to be a good, caring, God-fearing boy. She stopped questioning the timing and the circumstances of her life, and came to believe there was simply a plan in place for it all and grew happy in her contentment.

Carl was no longer working on a farm by this point, but instead had decided to seek a new career with the unions that organized the same year he was married. In 1903, the Teamsters had come about because of a merger between two other smaller unions of the time, the Team Drivers International Union and The Teamsters National Union. It was not easy work, though, and Carl had to endure long grueling days of up to 18 hours for seven days a week most weeks, to earn his place in the union and keep the goals for his family moving in the right direction. He was constantly feeling the effects of being overworked and had very little time to spend with his young wife and newborn child as a result, but what little time he managed to be away from work was spent with them. He figured this would be the way it would go until something better came along, and he would eventually find his way to better work and a more manageable schedule.

Phoebe enjoyed being a homemaker and used her time as best she could to manage the quaint single-family home they were renting, just south of the Mahoning River. She was certainly happy, spending her long days holding young Russell and dreaming of who he would become in time, and what his family would be like in the future. Phoebe wanted a large family, and not having Carl there much at all, children would provide a much-needed distraction in her life. Carl was onboard with this grand idea as well, so was saddened that he needed to spend so much time away from his wife and child. He was a hard dedicated worker and did not mind the work itself, but the lack of being present for his family was difficult for him.

He was out the front door before the morning sun rose and returned home late after the tired sun had set for the evening. Carl would watch as the sun's rays would dance off his windshield while he drove his oil truck, reminding him of the days he had spent courting his lovely wife. His mind would turn to a will to drive on, knowing that he was unquestionably preparing for a better, more sustainable life for them all and that this was his springboard. In his mind, something would come into their lives and enable him to make a few adjustments here and there, thus creating a much better, easier daily life than they all currently enjoyed.

Carl was not one to complain though. On particularly

hard days, he would remember that he had once survived a ferocious storm that possibly he wouldn't have if things were just slightly different. Had he fallen to the left just a foot or so instead of to the right some, he may not be here today to enjoy this hard work. Carl knew and understood that. He understood that life became a game of inches and feet, and that when it would be his time, it would be his time. Life was to be enjoyed, even with the harsh working conditions and long hours that people had to endure during the first part of the century. He was married, had a boy, a good steady job, and though he dreamt of more, he knew just how lucky he was.

The Mahoning River was a favorite place of theirs on the off-chance Carl was able to secure free time away from his truck. In fact, Phoebe tried to visit the riverbanks of the Mahoning at least weekly to get young Russell out of the house, and into the fresh air and sun. On her travels, Phoebe developed a curious obsession. When she would reach the lapping water, she would sit along the damp ground of the water's edge, with Russell asleep in her arms, gently breathing in the fall air, tired from the ten or so block walk it took them to reach their favorite spot. The first few times she sat there looking out over the dark water that splashed playfully towards her, as if inviting her to say hello in reply, she would notice rocks of different sizes and colors laying all around her feet. She began to look intently at one that called out to her. As she moved three rocks that were neighboring this specific one, it came clear to her that this was a unique rock. Its edges were smooth, and the shape undeniable. The rock that was just sitting there untouched by human hands, minding its business for hundreds, if not thousands of years, was firmly in her palm. As she made out the distinct heart-shape of the stone, Phoebe felt that this was a good omen. No one she knew had ever stumbled on a rock of this shape, or they had and never took notice. It may have not been of any importance to them, but to her, it had.

So began a practice for Phoebe. Anytime she was out somewhere with Russell, and there were rocks of different shapes and sizes that would fit into her tiny hands, she would study them, looking with purpose over each one. Some days she would return home empty handed, and other days she would find one, two, or even three rocks that bore the shape of love. She would place them in her pocket, and continue with her day, knowing that when she returned home to prepare supper for her hard-working Carl, the rocks would have a new home in her house. After all, these stones were too important to leave behind where no eyes would grace them.

As Carl began to see more and more of the plain, simple brown and gray rocks laying around their home, he decided to ask his beloved Phoebe the meaning behind them. Was she losing her mind, bringing in useless dirt-colored rocks that were meant for the outside world and were of no use inside? He did not want to sound as if he were questioning what she did to occupy her time while he was unable to be with her, because she absolutely worked hard maintaining their place and supper was always waiting and ready on his return. No, he just wanted to know what drew her to something that others saw as simple rocks. He wanted to see the world from her eyes, not just from his, as he explained to her. How did she see things? What did the color orange look like to her? Because he was aware of how the color appeared from his eyes already. He needed to see things as those big, beautiful eyes saw them.

She explained to him that she enjoyed finding the small heart-shapes the earth intended for those rocks to maintain and that nature had helped to form. She knew that most folks would never take notice again and felt it was her duty to share their beauty with others. So, she began picking them up, and with each one, gently running her soft hands across their smooth surfaces, wondering how long it had taken for the air to blow just right and the water to cut and sand down with exactly the right amount of pressure, to create a perfectly shaped heart that caught her eye and so easily and thoroughly captured her attention.

Carl smiled and told her he thought it was a swell idea, and that her rocks made the place look more like a home, rather than just a house. He knew Phoebe was a good person, and that she was proud of what she had stumbled across. She felt there was a reason those rocks had sat there, with people walking by them, over them, around them for so many years, she had been the one to discover them, possibly being the only person to touch them in all of Mahoning, or even the entire world. This became her pastime. Finding these curious shapes that no one else had bothered to notice, and bringing them back home for Carl,

Russell, and herself. Plus, as Carl had to admit, they did add a nice touch to the inside of the home.

Phoebe filled her time tending to their home, caring for Russell and searching for hearts, as Carl went at it day and night, working mostly alone, making his stops where instructed, and then off to the next. He tried to find quicker ways to do his work, only to realize, it did not matter. The faster he worked, the more work his job found for him to do. It appeared a never-ending cycle but appeared to be what everyone else was doing as well. So, Carl did as he was told, and knew one day things would be different. That he knew for sure. Things would somehow, one day, be quite different.

Chapter 3

Courting Phoebe

* * *

Carl enjoyed his simple farm life as a boy even after the incident, when temperamental Mother Nature stared him down and threatened his legs and his life. Growing up with his siblings and his parents working mere steps from his own footprints provided him a glimpse of true solid family bonds that he hoped to always enjoy. He was especially close with his younger sister, Cora. She was ten years younger than him, but Carl still enjoyed Cora's fearless personality as a child, even if she would follow him around the farm asking countless questions to learn all she could from her older brother whom she simply adored. She enjoyed a unique zest for life and had a calming way with her warm smiles whenever work got to be a little too much, as work on the farm often could. Cora was excited for everything she saw around her. She chased the goats through the same pen that had almost claimed her big brother. The roosters sensed when she was around, and quickly changed directions to avoid her playful spirit.

For his part, Carl had healed remarkably well and often casually forgot about the incident. However, whenever the sky began to close in, and the storm clouds grew angry and spit out their fury, he was compelled to relive that dreadful day. Older and wiser now, he knew if he were forced in that same spot again, he would handle things differently and be more aware of what was around. Carl intentionally tried to learn from life's mishaps and understood that to slightly alter the course life intended for him, he sometimes needed to adjust how he would have previously done things. This was a lesson he promised to take with him throughout his life. Learn from his mistakes and try his darndest not to repeat them if possible.

While Carl was living his early life in Alliance, so was Phoebe, just a short distance away. Her parents brought four girls into the world between the years of 1868 through 1874, then did not have another child until Hannah was born on February 2, 1884, some ten years later. She was the closest to Phoebe in age, so naturally they formed the strongest bond of the sisters. Phoebe had called them "bookend sisters". Hannah born the beginning of one year, and Phoebe born the end of the very next. Together, they, being the youngest of the sister group, grew up getting to know more about each other as the much older siblings married off and moved away from the homestead.

Through the late 1800's the population of Alliance had grown, and between the years 1880 and 1890, the population changed by a lofty 64 percent, creating a boom of sorts to the railroad and industrial town. More people enjoyed the banks of the 113-mile-long Mahoning River as trains brought in workers from all over the eastern coast along with their families, in the hopes of securing decent, wage-earning, steady employment.

The Mahoning River starts just North of Alliance, flows up and down, zigzagging along the Northeast side of town, and continues through Ohio and just into Pennsylvania. The hard-working folks of Alliance, however, cared only about the section of the river that organically cut through its soil. During torrential rains, the banks would flow over, and flooding could be found all along its shores. When the weather was not so temperamental, they fished, swam, and laughed while watching their kin smile gamely as they jumped from nearby red pine trees and into its sun reflective gloss-like waters. That was, until the large factories and steel companies along the waterways started using the waters for cooling and waste. Sadly, the river would start to turn for the worse for many decades, but it would take years for those living around to understand the monumental damage inflicted on their pretty river.

Both families were hardworking and knew their roles well. While Carl's family was preparing him to be the man of the house, Phoebe's was reminding her of her duties as a wife, as was normal for that time and how most people and the community saw it fit. Both unquestionably accepted the traditional roles expected of them and cherished learning about what life would be like when their time came, as it eventually did that cold December 25th. But for that time, they knew nothing of each other and were each hard at work on their family farms, in school, and attending church services with their families on Sundays, which is where they would eventually first set eyes on one another. It was important that the families knew about family bloodlines and history within the church. For Phoebe's father, he wished for his daughter to marry a hardworking, dedicated man, but also a man of vigorous faith. Community was to be considered. Meanwhile, Carl's father felt that he should find someone that brought out the best in him, a woman who would care for his son and one day for the family they would create together, as he had raised his son to provide completely for his wife and family.

As the century turned, life grew difficult. People worked long, exhausting, laborious days, and free time was considered a luxury for most. While the country was growing, the people of Alliance were more focused on the tiny, but rapidly growing community they had created over the last century. To them, it was more about self-respect. While they certainly felt a strong sense of pride for the country, they were simple. They were determined to ensure tradition and a trail of continued honor within their circle. The intention was to leave a legacy to proudly pass down to their children, their grandchildren and even beyond. The mindset was not just for the now, but to share a way of life for continued generations to follow. They wanted to create a blueprint on how people should live and expect to be treated, based on who they were and what they provided for those around them.

By the tail end of the 1800's, Carl's family had moved to Smith Township, Mahoning County, Ohio, which, as fate would have it, was where Phoebe had lived her entire life. It was inevitable that they would find love in one another and for that reason alone, Carl was content with having moved to the next town over and away from all he had ever known. His siblings were not so enthusiastic about the move, but they would eventually learn to accept and understand it as a necessity of sorts. His parents felt the move would open new opportunities for their ever-growing family and had prayed on the move for a long time before deciding it was just the right time. This was not a quick, easy decision for them. It required planning, patience, and a belief that it was the right thing to do.

Carl and Phoebe's relationship grew slowly. As Carl began to build the courage to talk with Phoebe on those warm summer mornings while at Church with his own family, he was also adjusting the direction for his future. At first, Phoebe was shy and did not take Carl seriously, but as time went on and Carl persisted, she eventually realized that the shy young man with the piercing grey eyes and slight limp was not going away. That was curious to her and so she decided to press on and get to know him better.

Their first date out was simply a walk around the grounds of the church. Both had decided to stay beyond the service after their families left. They talked about the weather, the trees as the leaves swayed in the gentle breeze, and about their siblings. Phoebe slowly built up more courage and decided to ask Carl about his limp. Had he fallen recently or was it something that happened to him long ago?

Carl smiled slightly at her inquiry, pushed his head down

towards the ground and kicked a rock below his feet gently away. As he told the story of the storm, Phoebe looked intently at the handsome man before her, and was mesmerized by his words. She hung tight to each sentence, and when he finished the story, she had tears in her eyes. He asked her if she was all right, and she just nodded and forced a smile. She had learned something about Carl's character in just a short walk that she would never forget, and she could not imagine wanting to be away from him again.

What both Carl and Phoebe did not know, however, was that they would be tested many times throughout their lives, and they would need to lean on each other more often than most and certainly more than they anticipated. But in those early days, all they knew was they loved one another, had committed to a life together before God and their families, and they intended to honor that commitment regardless of what life brought their way.

While their daily life could be mostly predictable, life as a whole rarely is, and there was the ever-looming possibility of events and challenges ahead that could alter their course as a couple. Carl and Phoebe simply had no idea of what to expect. Would they face obstacles and make choices together that would make their family undeniably stronger? Or shatter their alliance to each other as the weight of life's burdens piled on their shoulders becoming too heavy to handle? Whatever it was, they did not know what was ahead or when they would need to adjust to life's will, so they lived as if they had not a care in the world, outside of what they knew for certain in any given moment.

Chapter 4

Starting a Family

* * *

After the birth of their first child, Russell Carl, Phoebe was able to conceive as if at will. The following year, she had a daughter, and they named her Aletha Mae. Then once again, before the decade would close, she and Carl had a second boy, Emil Chester. The kids were healthy, and life was going much as planned. The extended family was proud of both Carl's dedication to working long hours to provide for his growing family, and Phoebe's never-ending will to ensure the family was well cared for at home. She had now birthed three children in as many years, and she handled it well. Motherhood suited her and she felt being a mother to her children was her destiny; Her calling, as she saw it, was to raise children and guide them along their own paths in life.

In 1910, a blow was struck to the family. Carl's father, John Emer Bradway, passed on April ninth due to complications from pneumonia. John was only 53 years old and left behind a wife and several children who still resided at home, as well as two young grandchildren living with them. His wife, Mary, was at least thankful that two of her sons, Charles and John, were back to help her once again. With the passing of their father and husband, the family decided it was time to move back to Alliance, so they packed what they had and returned to the town where John and Mary had originally raised their children. Mary felt it would be good to be back home where she knew her surroundings and had a sense of calmness, familiarity, and memories that she knew she would need.

Carl was feeling somewhat conflicted on what to do. He had set roots down in Smith Township and his family was learning to enjoy the area where Phoebe had grown. He and Phoebe considered their options and eventually they agreed it would be the best course for them to move back to Alliance, so that they could be closer to his mother and siblings. Mary was proud, and Carl felt that if he were closer to her, he would be able to give her the help she would naturally need, but that he knew she would not ask for. So, the decision was made, and once again, the brothers were mostly all back in the very town where their father had shown them how to be men.

Being back home in Alliance was different from how they remembered. For one, it had been a solid decade or more and things were changing in town. Not to mention, Carl's father was no longer there to be the head of the family unit and the responsibility fell to Carl. Harder still, the memories Carl had of working side by side on the farm with his father, and of that life-altering day the terrible storm came through and forever altered the way he saw him, all came back as if they happened yesterday. He felt everything differently. Even the ground beneath him felt different. Carl saw the earth as not just dirt, but soil that shaped who he was and ultimately helped create the man he became and allowed his family to grow. It was insignificant to most others, but Carl thought a little deeper about things like that. The dirt had been a part of his past, of his blood, and he never forgot that, and he never would. Not ever.

They decided to rent a house on East Garwood Street, and once again Phoebe would make a home for her family. The furniture they had was moved into place. The children's belongings all came with them. After Phoebe finished setting up the home, putting her last heart rock in place, she sat on the back steps, looked out over the flat rear yard and with Emil in her arms, she smiled, although a bit exhaustedly. It truly did not matter to her where she rested her head at night. It was the company she was in that made the difference. Having her family and creating a loving home for them was all she wished for. She was grateful this new home was still close to the Mahoning River, as her walks, although now with more children in tow, were still something she treasured and would be able to continue. Her heart rocks were with her, and she looked forward to adding to her collection; growing excited to explore with young Russel who had turned three and shared her excitement for the rocks and found the rock hunting a fun distraction.

Carl had no time off for the move, so he had to do the heavy work late at night. During the day, Phoebe would do what she could on her own. Her sisters were eager to help watch the young children and give her a hand, and she welcomed their help and their company, with open arms. Her siblings were much older than she was, except for her bookend sister Hannah, but they had all grown to know more about one another as they built their own families and lives. They loved growing their families and sharing that experience with one another became important to them all.

The year of 1910 was the first year Phoebe would not be pregnant, and she knew it was for the best. They had just moved, Carl had sadly lost his father to pneumonia, and they honestly needed a little time to get things in order, so they decided it best to wait to add to their family. She was settling into her routine and doting on her children as much as time would allow, and she cherished the short break.

The following year however, she learned she was expecting once again, and Phoebe could not be happier. She had a glow to her with this one, but Carl was feeling a little more nervous. He was already working tirelessly and trying to scrape together all he could so that they could stop renting houses owned by others and own a home of their very own someday. While he loved having children, he also was practical and was naturally inclined to worry more than he likely should have. It was his nature though, to go over all the pros and cons of life and to balance decisions based on probable outcomes. Not wanting to worry his beloved Phoebe, he kept his fears to himself and focused his attention on work as he had been doing all their life together. In his heart, he knew something would give eventually, and things would be much more manageable.

By the end of the summer of 1911, Phoebe was emotionally drained and physically tired, more so than usual. Caring for three children under the age of four, while carrying another was sheer exhaustion for her. She had handled all the previous pregnancies quite well, but this one made her wonder. Had they perhaps become pregnant a little too soon? Maybe her body needed more time to recoup from the three children she had already conceived and birthed. She was 26 by that point, and about to have her fourth child in just over four years. While she enjoyed good health, something felt different to her and worried her, as she was usually very attuned to her body.

She put her worries out of her mind, and continued to do her daily chores and tasks, which were not easy at seven months pregnant. Her walks to the river had stopped a few weeks back as it was fine getting there, but brutal returning home the ten or so blocks she had to travel. Her fear was that she would have trouble getting back home, or worse, that she would go into labor by the water with no one around. Her baby would not be birthed next to the water, she told herself. While the walks were exciting for the children and a good distraction for her while Carl was away working long hours, she knew to listen to her body and that she needed to rest, as best she could.

In mid-October, it was finally time. To both Carl and Phoebe's great surprise, she delivered twin boys. Their family of five grew to seven in just one delivery. The surprise of twins made sense to Phoebe, as she understood why she felt so different with their pregnancy. Her body had craved more nutrients than she had given it, and it all made perfect sense. Phoebe delivered two healthy boys, and as she laid holding them in her arms, Carl simply smiled at her. He was so happy and proud that she had come through once again and delivered two handsome boys to him. His thoughts and fear of how they would manage with the additions to their family were still safely tucked away. It was not a time to worry about what could not be changed. It was a time to cherish the gifts that had been bestowed upon them.

Russell was ever so curious when a new baby came into their family. Aletha wasn't sure what to think as they looked so real, but so little to her. Little Emil, well, all that mattered was he had two more little brothers to play with and that was all he cared about. Life was going to be different for the Bradway children, but they all felt that it would be for the better. Not one of them ever dreamt there could be any negative to come and they each welcomed their new brothers in a different way.

Carl and Phoebe had talked about possible names if they were to have a girl or a boy. But with two boys they were not prepared, as they had never imagined the possibility. They decided together. The first boy would be Keith Emmer, named after Carl's late father. The second child, they decided to name Kenneth William, named for Phoebe's father, who was by her side when she delivered their twins. The boys would each have the middle name of their grandfathers, and both families loved that they had done that for them. It was the right thing to do.

Keith and Kenneth were small little bundles. Phoebe knew they would grow to be close to one another and she felt deeply blessed. She gave it no thought that she had two more mouths to feed, and two more children to watch over. It was her purpose, and she was content in her soul with that knowledge.

Time, healing as it was, had moved them along and both Carl and Phoebe felt that things were returning to normal after the death of his father. His mother, Mary, was doing better, and his brothers and sisters were ensuring she had all she needed. Knowing his mom was cared for brought Carl peace and he felt more relaxed and able to put his mind back into his work. The work was still grueling and had only given him one day off for the births. He did not mind, though, because Carl was a worker at heart. He genuinely enjoyed the fact he was not sitting around and felt that he had much bigger things in store for him if he continued giving it all he had, day in and day out. He was determined that his Phoebe would have things she could only dream of one day. That he knew.

Chapter 5

The Loss of One

* * *

As the year closed out after birthing the twins, Carl and Phoebe looked back on the eight years of union they had shared. While it was not always easy, they had enjoyed what most would consider a normal life. They were humble people and enjoyed a comfortable, though modest life and despite the loss of Carl's father, their family life was strong and intact. On Sundays, Carl would attend church with his wife and children, and then hurry back home to work. His job was demanding, and Carl knew that he needed to give in for now and endure the grueling pace. What else could he do? Farming wasn't what it had once been. He loved to farm, but it wasn't always predictable. A bad crop could change everything over one season. The family had little savings and could ill afford that setback. He had seen his own father struggle when a storm rolled in and wiped-out crops. It was devastating when animals would take to being sick, or disease would spread, and they would need to put them down.

It was not a sure thing as it had seemed to him long ago. Carl always saw himself retiring doing what he loved, but times had changed, and he had to adjust, which is exactly what he did. Things were harder now, and he had given that up to pursue a new line of work that he could see a different path in.

Carl received word that a new opening for a better paying job had come up, but it would require yet another move. This time, to Salem, Ohio, which was roughly 15 miles east of Alliance. He was not sure how to tell Phoebe that they would once again need to pack their belongings and move to a town they had never lived in before, but he knew it was for the best. With a raise in his hourly earnings and a chance to provide a more stable future for his family, he would find a way to ask her.

The very night he learned of the job opportunity, after he had finished his long shift for the Teamsters, he proposed the idea to Phoebe. She sat back in her chair, looked blankly at Carl, and then to their children, wondering how on earth they would manage another move, one that would bring them further from his family that they had quite literally just moved to be closer to. It was her decision to move back to Alliance, so that Carl would be nearer to his dear mother, who was without her husband for the first time in 32 years. She thought of all of that, while also considering the one good part of the change, which was that the new job was working with William, Phoebe's father. She thought maybe it could work. After all, her father had recently moved to Salem and in fact, had a place that would accommodate their family, at least until they could find a place of their own.

She wanted to sleep on it though, which for her also included praying on the decision as well. She needed to be as confident as she could be that they were making the right decision for their family once again. When she arose the next day, Carl was already long gone on his way to work. Phoebe would let him know on his return what she felt when she awoke that morning. Her decision was not taken lightly, but she felt certain about it. She had thought, prayed, and rested with it and the decision felt right and she was good with it all. They would make a move once again, staying with her mother and father until such time as they could find their next home. She figured the short time with her parents would possibly allow them to save enough money to purchase a place of their own, where they would not feel the need or the urge to continue on to a new place each year. She wanted to set down roots in a place they could finally call their own.

When Carl returned that night, he was drained physically and beaten mentally from the vigorous workload. Phoebe had supper on the table, told him to rest, and smiled. He knew without asking. She did not need to tell him her decision, because he knew his Phoebe almost as well as he knew himself. Carl felt a great relief, knowing he could work just as hard somewhere new, but earn more for it. It was what he would do and knowing that Phoebe was behind him whole-heartedly brought him much relief. For if she were not comfortable with the move, he would have stayed in Alliance and continued as he had been.

Everything was set. Carl's brothers were to help with the move and give Carl a much-needed break from doing everything on his own. Phoebe had the children to tend to and went ahead a few weeks early to get them settled with her parents. She was thrilled to be home again. It had been a decade since she had lived with them, but they welcomed her with open arms, and she felt as if she had never left. The children entertained themselves, shouting and laughing about, and William just sat back and smiled. Watching his youthful grandchildren caused him to take stock. Life was good, and although he was still working, driving for the Teamsters as he had done for the past decade, he was home a little more. His farming allowed him to live a little easier in his older years and life was full and good.

In March of 1912, Carl and his brothers delivered the final items to the new home and finished clearing out the one they had rented in Alliance. As Carl looked around at the home they were leaving behind, he felt that one day he would return to his hometown, but for now, they had made the right decision. He was still young and had a lot to learn and give, so it wasn't goodbye, rather it was I'll be seeing you soon, when the timing is better.

Not long after settling in, Keith, one of the twins, fell ill. Phoebe tried desperately to control his increasing fever, but she felt something more was wrong with her son. He started to develop a horrible red rash about his small body, and so Phoebe decided it was time to take him to the doctor. Carl was out working and had no idea what his wife was dealing with back at home. He knew Keith did not feel well, but figured kids got sick. It was just part of growing up. Kids just got sick, and he would fight it off. After all, he came from tough stock.

Unfortunately, their otherwise young and healthy son, was not able to fight this particular illness. Keith passed away on a Monday night, April 29, 1912. The cause of death was the measles, which in 1912, had just been finally classified as a nationally notifiable disease. Keith would sadly be a statistic for the horrible disease that took him, and a void would be forever in his parents' hearts.

Carl was devastated and felt that had they not made the move, had he not pushed for another better paying employment opportunity and had just stayed with the job he had back in Alliance, that it may not have happened. His job in Alliance had been secure, and everyone was getting along fine. He had been close to his mother and that was Phoebe's intent for going back in the first place, but he went ahead and looked for more, making changes once again. This one though, possibly resulted in the loss of his son, and as a result of the unimaginable loss and guilt, he tumbled into a deep depression.

Phoebe was heartbroken, but she knew there were other children that needed her. She had no choice but to be strong for them, and not only for herself, but for both her and Carl. She knew her husband shouldered the loss of Keith exceedingly hard and most certainly blamed himself because the move had been his idea. Phoebe knew that was simply not the case. Children succumbed to the dreaded measles every day, and there was simply no way he could have known it would happen to their son. In her mind she did not need to understand why because it was God's will. She hated it deep in her soul, and yet she accepted it. Carl, though, did not. He never would.

The funeral was held in their family home, as was done in those days. Afterwards, they held a short meeting at East Goshen Church, where they attended services for many years. Carl and Phoebe buried their boy just two short days later in Bunker Hill Cemetery, which is in Beloit, Ohio, north of Salem. Carl stood stoically as the people that came to pay their final respects left. He stood there as the elder who spoke moments ago, said his goodbyes. As Phoebe tried to comfort Carl, he just stood there, in a daze of sorts, and she knew he needed to be alone for a while. She gathered the children, and along with her parents, they set out back to home. Carl needed time to reflect. Had his decisions cost him the life of his boy, Keith? What had he done to deserve such a horrible outcome? He wanted answers, but he knew he would not get them. After a short time, he looked down to where his young, innocent boy rested, and he said his final goodbye. Carl turned and walked away, wondering to himself, what if they had never moved? How would things have changed?

The year, though, was not finished just yet. There was more to come, and it was only a short time before they would be struck with tragedy once again.

Chapter 6

A Time to Move

* * *

Back home, Carl reluctantly went back to work. His job felt much more difficult because he blamed it for the loss of Keith, and he now had to face the weight of that loss every day. It was hard on him, but what he did not realize was that Phoebe was silently struggling as well. She was hurt and could not show it as he did. She had to dig deep and trust that there was a reason. Otherwise, she would feel the same guilt her husband did, and she too had a job to do. She was responsible for raising the other children. Not only raising them, but she had to explain to them why their brother was not coming home. She had to assure them that they would be fine, and just because their brother had died, did not mean they would as well. Helping her children understand that they would be ok was one of the hardest things she ever had to do. She wondered to herself how she could possibly make such a promise to them knowing what had happened to Keith and how they had such little control over it.

Phoebe's parents tried to help as best they could. Being elders in their church, they had a great deal of experience with loss and had some insight into what needed to be done. They had also lost a daughter of their own at a very young age. Phoebe's older sister, Sarah Luella, died in infancy and her mother had struggled with why for a long time. She warned Phoebe not to dwell too much on her guilt and thoughts. She had children that needed her to be strong and she warned her that her husband would need to find a way to cope and release himself from the guilt he carried, even though they knew in their hearts, he never would.

Over the next month, Phoebe got back into a routine and made peace with it all as best she could. She had no choice, or it would simply eat away at her. Her pain, she told herself, would still be there, but she would just find a way to push through it, as she did not have the time to be angry and sad. She had to accept things as they were for the time being.

Carl, he did the best he could. Work always took most of his days from him, but he came home each night in a sad state. He could not cope with the sorrow and move through the grief the way his wife seemed to. Phoebe was certain he just needed time, so she continued to do her tasks and allow Carl to just be. She prayed nightly that God would allow her husband to forgive himself for what he had not done, and she understood that if he ever would find that forgiveness, it would be in his own time.

Shortly after Keith's passing, William had to take some time off work due to a condition known as dropsy. His muscles ached and his body swelled as the condition worsened, and though his wife tried to make him as comfortable as possible, he just couldn't shake it. As he continued to deal with his illness, William watched as his grandkids ran about, wondering when he would heal enough to get back to playing alongside them. He longed to chase them in the street and bounce them off his knees. His grandchildren were what brought William happiness and he feared he would never be well enough to enjoy them as he once had.

On May 13th, 1912, William had a stroke at home and fell into a state of unconsciousness. He remained unconscious for an entire week, until the morning of May 20th. With his family by his side, William passed away quietly at 8:10 in the morning, less than one month after his grandson, Keith, had died.

Phoebe was once again devastated. How could it have happened? They had barely time to mourn the loss of their son, and then so quickly to have to prepare to say goodbye and bury her father was unfathomable. She was just not prepared. Who could be prepared for such loss? she wondered to herself. Her life was being altered over and over again, in such a short period and she just needed a moment to breathe. She longed for just a small break, feeling it was all she needed. It was not to be though. She continued to pray for answers and peace in her life. What was it He wanted her to do? Whatever it was she would do it. She was angry and was beginning to understand how Carl was feeling. Both had lost their fathers and a son in such a short period of time. Now they had to do whatever they could to keep the rest of their family safe. That was how they saw it. They had to do whatever was needed to keep the rest safe from harm.

They both had enough and decided Salem was not for them. It would take some time to figure out where to go next, but both Phoebe and Carl needed to leave the town of Salem. It had not been good to them, and they felt if they stayed much longer, it was possible even worse would happen. Carl began searching for other areas to work. He could not find immediate work back in Alliance, which was their first choice, so instead, Carl was able to secure work in the village of Beloit, Ohio. Beloit sat almost directly in between where they were in Salem, and where they wanted to be, in Alliance. It was also where they had buried their son, Keith, not long before. A move to Beloit was a step in the right direction they hoped, though once again Phoebe felt it was temporary, she resigned herself to accept it.

As they packed their things, Phoebe talked her mother Mary into moving along with them. She assured her mother it would be a good change of scenery, and besides, what would she do alone there in Salem? She needed someone to look after her, the grandchildren loved being with her, and Phoebe could use help with the children. Mary agreed to go along, although a bit reluctantly. Carl felt better about the decision. He was pleased to have his mother-in-law there to ensure his Phoebe was provided with someone to keep her mind occupied while at home with the children all day.

After they settled in, Phoebe decided once again to visit the river's edge in search of heart rocks. She felt that in the past, the search had brought her a calmness she desperately needed; however, she was rarely able to achieve it. It had been a longer stretch of time than she liked since she had gone in search of the pretty heart rocks she so admired, and she had just unpacked the last of the ones she had saved all those years. There was one particular rock she kept close to her. The very first one she had ever picked up and turned about in her hands as she examined its curious shape. That one rock was special, and in her thinking, did not belong mixed with any of the others. There was something about that rock and she thought maybe it would bring her family some much needed peace one day. That was how she felt anyway. Maybe, just maybe, it would.

While the Mahoning River did not run through Beloit, small branches of it did. There were also quaint trails to explore and walk around. Phoebe was able to talk her mother into those long walks with the children, and after a while, Mary began to see the joy in it. The walks took them through peaceful trees swaying in the light breeze, and the sun would drip through the tall pines, adding just enough sunlight to shine across their path. As Phoebe slowly walked, she would glance at the children, and then look intently at the ground beneath her feet. She was always looking for rocks in the shape of hearts. Each time she found one that looked as if it could be, she would examine it. If it were complete, she would place it in her pocket to bring home with her. If it were not, she left it there for Mother Nature to finish its shaping so that it could be found when the time was right. She often wondered if anyone would come along and see what she saw. Just how many more years would it take for that almost heart-shaped rock to complete its transformation? She figured she did not know well enough, and there was an odd comfort in not knowing, so she let it go.

Russell turned five over the summer. He was growing into a fine young man, and Carl was proud. While he was not able to go on the walks with his wife and son, when he returned from work, Carl would take Russell outside and just sit with him, looking up at the night sky. As they sat, Carl would tell his son stories about himself as a young man and even decided to tell Russell about the tremendous storm that had almost taken his life. Russell loved that story and always ask his dad to tell him it again and again. Carl did not mind, because he knew sharing the story was valuable to both himself and to Russell for many reasons. One, he found something that allowed him to bond with his child and forming a bond with his father was most important to a young man. Another, he saw it as a lesson in life he was teaching his son. He shared how his own father, Russell's grandfather, had felt the storm coming on, how he knew without fail to trust his instinct. Carl was always amazed that his father had sensed that storm long before anyone else. He just felt that old storm in his bones and always, his father had told him, always trust your bones. They have no reason to lie.

So, Carl taught his son how to trust his bones, what that felt like, and how he was to understand that when your body told you something, you had better listen. Oftentimes, the bones knew more than the mind did. That was a hard concept to understand, even for Carl, how our bodies would feel something before our minds could tell us. That was how he understood fear though. Your body would feel the effects of fear well before your mind could catch up and even consider the reason why.

Russell looked up to his father and swore one day he would work side by side with him, as Carl had done with his father-in-law. Carl did not want that though, as nice as it sounded. He had dreams for his son to do better things than he was able to do now. He worked hard so that his boys would have a chance at something greater, even if he did not yet know what that was. He just wanted more for them, so he would do his best to talk his boys out of the truck driving business. The hours were long, the days lonely, and the nights exhausting. Why would he want that, other than to be side by side with his father? Carl smiled at the thought. Here was his boy, wanting to be just like his old man. He was proud of that fact. It was the first time Carl felt absolute pride in his job. When your own son wants to be just like you, well, you feel a huge sense of pride no matter what.

As time passed, Carl began to feel himself come back from the depression he felt earlier in the year. He was beginning to see through the fog of grief and decided it was better for him to look forward to his children growing, instead of dwelling on what had unfortunately happened. He, like Phoebe, knew he needed to focus on their children and carefully store away the pain until it was time to visit it once again. It was just not the time for that quite yet.

Chapter 7

A History for Phoebe

* * *

Phoebe had a strong history in America. She had come from Heald blood, and she took pride in knowing her ancestors had touched American soil all the way back in 1703. John Heald had immigrated from Cheshire, England, with many other Quakers to escape religious persecution that had killed many of their brothers and sisters in their homeland just some 18 years prior. He had married a woman named Martha Foden, and together they set out to start a new life in Chester County, Pennsylvania, just along the Delaware border.

John and Martha had a total of six children, including John Junior, who married Elizabeth Yearsley. They in turn had five children during their lifetime and started to build a name for themselves as hardworking, good Quaker men and women, throughout the Chester County farms and communities. Of those five children, came Sarah, who would marry a man named John McFarlan in 1765. They lived just south of Kennett Square, in Chester County,

Pennsylvania, and were present for the Battle of Brandy-wine, which took place during the country's Revolutionary War. There is a book titled "Our Kindred: The McFarlan and Stern Families of Chester County", written by Cyrus Stern, in which Cyrus tells a story of what happened one morning, during the invasion:

> *The day preceding the battle the right wing of the British army passed near their home. Some Hessian soldiers entered the field where John was ploughing, and cut the three horses from their traces, preparatory to taking possession. The owners resisted this confiscation so far as he was able, but with no other effect than to induce the marauders to fasten a rope around his neck. To teach him, as they say, how to behave. And not only his horses driven off, but also his cattle, pig, and sheep, and all his poultry and grain were carried away. While the soldiers were thus engaged, the women following the army, entered the house and stripped it of everything they could lay their hands on; beds, bedding, clothing and victuals; not even sparing the family bible. They tore the cap from the head of the baby in the cradle, and the kerchief from the neck of its mother, telling her as they did so that they had come to stay. Yes, to find your graves soon, was her indignant response.*

Everything was lost, but their dignity. Sarah had refused to allow them to take that from her family. It was her family, and no one was going to remove their dignity without her approval. They spent years rebuilding their lives from that loss and continued to raise their children to be better people. It was their intent to raise good, hard-working people, and they did.

The small baby in the crib who the soldiers had so harshly greeted and removed his cap, was Enoch McFarlan, who later would marry Phoebe Cloud. Enoch was Phoebe Bradway's great – great-grandfather. She knew little about him, other than the stories that she heard told by her family. Her mother, Mary, kept impeccable records that were handed down over the generations, even though the bible that John had was removed from his care that fateful day.

Mary had been born in Pennsylvania as well, and after her father passed away in August of 1856, she moved in with her Uncle Samuel. Somewhere between 1870 and 1880 she met her husband William and moved to Ohio, where Phoebe was born.

Phoebe knew her heritage was rich in tradition, and her ancestors were strong in their desire to pass down to each generation the lessons they had learned and been taught by their predecessors. She felt the same. What she had learned from her parents, she desired to pass along to her children as well. She had always wanted a large family, and she had been able to enjoy that privilege. She could not allow it to stop there though. Traditions, after all, deserved to be passed down.

In 1913, she would have another child. On October 20th of 1913, she introduced Mary Elizabeth Bradway to the world. Carl had lost a son but gained another daughter. He tried not to believe she was born because of Keith's death, but he wondered if God had intended him to have this little girl to help ease his pain. Carl lit up when he first set eyes on Mary, and he settled on the notion that all would be all right from here on out.

Life was beginning to get back to normal once again, and they made plans to continue with their hopes of owning a home of their own. Carl worked all the time that he could. He knew it would wear on him and limit his time with his children, but he held out hope that it would be for only a short while. It was his intention to work hard for a time, so that he could eventually enjoy and give all he could of himself and his time to his children.

Phoebe too felt a special bond with Mary Elizabeth, possibly for the same reason Carl did. She would never get over the tragic loss of their boy, Keith, but she had others to care for and now a newborn once again. So, she devoted her time to the children while her husband was hard at work building a future for their family. She missed him terribly when he would work all day and night, but she too felt that there was a better plan in store for them. She held firm to the belief that their sacrifices and hard work would eventually be rewarded and had faith that even though she did not know what the plan was, that it would all one day work out as God intended.

Chapter 8

The Ice of the Mahoning

* * *

Carl asked both of his girls where the boys were. It was getting late, and supper was set on the table waiting for them all to sit and talk about their day. It was 1919 and Aletha, at 10 years old, had worked a hard day for a young child. Her chores included cleaning the home, ensuring the family was fed, and keeping watch over the boys as best she could while Carl worked his long days. Carl had decided to leave her in charge because he knew she was the best of the children suited for the task. Aletha took naturally to caregiving and cherished the responsibility of caring for her siblings and family, even while trying to enjoy what childhood she had left before her. She had learned a great deal in an extremely short period of time, and Carl was proud of her.

Aletha told her father that the boys had decided to go out for the day, even though the temperatures were below freezing. It was January 18, 1919. The white snow covered everything in view, and the rivers and streams appeared frozen as far as the eyes could see. Earlier that day, Carl left for work as he always did, and he reminded the boys to listen to Aletha, and to be careful. On that particular morning, the boys had mentioned something about ice sliding. It was a game they enjoyed playing, where they would take each other's hands and fling one another forcefully from one point to the other, and then back again. When the river froze, it was a great deal of fun for the small children to entertain themselves on its slippery surface, and his boys were no different. But that morning, Carl made it a point that the boys were not to go as far as the river. They were to stay around the house and enjoy the snow there. The lack of the sun recently made it appear as if the ice were thicker than it actually was, and Carl knew it could be difficult to tell just how thick or thin the layers were beneath its glassy veneer.

He asked the girls if they reminded the boys what time supper was before they left. Aletha acknowledged that she had indeed, and that Russell had promised her that they would be back well before their dad returned from work. Even though Russell was slightly older than Aletha, he admired and looked up to her. Here she was, a ten-year-old girl, taking on the responsibilities of a grown woman. She took on so much around their home, that even as a young boy, he had to be impressed.

Emil and Kenneth looked up to both Russell and Aletha, but they were certainly not opposed to finding a little trouble on their own from time to time, as often happens with young boys. Plus, it was a Saturday and schools were not in session. The lure of the iced river made it hard for the boys to listen to their father's words, even though they had promised him they would not venture out to the water.

After Carl ate his meal, Aletha could see his frustration mounting. She had watched her father change considerably during the previous year and a half and witnessed as his happy, hopeful, once cheerful self, disappeared noticeably. Despite being considered poor, their home had always been filled with laughter and happiness, however, that laughter and happiness was abruptly replaced with quiet awkwardness. Most days Carl came home, put his shoes by the door, and sat at the supper table, saying no more than a word or two for the most part. The children wanted to tell him about their days, but he would become lost in his own thoughts, almost as if he could hear them but could not comprehend the words that they spoke.

After about another hour of waiting, Carl decided that it was time to go and bring the boys home. He was disappointed in them that they would stay out late, when they knew he needed them home to help with the chores. Just because it was a Saturday, did not mean it was time to rest. There was a lot to do, and Carl would see to it that the boys learned the value of hard work as he had. He was not pleased at all, and the girls knew the boys were in deep trouble. Mary was only five, but she too knew when her father was upset, as he so often seemed to be as of late.

After asking Aletha to clean up from supper, a job meant for Emil that Saturday, Carl laced his brown weathered boots back up and pushed open the front door with force, allowing it to slam behind him. As he looked up and down the street, he imagined the boys coming back down the road, with a scared look on their faces, because they knew they had broken the rules. He tried to calm himself in that moment and took a deep breath in, held it, then let out a sigh. He was upset with them, but not angry. Carl understood boys needed to be boys, which included breaking the rules set before them every now and again. He just wanted them home so that he could rest for the evening.

Rusty was scratching at the door trying desperately to get outside to be with Carl, but he did not pay him any attention or perhaps he simply couldn't hear his scratching and whining over his own thoughts.

As he walked left, Carl felt that maybe the boys had gone down the road to a friend's home. The Brantinghams lived only a block or so down the road from their house, so he would be able to quickly retrieve them and give them a talking to on the way back. He bundled up just a little tighter as the cold air from the darkened night stung him a little more than it had earlier in the day. A gray ghostly smoke escaped from his mouth as he called their names over and over and then listened intently for a familiar reply.

When he decided that he had gone far enough left, Carl turned around, looked up to the sky, pausing again, and then as if his head were growing heavy, dropped it, downward to the snow-covered ground. He kicked at the snow on the tips of his boots, and then sighed again and walked on. As he passed his house, he gave a shout to the front door to see if they had arrived home while he had been in the opposite direction. Aletha did not say a word. She only needed to shake her head side to side and put her head down. Carl knew his boys had not yet returned home.

Aletha was growing worried. Not that she felt the boys had stumbled into trouble, but she was concerned with what her father's final reaction would be the longer he was forced to search for them. His patience was gone and had been for more than a year. Carl had seen his life altered in a way he never imagined and all he wanted to do was find his boys, get them home and rest. That was it. Nothing more. But he was struggling to locate them, and it was dark, cold, and the temperatures were dipping even lower.

As his search continued, Carl felt a growing sense of dread come over him. He just wanted his boys safely home. His anger had dissipated and been replaced with fear. It was fine that they had disobeyed this time, he told himself. He just needed to get everyone home and forget about the entire night. In fact, he bartered a little with God promising to just be happy for the boy's safe return and to let it go as if nothing had happened. Carl had long since become worn mentally and emotionally and he did not feel the need to focus on his anger but instead shifted it to one of concern. As he walked, he felt his legs moving quicker beneath him. His voice was beginning to crack some from shouting the boy's names over and over in the plummeting temperatures, though he barely noticed the cold as he had become so overcome with worry and his body had filled with adrenaline as he moved swiftly along. He did not even realize that he had forgotten his hat and his head was starting to freeze over from the snow as it dropped silently from the sky once again.

Up the road, he saw some boys in the street, and for a moment his fear turned to relief as he rushed over to them. As he drew closer however, he realized they were not his sons. Anxiously, Carl asked them if they knew where his boys were, but they just shrugged him off with a response that sounded as if they neither knew who his boys were or where they may be, nor did they seem to care.

Back at the house, Aletha was getting Mary ready for bed. She was scared for her brothers and now her father. He was out alone searching frantically for her brothers, and God only knew where they were and when he might find them. Aletha started to sing to Mary to calm her down, and probably herself as well. Her father had been gone over an hour, and she felt a heaviness in her chest that told her something wasn't right. She looked at Mary laying there peacefully at last and stroked her hair to ensure she rested for the night. Aletha did not want to go back downstairs, because she felt that her nervous energy would take her outside to find her father. All she wanted was to have him come through the front door with the three boys in tow, hollering at them to get to bed and they would discuss their actions and punishments after supper the next evening. By this point, having her father home and angry was better than his absence and her worry.

It was getting late, and Aletha was exhausted. As she lay with Mary, she inadvertently put herself to sleep too. About an hour into her slumber, she awoke and frantically looked around, forgetting for a moment where she was and just how long she had been there. She gathered her senses, and realized she was with Mary and that shortly before she had put her to rest for the evening. What bothered her was that she did not hear anything in the home outside of her breathing. Where was her dad and where were her brothers?

She scampered downstairs and quickly glanced around the main room. It appeared her father had still not returned and neither had her brothers. Maybe the police had picked them up. Maybe they had gotten into trouble for causing some ruckus somewhere in town. It was not farfetched. As Aletha started towards the front door and grabbed the knob, it opened at the same time from the other side.

Her father was standing there, shivering and snow covered from head to toe. He said not a word, nor did he so much as look at Aletha. Carl walked past her, laid his coat down on the floor, and slouched down in his chair, letting the melting snow drip onto the hardwood flooring below. He had a terribly blank, but still confused look on his face, and Aletha was unsure of how to ask him what she already knew the answer to. He had clearly not found her brothers.

"Pa, what time is it?" She inquired, hoping to coax anything from her father's mouth.

Carl just sat there, staring straight ahead, and did not mumble even a word. His demeanor frightened Aletha and made her feel concerned even more than she already had been.

"Pa, where are they? Pa? What can I do?"

Carl looked blankly at Aletha, took a small rock from his pocket that he had kept with him for some time, and opened his mouth.

"Pray."

Chapter 9

A Heart of Stone

* * *

In the Summer of 1915, Carl and Phoebe traveled to Wheeling, West Virginia, to take part in the wedding of Carl's sister, Cora Bradway. Her soon to be husband, a man named Lorenzo Dray, was working in West Virginia and Cora decided to get married there in the foothills of the Appalachian Mountains. Phoebe was very fond of Cora and was terribly excited to be with her on her special day. Carl knew extraordinarily little about Lorenzo, but he was an easy-going man, so if Cora was happy, well, then he would just be happy for her as well.

On her wedding day, Cora wore a simple dress of white. She was not the type to consume herself with the fashions of the day, nor was her husband to be. Lorenzo was a potter by trade and enjoyed the simple life over a complicated one chasing the designs of the day. It made sense that the pair would find each other and get married. They had fallen in love quickly and decided that marriage was the next logical step. With her father gone, Cora asked Carl to give her away, and he felt great pride in carrying out that request. He first talked it over with Phoebe, who did not hesitate to give her enthusiastic reply. She was happy that Cora thought so highly of her brother that she would ask him over the others.

Lorenzo was originally from Ohio. He had been born in East Liverpool in March of 1893, which was just across the Ohio River from West Virginia and just a short distance to the Pennsylvania border to the east. A tall, slender man with deep blue eyes and brown hair, one could see why Cora fell in deep. Besides his attractive outer appearance, Lorenzo was also a modest, hardworking man and came from good stock, and Carl believed he would be a good partner and provider for Cora.

The wedding was a simple ceremony, attended by only close family. The sun peeked its warm light through the trees, and the mountains exhaled a gentle breeze that lent just enough coolness to keep those in attendance comfortable. When it was over, Carl and Phoebe hugged Cora, told her they were happy for her, and that they would look forward to seeing her soon. Lorenzo shook Carl's hand and thanked him several times for being a part of their new lives. He felt blessed to have such an honest and caring brother-in-law.

On their way home, Carl and Phoebe discussed their plans for the next few years. Beloit was becoming home, and Phoebe was feeling at ease there. Her sister Hannah lived there as well with her husband, Walter Toole, and so as time went by, the trips back to Alliance had become much more infrequent than they had once been. In fact, Carl had agreed that placing roots down in Beloit, Ohio was the best decision for their family, and they all needed to make the necessary adjustments to make it as much home for them as Alliance had been. He missed his mother but knew he would get back home to see her when time allowed, and he felt comfortable knowing that she had his siblings there to help her and keep her company. Carl felt that even though funds were always tight, the day would soon come when opportunity would arise for him and he would get the break his family deserved and the freedom that came with it, allowing him to visit his mother and family whenever he desired.

At the close of 1915, Phoebe and Carl celebrated twelve years of marriage together. Their union had brought six children into their lives, and although they had lost Keith at such a young age, the others were all healthy and enjoying life. Things were back to as normal as they could be for having had a series of losses in such a short period of time as they did. The dark storm cloud that loomed over them for a time had seemingly moved on and they had finally grown comfortable enough to allow some happiness to seep back into their lives.

Phoebe had a favorite heart-shaped stone that she carried with her everywhere she went. It was a good luck charm of sorts for her, and she made sure on long trips she did not leave home without it. Carl would watch as she played with the stone mindlessly, tracing its rounded edges with her fingers as she turned it over and over in her small hands.

As he watched her, he felt a warmth in his own heart and smiled at the thought of how his beautiful wife saw the world. Even after suffering significant loss, she still saw beauty in things no one else did, and for that he felt truly blessed. When he had a longer shift at work, more so than his usual already lengthy shift, Phoebe would slip one of her rocks into his jacket pocket, thinking it would keep him safe and bring a smile to his face if he happened to discover it. Carl never let on that he knew she did that. He wasn't certain why he never told her. He just didn't. It was her quiet way of sharing the joy of her heart rocks with him and ensuring he would come home safe to her, and he enjoyed the quiet happiness it brought her. Perhaps, he just did not want to interfere with her enjoyment.

Beloit is a small village that in 1915 had less than 600 inhabitant's total. The quaint small-town feel suited the Bradways just fine. Close knit was exactly how they lived their own lives so for them, Beloit felt like just the right place to purchase their first house.

At home, Phoebe's sister, Hannah, would help Phoebe with the children when she could or watch them so that Carl and Phoebe could have a night to themselves, which they rarely had, if ever. She was grateful for the opportunity to spend time with her nieces and nephews and enjoyed playing with the girls and watching as the three boys, Russell, Emil, and Kenneth, began to grow into fine young boys.

Kenneth never truly knew his brother Keith that had passed, so the only fear the family had for him was the bond that twins often seemed to carry. Would he one day feel a sense of loss that he could not explain? Maybe. Only time would tell, but at just four years old it seemed he was fine and developing his own personality, different from the others. His gentle eyes seemed to look right through you, as if he were able to see something others could not. He had dark hair that shined in the light, and his skin nearly had a glow to it. His appearance matched his growing personality being both magnetic and intriguing, and it was easy to see he would one day grow to be an interesting and charming young man.

Emil was the curious one of the three. He had to know how everything worked, but he had a shy way about him. So, often instead of asking questions, he just observed silently but intently. Emil loved watching Carl and the men of the neighborhood work. If they were working on the roof of a home, Emil was the one sitting in the grass, watching each step the men took. At times he would sneak up on the ladder, shift silently to the top, and with just his eyes above the roof line, watch in awe. Nothing seemed mundane or ordinary to him, and Carl appreciated this curiosity in his middle boy.

Russell was the oldest and it showed. He was in charge without a doubt. The other boys followed him with great fascination and wonder deferring to him in all things and letting him take the lead. His charm was ever apparent and his smile quick. If something was going on, Russell was either behind it, or knew how it started. His leadership skills were apparent at a very early age, and by the age of eight, one could tell the was destined for massive things. Phoebe would often laugh when they were not around, because she did not want to believe she encouraged his behavior, but the truth was she loved how he oozed confidence. Even from a young age, she knew he was never going to settle for ordinary and that he had the mind to change the world.

The boys were always involved with things together, and their parents loved that. It was their wish that the children would grow to be the best of friends, because when life had trouble in store for you, it was family that was there for you to rely on. Both Phoebe and Carl had seen that time and time again. They knew they always had family to fall back on, and providing that same safety net to their children was of the utmost importance to them.

As far as they knew, the boys and their sisters would always be close, and never abandon each other regardless of life's circumstances. It was a lesson they impressed on them each night. As Phoebe would lay them down to bed, she would place a gentle hand on their heads and look at them as she prayed. Her prayers always included a story of how the children would need to be there for each other, no matter what. Through good times and troubled times, they needed to promise her they would stand together, firm and tall, when necessary, even when it was hard. Each of them always promised her, and in her heart, she knew for absolute certain that they meant it.

Chapter 10

Needing Charlie

* * *

One thing Carl was able to keep in perspective in his life was that he felt he had only one direction to go from where he was, and that was up. Life had not been easy on him, but he always seemed to find the positive in everything around him. That was until he lost his young son. Still though, he was determined to continue his pattern of looking for the good in life. As time passed, he began to slowly find his peace. Each month he paid a visit to his young son and continued to heal from the pain he had so viciously felt. Carl forgave God and tried desperately to forgive himself. Phoebe often had to remind her husband that he had done nothing to cause what had so tragically happened to their family, but Carl needed to work through his guilt and pain and find his way to peace in his own time and in his own way. Understanding the complexity of her husband, Phoebe simply reminded him daily of all he was doing to give his family a better life, even if they were poor still. She knew so many people were in fact in the same position, but that one day, things would change because her Carl was willing and working towards a change. If only he could catch a break, they could look back on all the years of struggling and scraping by as a blessing and a lesson to pass along to their own children. That even when times were tough, having a loving family and finding some small piece of joy in each day was really all that truly mattered.

Phoebe often thought back to when they were young and first married. It had been her favorite season of life. Life was just beginning to get underway, and she had found a hardworking man and fallen head over heels for him. She remembered every perfect detail of seeing Carl standing before her, dressed in black and white, simple yet handsome. His shy smile caught her attention in a way that formed a memory so vivid, she would never be able to forget. Even when things were tough, she was always able to go back to that time in her head and her concerns would melt away. Those early memories of their time together were hers to keep close and to cherish. When she would see her sisters, they would giggle together at Phoebe in a playful way because she was just so overly in love, and they had been slightly jealous of how she knew from the first time she met him, that Carl would be all she ever needed.

Carl had fallen just as quickly and just as deeply in love with Phoebe's gentle ways. She had a naturally caring nature and was always able to feel gratitude for all she had, rather than regret or desire for what she did not. This impressed him because there were days when he wanted to be happy and accept things, but it was just a little too hard. But Phoebe was different. Whenever things got a little overwhelming, or Carl came home from work a little short of money or patience, Phoebe would greet him with her warm smile and remind him that better days were coming, and that the many good days they had in the past could be revisited in their memories whenever they liked. She was right and Carl knew it, he just wasn't able to see things as clearly as she could. However, he did, have faith, in her and was positive things would get better, because his beloved Phoebe was by his side, and she was certain that there were good things ahead for them.

One evening, about a year after Keith's passing, Carl sat down with his brother, Charlie, who was three years older than he was. Charlie had been living with their mother, Mary, as she helped him raise his two children. His wife Maud, and his son Charlie Jr., both passed in 1907 just 21 days apart. They had been married for a short five years when he lost both his wife and his child, yet somehow managed to move forward with living. Carl was in search of something, and although he was not quite certain what it was, he felt a strong need to sit with Charlie and learn from him. How had he handled the loss of two people so close to him? What did he feel was the reasoning behind the loss? Was it hard to carry on, or did he just accept it because it had already happened, and he had literally no control over that period of his life?

Charlie enjoyed his brother and knew how difficult facing the loss of a child was. To share that experience with a brother was an unusual gift of sorts, so talking to him about the incredible blows that life had struck him, came naturally. He sat back and looked at Carl as his younger brother asked the questions that had been churning in his mind for far too long.

"Charlie, how do ya do it? I mean, were you angry for long?" Carl asked. Before Charlie could answer, Carl continued on with a barrage of other pained and inquisitive thoughts as though a flood gate had opened, releasing the intense rushing water in one quick blow and he could simply not keep the inquiries inside his mind a moment longer.

Charlie sat there and listened to the questions as a small awkward smile rose from the corners of his mouth. He knew what Carl was searching for, and he wanted to give his baby brother good solid advice. It had been a few years since his loss, and Charlie had plenty of time to understand how he felt. He had lost a child as Carl had, but he had also lost his wife. In his mind, losing a wife may have been a different process of healing from losing a child, but loss was loss. Carl was clearly struggling and hurting from the loss of his son, and so Charlie offered him the best advice he could, from the perspective of someone who truly did understand.

"Listen Carl, you never truly get over a loss as deep as losing a child. Never. I wish I could tell you different. There are plenty of days I wonder where I would be and who I would be if Maud and Charlie were still with me to help determine my path," he began. "Maud was a good wife and a better mother, so trying to fill those shoes of hers is plain impossible, but you know, little brother, all I can do is carry on as she would want me to. I need to be the father she knew and the man she loved, and I try my darndest to do just that. Otherwise, what would be the point?"

Carl listened as his brother spoke with passion and intent and watched his body language as he did so. Body language was important to Carl. He felt you could learn more from a man by observing his body movement as he spoke, more anyway, than you could decipher from the words that escaped his mouth. He knew his brother well, of course, but it was a hard habit to break and so, he watched, listened attentively, and felt deep in his core the words his big brother Charlie spoke to him. Carl's appreciation was genuine, and his understanding of what Charlie told him was stronger than he anticipated. At no time did Charlie give an indication with his short movements or his piercing eyes, that he was trying to get Carl to trust something he did not trust himself. The meaning behind his words was pure, and it unexpectedly helped Carl begin to heal the wounds of guilt and grief he had been carrying for so long.

When Carl told Phoebe that he felt some relief from the pressures he placed on himself after speaking with his older brother, Phoebe felt lighter. Her heart was crying with joy for her husband, and she placed her arms around his neck, looked deep into his eyes, and smiled. Phoebe had prayed for the day when Carl would release the blame that he had inadvertently placed on himself. She knew he did not want to suffer with that guilt, but it was just who he was. He was a man of pride and responsibility, and in his mind the death of his son was his to bear. The guilt he carried made him feel more alert and even more responsible for the other children, and for his actions, his reactions to situations, and the potential impact the choices he made had on those he loved. It was as if he needed to place that blame on himself, and now, he was finally able to let some of it go and allow his broken heart to begin to heal.

Charlie remarried in 1914, and that gave Carl even more hope that with time, even the deepest of heartbreaks could be healed. His second wife happened to also hold the same name as his first but had an E on the end of her name. She became Maude Bradway as well. Carl wondered how that felt for Charlie to call her by the same name as his past wife, but Charlie seemed to pay it no mind. He had two more children along the way with Maude, and life went on for old Charlie just as he had told Carl it would.

In 1914 the world was also experiencing a great change. The start of "the war to end all wars" had begun and the United States was at attention. The men and women of Ohio and all the other states for that matter, wondered if or when the U.S. would get involved. Carl wondered what it would mean for him if he had to leave his family and go off and fight. He had little savings. They were barely surviving on what he was able to bring home as it was, and if he lost that, he feared for what would happen to his family. Where would Phoebe and the children go? Carl was not alone in his concern. Many young men carried the same fear, not only in Alliance, but around the country. As Carl carried on with his daily routine, murmurs could be heard among the townspeople. The what ifs surrounding the war occupied the minds of the good folks, and Carl was certainly no different.

For a time though, the United States watched from a distance. This war was not being fought on U.S. soil. It was not like the Civil War that William, Phoebe's deceased father, had fought in for a cause he truly believed in. It was also not like the Revolutionary War that her ancestors had seen up close and personal, freeing themselves from a country that had no intention of letting go of her grip. Those wars were fought on the same soil that now was ripe with crops and homes built on the memories of those who had fought for it. Blood had been shed, and men and women had died, staining the lives and the lands of those around them and all who came after. It was impossible to avoid the tangible impact and memory of those wars, unlike this one that was thousands of miles away in places most knew little about, making it seem nearly unreal.

Eventually Carl once again found a zest for life. He decided that on the visits to see his mother and brother back in Alliance, he would bring the boys along with him. He and Charlie could teach the boys fishing. Carl loved to fish and had been doing so ever since he could remember. It was important to him that his boys learn the proper way to fish, but it also served as a second chance to bond with them after he had retreated so far into himself following Keith's death. Plus, he had not been able to spend much time with Charlie and the fishing would allow for that as well.

The two brothers had enjoyed trips to the Mahoning River as kids and were excited to bring their boys with them and show them what they considered the best fishing holes around. John Emmer, their father, had spent so much time up and down the muddy riverbanks, marking spots where he had found "fish for days," as he would say. The boys remembered those days well, and when they first arrived with their own boys chattering along behind them, they smiled as they smelled the warmth of summer in the air. The river and its banks had changed, as factories came in and altered the surrounding landscape, but that did not bother them any. They weren't there for the views. They were there for the experience they were providing the next generation, and maybe to relive some of their own memories that had long since escaped their minds.

Charlie was an excellent fisherman, and Carl was no slouch himself. The boys were impressed as they watched their fathers play with the lines, scouring over the rippling water, appearing as if they had heard the fish call to them. They were patient, as if they knew patience was required to catch the particular fish they were waiting on. The lines danced gently on the water, teasing the fish below. Carl had never told Charlie, but he admired him greatly for the man he had become. All the tragedy he endured, and yet he had not allowed it to change his outlook or his ultimate path. As Carl fished side by side with Charlie, he wanted to tell his brother how this trip, this fishing trip of the boys and men, wound up really being for him. It was a trip that showed Carl, it was time. Time to welcome healing and become open to learning how to do that. Time to teach and time to enjoy laughter again. On that trip, the river began to heal Carl, and for the first time he was able to allow himself to really feel it. As he watched his boys studying Charlie casting over and over in a smooth pattern, he smiled and felt peace. It was all he had hoped for in the day, and perhaps even far more.

Chapter 11

A Stone for Phoebe

* * *

Phoebe filled her time at home teaching her girls about life as she had lived it. Aletha was especially interested to hear her mother's stories of growing up on a farm. Life was different on the farm, and so those stories intrigued her. She was curious to learn about the process of planting, the long hours required to ensure that a good crop was brought to fruition, and how a family could live off the land. It seemed like farming required a type of consistency that she had never experienced as her family moved from one rental to the next. So as her mother shared her stories, Aletha would sit and listen intently. She wondered if there would be a day that her mother and father would once again own a farm and allow her and her siblings to work and learn until it would be their time to take over. She hoped so.

As 1917 came, things were beginning to change, and the war became increasingly real and worrisome. When it was becoming evident that the U.S. would need to enter the war, men began to fill out draft registration cards and plan for when their number was called, and they were sent to serve.

Carl filled his draft card out as follows:

Age: 34
Date of Birth: Oct 28, 1883
Present occupation: Teamster
Employer name: Standard Oil Company
Place of Employment; Alliance, Stark County
Color of eyes: Gray
Color of hair: Brown

Carl figured it was only a matter of time before he was called to duty, and he made plans as best he could to ensure his family was well cared for. While he was still working, he spent any downtime he had fishing with the boys, sitting on the backsteps with the girls answering questions as their curiosity got the best of them, and kissing Phoebe a little more than usual. Phoebe knew her husband carried the weight of what may happen if he was called to serve, but she decided to not worry until there was a tangible reason to be concerned. Maybe the war would end suddenly, and her Carl would be here safe and sound without having to ever travel overseas or step foot on foreign soil. She prayed daily, and her faith was strong. She knew that if there was a good reason her Carl needed to go, he would go, and they would somehow manage, but held out hope that he would not need to.

The same was happening all over in other counties. Men were registering and waiting for the call. Some had simply enlisted to take fate into their own hands, and Carl wondered if he should just get it over with or wait. The waiting was what scared him. He was a man who would rather deal with things head on, rather than let fate take him by surprise. When he was a boy and that storm came crushing through, Carl knew he was powerless and had little control of how that all played out. With the war though, he could enlist, avoid the draft and the unknown, and serve his country. Then hopefully, by the grace of God, be back home quickly with his wife and family.

Carl was getting older and growing frustrated that things were still not panning out as he had intended. He continued to move forward with hope that maybe by 1920, things would change. Maybe the world would settle down, and new opportunity would present itself and pull him in a better direction. He was not going to give up. After all, he and Phoebe had plans and he would be damned if he would not give it a go until he had no go left to give.

Fate, however, was not concerned with the plans this young couple with a growing family had for themselves. Without notice, Phoebe fell ill. On May 1st, 1917, Phoebe was taken to the hospital, complaining that she was feeling faint and unable to catch her breath. At first, she resisted going, but Carl had none of it. She needed to have herself checked out and honestly, she could use the rest, he told her. He convinced her to go with the promise she would only spend a night, have the doctors look her over once, get whatever medicine she needed and rest. The following day she would certainly feel better and simply get up and head on home to take care of her family as she had always done. So, she reluctantly agreed.

Carl had his sister-in-law, Hannah, come over to give him a hand with the children and did what he could to get off work early enough so he would visit with his Phoebe in the hospital and check on her. She was surprisingly ill, but she was from good blood, so Carl was confident that she would be fine. Phoebe gave all she had to her family and had worn herself ragged. All she needed was some much-deserved rest and to know that when she returned home Carl would help more around the house. That is what he promised his beautiful bride and so she rested.

For three days Carl visited with his Phoebe and sat by her side, talking to her, and telling her about the kids, and how Russell was eating so much food while she was away. Aletha was doing a fine job of helping Aunt Hannah around the house. Emil was quiet, trying to understand what was happening and wondering when his mother would be home. Kenneth spent more time with Hannah's husband, Uncle Walter, learning about knot tying and asking him what seemed like a hundred questions about anything and everything. Walter enjoyed Kenneth's attention and did not mind helping to distract him from thinking too much about Phoebe's absence. Little Mary, she fussed about, missing her mother greatly. Carl had held her more in the few days Phoebe was in the hospital than he had for her entire first four years. Once again, fate had forced him to bond with his children a little more and a little better than any of them were accustomed to.

May 5th was just like any other spring day. It was a Saturday and Carl was able to secure some time off work to help around the house in the morning, before heading out to visit with Phoebe. He left at about 7 am and remembered that Phoebe had asked for him to bring her the one heart rock she treasured so dearly. He tucked the stone into the front pocket of his pants, told Hannah and Walter he would return in the afternoon, and set out. On the way to the hospital, Carl remembered that the children had made her a gift out of some sticks they had found in the rear yard. Using the new knot tying skills Walter had taught Kenneth, the children fashioned a star of sorts for Phoebe, and asked their father to give it to her to let her know they were thinking about her. Carl had forgotten to grab it on his way out but would surely tell her all about what they had done. Besides, she would see it when she returned home.

As Carl approached the hospital, he reached his hand deep in his pocket to once again ensure he had not forgotten Phoebe's rock. With all that had been going on, he was forgetting small things and knew how important having the rock was to her. It was bad enough he had forgotten the kids' gift they made her, but the stone was something she had specifically asked for. So, he double checked and let out a sigh of relief when he realized he had indeed remembered the curiously shaped stone. Leaving it safely deep in his pocket, Carl went into the hospital and blindly followed the same path he had each day prior to where his wife rested.

Chapter 12

A Loss so Loved

* * *

"Storms are interesting creatures, that sometimes leave you small hints to their impending arrivals, and other times give you not a dang clue," Carl's father had told him once. He knew his father's words to be true, after-all, that storm that had almost chased him from the world had offered just the tiniest of clues to its landing. His father's acute awareness and ability to note the tiny warnings that storm had offered, probably saved lives on the farm that day. Other times, a storm could be cunning and move in swiftly and quietly, leaving even the keenest and attuned folks unsuspecting. Those storms don't give you even the smallest of clues, not even a soft breeze growing a little more impatient, or a tree with its leaves dancing erratically in an almost fearful way. Storms don't always leave havoc in their wake. Sometimes a storm can be a gentle reminder to be mindful of the complacency we tend to enjoy. Perhaps the storm witnessed something others could not see and was there to lend a hand and give a push to those in her path to make a change before an even greater storm blew through. Or maybe, just maybe, a storm comes for reasons we would never truly understand. Maybe for reasons we would not want to understand.

Phoebe suddenly and without warning, left like a storm that fateful morning at 5 am, just a few hours before Carl arrived, and only four days after she had gone to get some rest. Carl was stunned and stood in the hall up against a wall wondering if it was real. It had to be a mistake. Phoebe was young, and in good health. She had children at home who needed her so badly. She had a husband who absolutely adored her and was ready to bring her home. Plus, he had brought her the heart rock as she had asked, and he remembered. The children had made her a gift she would need to see at home because he had forgotten to bring it. How could she possibly be gone? What would he tell their children? Carl was dazed and did not want to move. He needed time to lay against the wall, catch his breath and figure out how he could possibly leave the hospital without his Phoebe by his side.

As he slumped against the sturdy wall his mind went right to his brother Charlie. How he had lost his son and wife within 21 days' time. How, now he too, had now lost both a wife and a child, after he was feeling as if he had finally begun to heal from Keith leaving him so young. How could he possibly heal from losing his best friend? What did he do so bad in his life that his entire future was changed again, forever?

Carl went home later that day and when he arrived at

the front door, Hannah had already heard the terrible news. She tried not to cry, for the children were all playing in the room directly behind her. It was impossibly hard. Walter entertained the children while Hannah stepped outside to console Carl. She was unsure what to tell him as he stood before her broken from all he had lost in the past seven years. His father, then his boy, and now his wife. What could one tell a man that had suffered so deeply that could possibly make him feel any better? So, she did not say a word. She just put her arms around his shoulders and held him as he placed his head down onto his lap. Carl was weary, both mentally and physically and was desperate to understand why he could not seem to outrun loss, yet knew he may never find the answer.

Phoebe was laid to rest beside her young son, Keith. She was outlived by her own mother, four of her sisters and her beloved husband, Carl. As Carl saw it, it was not how it should have gone. He should never have outlived his darling Phoebe, of that he was certain. But somehow, he had.

It never dawned on him that he would need to raise their five children alone. His mind unable to consider the depth of loss and the hole Phoebe's absence would leave in their lives, for he was far too consumed with the hole in his heart. The days after Phoebe's death and through the funeral, Phoebe's sisters and mother stepped in seamlessly to help Carl and the kids. They too were suffering, and helping Phoebe's family was a way to begin their own healing, but they all knew after a time they would need to step back, and Carl would need to step up. How, they wondered, would

Carl manage it all on his own? The day was coming that he would need to, and yet it seemed he had not yet given it a single thought, and who could blame him?

After the funeral and settling in at home, Carl studied his children. He scanned their tiny faces in an attempt to read what they were feeling. None of them had said much to that point, or if they had, he did not hear it. It could be because he was so confused and scared. But he knew he needed to be there for the children regardless. Phoebe had always been there for their children, and now that she was not, he had to, filling her role while keeping his.

Carl could see that Russell, his eldest son, was clearly not himself. His normal jovial ways were hidden behind a sad face that showed no signs of understanding. It was as if he were questioning the very same things Carl had questioned, without speaking a word. Russell just sat there, silent, dealing with his pain internally as best he could. Aletha occupied her time and her mind trying to keep things up as her mother had always done. She buried herself in keeping busy as if thinking that if she could still handle the daily chores as Phoebe had, she could escape the pain of missing her mother. All she wanted to do was cook and clean and take care of her younger siblings. Mary was not even four yet and needed almost constant attention. Aletha was strong and needed to stay busy. The household work helped her, as she became completely engrossed in being a caretaker to not have time to wonder what would come next.

Hannah observed from a short distance, trying to give the kids the space they needed, but at the same time, wanting them to know she was there for them. Her sister was such a tremendous mother, that Hannah wondered how the children could possibly get along without her. Carl was a good father, hardworking and dedicated for sure. He loved his children dearly, but five children alone while he worked almost around the clock would be a challenge to say the least. How would he be able to continue that schedule and take on so much more at home? Her greatest concern, however, was for her nieces and nephews, and so she decided to offer to keep them more if that would help. It was her hope that her help would allow Carl to get back to work and begin to gain some normalcy as quickly as possible. She knew that it made the most sense and that there would not be a lot of time for questioning all that had happened. Not now, anyway. Not now.

Carl had a lot of decisions to make. There was too much pain in the place he called home and had shared with his Phoebe. She was no longer with him, but rather in the ground buried beside their son. It felt like too much, and while he still continued to work for the same company he had been, he felt maybe it was time to move on once again. The pain of staying was getting to be too hard, and he could surely use some family a little closer. Not that Hannah and Walter weren't family. They were, but Carl needed to have his own family closer. Carl also thought of the children. Perhaps a change in scenery would allow them to leave at least some of their pain behind and begin the process of grieving their mother a little sooner. He knew he could never forget, but he also knew staying would create an intense tension within himself and that would do no good. Timing was complicated, so he would need to deal with all the changes as best he could, but he ultimately knew his direction needed to be adjusted. And soon.

In June of 1917, Carl decided to take a day off from work, and asked Hannah to watch the children so he could travel back to Alliance and see his mother for a short while. Russell begged his father to let him go along, and Carl agreed it would be nice to have him by his side. It was the first time Russell had smiled since the passing of his mother. The trip would be good for both father and son, Hannah felt. Russell as the oldest, needed to free himself from some of the burden of feeling as if he needed to be the strong one. His siblings looked up to him, and so he felt an overwhelming desire to act as if he had accepted his mother dying and had moved on because that is what people did. The truth was, though, he had not. Time had not allowed his pain to pass, though he pretended that it had. Carl knew better, and so he decided to take Russell along and told him to pack his fishing gear. They would spend some time on the river and catch fish.

On the way to Alliance, Russell and Carl talked more than they had in the preceding thirty days combined. It was as if some time together was exactly what his oldest boy needed, and Carl managed to provide it to him without really even knowing. Carl was happy to listen to his son talk about the other children, because truth be told, he had not really paid much attention to them. Life continued to move along, but not for Carl. He had become

PHOEBE'S HEART OF STONE

stuck on the day his wife passed and had failed to realize the children still moved forward and needed him to move forward with them.

At one point, Carl interrupted Russell and asked him how he would feel if they moved away from Beloit, and maybe back to where they had started. Alliance was home for Carl, and he needed home more than he could let on. Russell thought for a moment as he looked around, and then answered his father with an almost excitement. He agreed and asked if they would be close to their grand-mother if they moved. Russell grew enthusiastic at the idea as they did not get to see her often and enjoyed her very much. While talking with Russell, Carl warmed even more to the idea. A move to Alliance would allow all the children to feel a bit more at home once again, and if they were going to leave the place where they most remembered their time with their mother, it should be to a place that brought them family, comfort, and a feeling of peace.

Alliance. Carl had dreamt of moving back with his Phoebe and his children. Back to where he could feel more at home. A place he felt connections. Where his family had raised him, and to where he felt his best chance for owning a home would be. Since Phoebe had left, he had not given it a thought. Owning a home had been their dream, not just his, and he wondered if he could find that excitement once again without her. He was not certain, but he knew in that moment, listening to Russell with some joy in his voice, that his children needed him more than he could understand. He would need to continue to be the father he was, and although he could not be the mother Phoebe had been, adjustments still had to be made.

Carl was still devastated and a long way from understanding why once again, tragedy had struck him and his family, and yet he still remained hopeful. Phoebe had always been so positive, and he wanted to remember that. She would want him to move on, and in fact she would expect him to live his life as best he could. She loved him and she loved her children. To let that go away without enjoying all of it would be a sin in her mind. Carl knew his Phoebe better than anyone. She would want her kids to have the same chances they had promised to give them when she was alive, so Carl needed to find a way to ensure that the plans he made together with his wife, his Phoebe, still came to fruition.

Chapter 13

Back to the Beginning

* * *

One unexpected result of losing Phoebe was that Carl would not be asked to go to war. As badly needed as able-bodied troops were, the country would not call upon a man who was the sole-provider and caregiver of five children, risking them being left with no parent at all. At least it meant they would not be orphaned if something terrible happened to Carl while overseas fighting. So, that particular worry was taken from his mind, and he was able to focus on work, finding a new place to move his family into, and determining a way to get ahead as he and Phoebe had always hoped to. Time was not slowing down, and Carl began to feel a great deal of pressure with that realization.

In 1918, it was decided. Carl would pack up yet again, and move his family back to Alliance, Ohio, and start over. While he had no idea what starting over would mean for them, it was something he needed to do regardless. Hannah and Walter once again pitched in and helped where they could, watching the children or helping them load up. Whatever they could offer, they did. They were sad to see them go, but they also understood the importance of the move for Carl and the children. It was time.

Just as they were getting settled in, the Spanish Flu was beginning its sweep through the country. Carl wondered when it would all stop for him. What else could possibly go wrong in his life? Not only was he mourning great loss and trying to start over completely while being the sole provider and parent to five children, but he also had to worry about protecting himself and his children from yet another threat to their lives.

Measles had taken Keith. He feared the deadly new flu would take another of his children, but he would not have it. No. He insisted enough was enough. The children would follow the rules and stay as safe as they could. He would work but be more cautious of things. It was not for him, but for his children. There was no way was he going to lose another child. It brought back all the painful memories of Keith and how he saw his boy die before his own eyes. Carl knew he could not bear that pain again. He would never survive it.

Despite his fears, Carl was still happy to be back in Alliance, and so he made a firm effort to focus on all that was good in his life. He was back close to the river where he fished as a young man and had gone with his brother and sons. He thought it would be great to include Aletha on trips to the water and introduce her to the river. She had asked about those trips and Carl thought she would not have enjoyed them, but maybe he was wrong. Maybe she just needed to see what the boys were doing, and she could decide for herself. It was new for him, bringing a daughter along to do what boys did, but it just felt right. So, Carl told them one Saturday to pack a lunch, grab some old boots, and they would head out early to catch some fish.

Aletha was so excited to share the day with her father and brothers that she nearly forgot to grab shoes on the way out the door. The weather was warm, and the morning sun felt good against their faces. Each of them carried something and enjoyed the stroll up the road kicking rocks along the way. They smiled, and their smiles warmed Carl's heart. His children were all happy and he could not remember the last time he had seen them with joyful expressions. It had to have been before Phoebe had passed, he was sure.

Emil was keenly aware of everything on the way to the river. He even loved to imagine the fish under the glassy water and wondered what they did when they were not on a hook. How did they pass time? He was fascinated by every detail of each thing he saw. This fascination with his surroundings was not new to him, as he had done this for as long as he could remember.

As they approached the end of their morning walk, they could see through the trees the sunlight flickering off the top of the water. It was incredibly quiet, and they appeared to be the only ones out that morning. The silence was perfect to Carl. He enjoyed talking with other folks, but that day he preferred to just watch his children fishing without distraction. It wasn't even the fishing he cared to watch.

It was them. Smiling and laughing and splashing as kids are supposed to do. Only they had not been able to do much of that. With no mother around, they each had a set of new chores to handle, and it took so much up of their free time, there simply was not enough left to just be kids. Chores could wait though. Carl figured all that needed to be attended to at home could wait so that they could all focus on just having fun and being together. Work and chores would keep, and that was all right by him.

Carl thought perhaps a weekend fishing trip would need to become a regular event for them. There was surely a lesson to be learned. If they could ensure all their chores were done during the week, then they could return to the river each Saturday morning that Carl was not working, and fish. It would teach them discipline, patience, and to look forward to the rewards that came with hard work. That was how Carl wanted to have things be once again. To look forward to something, just as he had done before he lost Phoebe, and he felt the special day of fishing and laughter could be the beginning of that.

Sitting on a large gray rock hidden by some overgrown grass and weeds, Carl looked on as the boys showed Aletha what to do. He smiled softly to himself without them noticing. Kenneth was tossing rocks high into the air and watching as they splashed down into the river below. Russell was telling him to quit scaring the fish, without looking his way. Kenneth just kept doing what he was and laughing as the ducks went one way then another to avoid his attempts to scare them off.

Aletha intently studied each thing Russell pointed out to her. Carl watched her, knowing she was hit hard when her mother passed and that she had since tried desperately to remain so busy that she would not need to face what had happened. Watching his daughter learn to tie a fishing knot was the first time Carl had seen Aletha enjoy herself and take a break. He had wondered how she would handle the loss, but she seemed to be doing as well as anyone could expect. Carl looked on as her head tilted slightly while the boys showed her how to tie a knot and pointed out where she should cast her line in the river. Aletha looked and nodded but said nothing, just taking it all in. She was becoming a young woman and Carl had simply been so consumed with his own grief that he had not noticed. He was proud of her. She reminded him of Phoebe so much and he wondered how she had grown so much without him realizing.

Carl soaked in the moment and took note of the details. The trees swayed gently in the soft breeze that greeted them that morning and accompanied them throughout the day. A hint of sun reached Carl's hair and the warmth made him tip his head back as if he were bathing in the sunlight. He smiled, not opening his eyes at all. In his mind, he was imagining his Phoebe there with him. Watching over the kids as they played and fished and tossed rocks at unsuspecting dumb ducks. He had to wonder if she was watching, or if she was simply not aware. Carl had tried not to envision where she was, because it hurt him. But that day he was curious if she was looking down on him and smiling as he raised their children as she had hoped for. Maybe she was. Maybe not. But in that moment, he allowed himself to imagine she was. It was a perfectly simple day.

Mary had stayed back home with Carl's mother who had come over the night before to visit. Carl wanted to bring them all, but he was not sure she would appreciate fishing at her youthful age, so he would wait some before bringing her with them. Maybe next time he would, he thought to himself.

The ducks started to grow angry at Kenneth and would splash their wings as if they were about to take flight, but did not. Russell now was ready to toss his younger brother headfirst into the water because he was starting to scare anything close by, and they just wanted to fish. Emil smiled widely at it all. He was just sitting back studying the water and trying to figure out if he were a fish, where would be hide? That is where he would fish for certain. There were dark shades on the water because of the pine trees above, and he could see small air bubbles rising to the top. There, he told himself, is where he was going to fish.

And so, Carl watched his boys and Aletha fish that morning. They did not catch much, but that was not what it was about anyhow. What they did catch, Russell reminded them they had to give back to the river. They were small fish, and the river was not quite ready to let them go. If they returned them for now, she would ensure they grew into much larger fish and were ready for them when they came back another day. Kenneth wanted to pet each one first and give it a name. Emil teased him and encouraged Kenneth to give them a kiss, and he would. It was all so funny and perfect. A perfectly wonderful warm Saturday away from life for a short time, though somehow just long enough.

Chapter 14

An Aunt for the Season

* * *

The rest of the Summer went pretty much the same way. Carl would work long draining hours all day, and the kids would pick up around the house, have supper ready when he returned, and on Saturdays, they would most likely be found by the shores of the Mahoning River. Usually, they went to the same exact spot, but occasionally they would venture down the banks some, imagining they were on an adventure. Different spots meant different fishing. Sometimes they had great catches, while others were filled with more laughter and chatter and not a single bite.

Emil wondered if the fish were on to them and tried to come up with inventive ideas and changes in tactics. He was always thinking, trying to outsmart the fish. He knew though, that fish were not dumb creatures. Just because they would find themselves on the end of their lines at times, didn't mean when it came to other tasks, they were not proficient. He knew it was only a matter of time before they caught on to them, or the shiny hooks they left out to dangle.

Carl could often be found kicking the dirt with his old worn boots, moving a rock here or there. It was his way of remembering Phoebe and her passion for heart-shaped rocks. There in the dirt, he would sit at different angles to see if he could see what she once did. Sometimes he'd catch a glimpse of a heart, but on closer examination found he was mistaken. How on earth did she find those things anyhow? He looked all summer long on the banks, but his search had proven to be fruitless. He thought she had found them all. Or maybe she just had something special about her that drew her to the stones, or the stones to her.

Either way, sitting on the banks of the river with their children nearby and searching the ground for Phoebe's hearts, the way she once had, made him feel close to her. He knew he would always look for hearts wherever he went. It was his way of keeping her with him, much like the rock he still carried in his pocket. Her favorite and most treasured heart stayed with him daily. Wherever he went, so did it, and so the memory of Phoebe. She was never far from Carl's own heart.

Smiling more became something he strived to do. His boys were learning so much from him. His girls were making him so proud; how they were handling the loss and not allowing it to slow them down at all. His greatest fear was that they would languish because of losing their mother. To that point, and to their credit, they had done well not to.

Even Charlie, who had married once again and the year before had had two more sons named Jack and Billie, came around a little more to see that his brother was getting along okay. That was what big brothers did, Charlie would tell them. Besides, he loved fishing with the boys and Aletha. It reminded him of times gone and a father who had passed before the boys were ready to say goodbye.

Cora, who had married three years prior, had made a few trips to see the family too. She wanted to especially check on her niece Aletha. Cora knew that being a ten-year-old girl with so many added chores and responsibilities could be hard for anyone. She knew Aletha was putting on a strong front, but she still wanted to check in from time to time, just to be sure she was actually dealing with her emotions and missing her mother. If Cora could help, she certainly would. Lorenzo would often make the trip with her, and spend time sitting around at night with Carl, talking of his pottery days or asking about a recent fishing trip Carl had gone on. He loved to sit and listen to Carl talk under the stars until late into the night. Carl enjoyed the company as well. It reminded him that he still had a great purpose.

Lorenzo once even asked Carl if he could tag along for one of the fishing trips. Having no children of his own, Lorenzo thought he would get to see a different side of the world, one where children learned from their father, and one where they would fail but still find enjoyment in the lessons they learned in those failures. That fascinated Lorenzo. He had worked so hard and did not always take well to stumbling, but if the boys could fish all day and catch nothing, yet still head home laughing and skipping along the street, he wanted to be a part of that.

In July of 1918, Lorenzo, like many young men, was deployed. Cora decided to stay with Carl for a little to help him with the children and occupy her time while her husband was overseas fighting in the Army. Carl greatly appreciated the help and the kids, well, the children were excited to have a woman around again, even if it was only temporary. Cora was a good cook, and while Carl worked, she was able to handle things at home to ensure that when her brother returned, he had just a little less stress to deal with.

Mary Elizabeth was smiling like she had not in sometime. She was only four when her mother left, and having Cora around made it seem like the family was whole again. She did not understand that Cora was her aunt, and it did not matter to anyone. What was important was that the family was getting a little break from all they had to do in the wake of their loss.

As the summer gave way to the cooler weather of the fall, the children knew Cora would be heading back home. They begged the warmth to stay around, but she did not listen. The ducks were still around, but they acted differently and came less often. Carl still took them to the river, but they did not stay as long, as the days grew shorter and the temperatures lower. Everything was altering for the seasons, and the children could feel it. They pleaded with Cora to stay just a little while longer, but she just smiled and told them she would be back to see them just as soon as she could. Her own home needed tending to, and with the fall approaching, she would need to be there.

Carl knew that Cora going back home would set the

children back some, so he made sure to spend a little extra time with them, just sitting around and talking. He would tell the kids about the farm life and the animals they raised. The storm he had survived was always a favorite story of theirs, so he told that one often. Funny, he still thought about the small goat he did not manage to save, and sometimes during the story he would pause at that particular part and drift off for a second. It was if he were searching in his mind for a different ending, wondering if there was a way that he could have possibly done something to save that tiny animal.

Occasionally, Carl would tell stories about his Phoebe's family. They had handed down stories for generations, and the children wanted to learn more about where they had come from. Emil was especially interested in learning about the ones who had first arrived in the country. His fondness for adventure never ceased to amaze Carl. It was as if he could never hear enough about anything, and was always so intent on hearing every detail, not missing a single word spoken. He hung onto them as if he were writing his own story about the tales of his life and the lives of those around him.

As the fall began to creep in more and more, the leaves on the trees began to color and lose their hold, and life began to change as well. The trips to the Mahoning River were just about finished for the most part. Cora had promised to return by Christmas, but that was still a few months off. Charlie was busy raising his kids and his wife needed him home more than she had before. So, the children leaned on each other once again, and got back into a groove of dealing with what life had given to them. Though they missed Cora and longed for the freedom and joy summer had offered, they knew things needed to get done and they had grown accustomed to doing for themselves.

Aletha developed a routine for them all that really seemed to work. She made a list of chores that were to be completed each day, and she rotated them so that no one felt like they were getting more than their share. It was brilliant. If anyone complained, she pointed out that the next night another one of them would be handling that particular chore. It for the most part, eased any frustrations. They got to the point where they would trade tasks and Aletha thought if it kept them all happy, so be it. She was not looking to run the ship; she was just doing what she needed to take some burden off their father. She worried about Carl and felt his pain and all that he was missing and taking on.

Work was busy once again for Carl in the fall, and as the winter quickly approached, he began to work even longer days, and was back to seven days a week. As always, he did not mind work because it kept his mind off things that he had pushed away deep down, but the days were getting shorter, and the children were home alone so often. He, however, could not do much for the time being. Still though, he kept feeling like a break was coming and he would be able to slow things down some for them all. All he needed was to be patient and stay the course.

On top of this, the Spanish Flu continued to rip through

the country, and he had to be cautious not to bring anything back home with him. He still carried the guilt of Keith having contracted the measles, so he was acutely aware of what ramifications potential carelessness could bring. It was something he had to keep in mind while out working. Thankfully, he packed a lunch daily and was in his truck most of the time by himself. That at least made him feel he was doing all he could.

Chapter 15

A Poor Dog's Cry

* * *

Christmas 1918 would have been fifteen years for Carl and Phoebe. It was certainly a milestone he had anticipated reaching together, and he had truly believed by that point they would be in a much more comfortable position. Neither of those things were to be, unfortunately, and Carl decided to face the emotions of that day prior to its arrival. He wanted his children to enjoy Christmas and not have to think about more than children should. He did his best to provide for them, give them joy and make their childhood as normal as possible.

Carl was clearly not ready to move on. As others died off around him, he saw widows and widowers marrying quickly once again. Perhaps it was the fear of being alone, or the need to have someone to help with the children now that they were left with no mother or father. The devastating flu created voids in families all over, as had the war. Thankfully on November 11, 1918, it ended and the boys and girls who had given their time, were coming home. Now if they could get past the flu, hopefully the next century would be one of peace and calm.

Earlier in the year, Carl brought home a dog for the kids to keep them company, but also to serve as a protector. Russell had come up with a name for him: Rusty. He was not a young pup by any means, but he was not on his last leg either. The children had no idea where exactly Carl found the poor dog, but they loved him immediately. Each night they would take him outside for a walk, and on weekends when they weren't in school, the boys would run him all the way to the river and watch as he splashed on the banks or in the shallow puddles left over from the previous night's rainstorm.

Aletha would get upset when they would return and Rusty would track dirt and whatever else he had all over his paws, into the home she just spent all day cleaning. Kenneth would tell her to quit making Rusty sad, and then run him straight through the once clean house, laughing all the way. Carl tried to tell him to quit making his sister so dang upset, but it was funny still. Even Aletha would laugh after a while.

Even though the boys had plenty of other friends in town, they preferred to spend time with Rusty and each other. They did not fight like most brothers did, but rather had a unique bond between them that was probably due to a few factors at least. One, they had lost their mother, and to deal with that loss, they needed to rely on one another more than other children their age. Plus, Phoebe had ensured they developed a deep friendship and appreciation of each other as well. She had instilled in them the importance of family early in life, since she understood how badly she had needed her own family when she and Carl endured hardship after hardship. The boys, while very close, were also all very different. They actually complimented each other well. It was a fascinating dynamic.

Rusty was a strong dog and at times would dart quickly if he saw a squirrel or another dog, making it difficult to walk him. Emil was crafty, however, and worked out a contraption to use to walk Rusty allowing even Mary to manage him. He devised a latch that went around Mary's wrist and continued through to his. In the event Rusty attempted to dart off, Emil would be the backup to hold him in place. Mary felt she was walking him alone and that made her smile broadly from ear to ear, making her feel as strong and capable as her brothers on those days. Emil was proud, knowing he had been able to bring that joy to her, and even Carl was deeply impressed with his son.

Carl would sit and tell Charlie about all his boys, and when he came to Emil, he almost would be at a loss for words.

"That boy of mine, Emil? Shoot. Ain't nothing he can't do. Why I bet if I asked him to come up with a way to fly, he could do it."

Charlie would just smile, looking at his brother's pride for his kids. All of them. He would also talk about how Aletha had done this, or Russell did that. Carl would go around speaking of them all and Charlie would just sit and listen. He knew his brother needed to brag about his children and was happy to see him doing well. That was important to him, that he was moving on from something he had not known he could.

As Christmas 1918 passed, the weather took a turn for the worse. It grew bitter and ice covered anything it could dig its claws into. The steps to the house would cause Rusty so much trouble that the boys would need to pick him up to get him inside. Rusty didn't mind the cold, but he could not get a decent grip with his paws on the icy stairs.

The children looked to the new year with excitement for new changes and a hope for something great. Nothing would really be different from day to day, but there were plenty of weeks in the year to see change, and each one of them wondered how that change would look. None of them could've actually ever imagined what was to come though.

January brought snow again and the boys stayed outside as much as the cold would permit. Carl consistently reminded the boys that the Spanish Flu was still running amuck, so he just asked they not wander off with others for the time being. That suited them just fine though. The three got along splendidly most of the time, so they were perfectly ok with just throwing snow at one another and chasing Rusty through snow piles while falling over. Rusty always ran right to the boys as they fell, as if to make sure they were ok. Then he would run off again with his tongue hanging out, and the boys trailing not far behind.

As they ventured a little further each day, Rusty stayed by their side. The snow did not seem to bother him as he ran, mouth wide open with teeth the same color as the fresh fallen snow peeking out. The snow and cold certainly did not bother Russell, Emil, and Kenneth much either. They would stay outside all day if they could. Chores would be done quickly after school, or first thing in the morning on the weekends, and then they would dash outside and find something to get into.

"Boys will be boys," is what Carl always told Aletha. She would be home trying her darndest to keep the house in order, and of course keep an eye on Mary. The boys would simply not listen, and so Carl was sure to let Aletha know more often how well she was doing. He could see that the boys sometimes frustrated her, and she needed a little extra encouragement from him, which he was more than happy to give to her. After all, he was incredibly proud of all she had taken on, and appreciated how hard she worked to help him keep up the family home and take care of the boys and Mary.

During the winter when Carl was leaving for work, after lacing his boots up, he'd throw on a little extra clothing to combat the brutal cold on nights he had to walk home from work. He would walk by the river, down south about ten blocks, and then head east to where their home sat. It was a modest house, and though they were fairly comfortable, the walk allowed Carl time to think about their home, the kids, and what he wanted in the future for them all.

Saturday January 18th started off just like any other cold Saturday. Carl got up early, checked on the children, grabbed his clothing, and walked down the steps, passing the dog on his way out, and giving him a pat on top of his head. Rusty, as always, wagged his tail and placed his head back down to finish his slumber. Then Carl walked out the door, turned right, and headed to work as he did every day. He felt nothing special about the day. Just the beginning of an ordinary day and then back home later for supper.

He had reminded the boys the night before that if they ran to the river, even though he preferred they not, that they were not to go on the ice, despite the fact it looked frozen over. Carl assured them it was not, and told them that they were to just stay on the bank, or better yet just stay near home. Besides, he told them, it was cold, and they didn't want to be too far from home if another storm came through. The boys nodded showing they understood and went on their way back to playing.

And so, Carl went about his day. He made stops all throughout Alliance, and then went east into Salem. His day was just like the others, with a few different stops, but not much else.

As lunch came, Carl sat in his truck and opened his container to grab what he had packed. A drumstick, some carrots, and a slice of white bread. He looked out the window at the snow lightly falling and drifted off into a different time. He was back on the farm with his father, before the storm that fateful day. Before chasing animals to get them to a safer place. He was right at the start of the day enjoying the morning sun with no clue about what was to come, and without a care in the world other than to finish his next task. That day on the farm started off feeling not much different than that January 18th, nothing to concern himself with other than to finish his daily tasks and get back home.

His day wound down in the late afternoon as his truck pulled back into Standard Oil. Carl exited, went in the office, and then back out, to start his walk back towards home.

The seemingly normal, mundane walk took him by the icy Mahoning River, to where for some odd reason, Rusty was barking. While he had gotten away a few times and ran this far, Carl thought it odd with the cold, damp weather. He began to drag him back. Back towards home and inside before that poor dog froze himself stiff. The boys would need to explain why they had not been with him. Rusty would never leave their sides if the boys were outside with him. He wasn't that dog.

Chapter 16

"Pray". His only word to Aletha.

* * *

Aletha pulled back, and an unsettled feeling fell over her. She knew her father was worried and that was not good. Not at all. She tried desperately to remember if her brothers had said anything to her that would maybe give her a clue as to where they were headed. Had they told her they were taking Rusty? Was he with them when they left?

As time passed and the night went on with no word from the boys, Carl understood the gravity of the situation. At nearly 9 pm, he decided to go to the fire department not too far away, to inform them something was wrong. Hoping that maybe they could help.

"Aletha, get some rest dear. I'll be back. If the boys return, well, just have them sit tight."

As Carl opened the door, Rusty bolted out past him, escaping Carl's attempt to grab him back again, and off he went into the dark. Carl had no time to deal with a wayward dog though. He needed to get to the Fire Department and get help. The dog would come back when he was cold and ready to warm up and Aletha would be home to hear him barking. He would be all right.

Carl walked through the damp air and finally reached the brick walls of the fire department. He looked to the entrance, and took a deep breath in, wondering if he should have looked some more first, before coming to bother these fellas. But Carl was tired and cold, and the night air was unforgiving. So, he walked through the doors and began his plea.

Eventually the good men at the fire department convinced Carl to head back home. It was blistering cold, snowy, and he was doing no good. Running all different ways and trying to explain to the firemen who all the boys knew in the neighborhood and where they typically could be found. They figured that the boys had probably got stuck at a friend's house and would return the following morning, expecting a whipping for being out all night.

Aletha was half asleep downstairs waiting for her father to come through the door with the boys, and when he came in alone, she immediately cried. Aletha was not one to cry, and in fact, Carl could not recall having ever seen her cry, even when her mother died. She had been so strong, and if she did cry, he had not known. But on that night, with her brothers missing, she stood before him sobbing, and Carl wanted to tell her it was going to be ok, but he could not. He didn't know that himself. So, he pulled her in and held her, telling Aletha he would find them. Then he softly cried to her as well.

He sat up all night, as tired as he was, and each time he thought he heard a noise at the door, he jumped. And each time, it was the wind, or the cold snow scratching at the door as it fell from the dark sky.

Carl must have dozed off at some point as he was awoken by someone knocking on the door. Carl sprang to his feet, shook off his body that was still in a daze and looked over to see Aletha fast asleep. Not wanting to startle her, he walked quickly to the front door and pulled it open to see who was on the other side. As it opened, he could see daylight coming through and he quickly realized it was morning now. Shading his eyes with his left hand from the brightness, three figures came into focus. He realized in that moment he had gone the entire night without a word about the boys, and he grew more concerned not knowing what he would learn shortly, if anything.

"Mr. Bradway, may we come in?" one of the shorter men asked.

He was dressed in a dark coat that hugged his neck tightly. His eyes were facing down ever so slightly as he tried his best to be respectful but could not meet Carl's eyes even if he tried.

Most of the town knew about the Bradway family. The family had long-standing roots in Alliance, and despite moving from here to there, Carl was still well-known. It was, after all, a small town, and his family had deep ties. Good ties in fact. People respected the Bradways for their honesty and hard work. It was no different for Carl. They knew he worked hard and was a dedicated family man.

They also knew about Phoebe and how hard losing her had been on all of them.

The three men, wearing somber looks on their faces, removed their hats and stepped inside without another word. Each one glanced at Carl, but not one of them would meet his gaze. It made Carl uneasy as he braced himself for bad news.

Aletha was still asleep in the room, and had not heard the knock, nor the men enter the room. As they saw her, they asked Carl in a voice almost impossible to decipher, if they should go somewhere else.

Carl was unable to answer them, so he just slowly shook his head to tell the men no, this was where he needed to hear what they had discovered. He hedged toward a wall to give himself some type of brace just in case the news was unfavorable. In the past decade he had heard repeated news that would make a tough man drop without thought, and here he was, bracing once again as he studied the men and their demeanor.

The shorter man seemed to be the one in charge, and so the others just held their hats in their hands, stood a step behind him, and patiently waited for him to speak up about what they had found. They were cold for certain, but none of them appeared to notice the ice and snow that hung from their gloved hands and dripped onto Carl's hardwood floors, as the warm air from inside tried to chase the cold away.

They had found Rusty. He must've run clear to the river as soon as he left the house that night before. Late into the evening the men searched high and low for the boys, and as day broke, folks getting up in the morning hours began answering their doors as men scoured everywhere that they could think of to find a clue about the boys' whereabouts. Some had gone door to door to ask neighbors if they had seen them. A few searched vacant lots for a sign someone had been there recently.

Eventually, an alert neighbor said he heard a strange noise, almost as if a dog was in pain, coming from the banks of the Mahoning River, just a hop north from his home. He didn't think much of it, being that they had heard many animals from their home crying in the night. It was cold, and he suspected the dog was just complaining about the frigid weather and his owners would find him shortly as the sun rose. The day was to be a little warmer for a change and the sun was a welcomed sight in the sky.

As the search worked its way to where they heard the dog yelping out into the morning, they could see just beyond the trees, along the edge of the Mahoning, the animal barking feverishly at something not far from him. The men continued walking through the snow and brush, pushing away anything in front of them, so that they could get a better look at what the poor creature was crying for.

As the short man stared into Carl's chest, he realized that he needed to do him better. Carl deserved better. He steadied himself, took a deep breath in, let it out, and focused his eyes on Carl's. Then, he knew he could not delay longer and had to deliver the news that would break any father.

"Sir, them boys of yours were located," he paused as if

trying to figure out what he would say next. "I'm sorry sir. I truly am sorry."

That was all Carl heard. If the man said anything after that, he was completely unaware. Nor did he care in the moment. Carl knew what it meant, and although he knew no details, the details didn't matter. Details would just be wasted words from the lips of a stranger, and he was not ready for them. He wasn't ready for any of it, though no man or woman would be. There wasn't a mother or father alive who could ever be ready to face the terrible truth of that moment.

Aletha had started to toss some, and then she opened her eyes slightly. For a second, she too was not sure where she was and what had happened, but as soon as she understood, Aletha knew why the strange men were there and her brothers were not. She swung her head over to her father and saw him hunched down against the wall. She tried to read his face, but Carl was blank. There was nothing to read, or perhaps amid the blank stare was a sorrow she recognized all too well. Aletha got up and asked the men if they wanted coffee or something and they politely declined. Like Carl, she too, did not want to hear anything more. Why? It would just be more horrible news.

Moments later, Aletha heard Mary talking to herself from upstairs and excused herself, walking quickly up the stairs, looking back at her father one more time, before disappearing. As she tended to Mary, the men on the floor beneath her, could hear her praying. She prayed just as Carl had told her to the night before. She prayed with no fear of being heard and great hope of the same, and the men all looked at each other, and knew it was time to pray as well.

One of the other men, lanky and tall with a long face and nose, went over to where Carl sat slumped, and placed his hand on Carl's shoulder. He asked Carl if he could pray for him, and without an answer, began.

The other two men bowed their heads, and the moment the man was finished, they all said a collective,

"Amen."

The three men then walked back out the door they had moments ago come through, saddened, and pulled it closed behind them. Carl dropped the rest of the way down, now in a half-seated position, and was completely lost. What was he to do? He had honestly not heard more than "I'm sorry," from those men. While he knew his boys were gone, he did not know the how or why. Did it even matter, he wondered?

Aletha. Where was Aletha and Mary? Carl began to get up just as they descended the stairs and his panic about his girls subsided. Aletha had a slow pace as if she were checking out the situation before committing herself to going all the way down. Her father looked over at her, and with such a sad look, he just cried. He could not hold onto his strength any longer. Although he tried to be the strong one always, no matter what was going on around him, he was spent. There was no longer an ability to see through his anguish and continue on stoically as he had always tried to.

As they sat there, embracing, and shedding tears, Carl

remembered something the man had said. He would need to go identify his boys. There was a pause in his thinking as he struggled with the timing. Should he go now and get it over with, or should he wait and try to come to terms with this all first? It was not a decision he could take lightly. He had no idea of what his reaction would be, so he wanted to try and do right by this.

In the span of just ten years, Carl had seen a world full of hope and dreams go from wishful thinking to shattered chaos. His father passed. Then he buried his son, Keith. His father-in-law just after that, and then, his beloved best friend, his wife Phoebe. Again, without notice. Without a cold or rash or sign of sickness, his three boys, Russell Carl Bradway, Emil Chester Bradway, and Kenneth William Bradway, were gone. Carl knew that it would be too much for him to handle. In that moment, he did not know much of anything. But that one simple fact? That he knew.

Chapter 17

The River Held Tight

* * *

The news of the day could sometimes carry over from town to town, or county to county, and although at times the wording was different, the message was the same. Sometimes it was simple. Mr. Smith and Mrs. Smith traveled to Akron to visit with friends. Maybe three newspapers would print this to fill space. Sometimes it was a little more, like the time when the first death from the Spanish Flu had found its mark in Alliance. The counties would carry that news and more throughout the State.

Then, there was the story of three boys, who had gone to the semi-frozen Mahoning River. Intending to slide on the ice near the edge of the bank and laugh and play and fall as children often did. Escaping the daily rituals of life for a few moments and pretending to be someone else, while whistling past each other on the ice, feeling they were going a speed far greater than they were going.

Life was good in those moments, until it wasn't. Mother Nature could be moody and tricky to the comfortable and unsuspecting. She didn't worry about expectations; she just did as she pleased. And when the river wanted to give or take back, it would do just that. You could not control the outcome of what it was ready to dish out. You could though, have a say in how much you tempted the river.

As Carl and his father had done years ago on that farm, so had the boys. They took life into their own hands for different reasons, but both had tempted the elements. Both situations, though vastly different, produced the same dangers. If you test yourself against what Mother Nature had created at her will, you placed your life into her hands. That was a lesson Carl tried to instill into his children. Be respectful of everything around you, and know that at a moment's notice, things could change quickly and mercilessly.

And things had indeed changed. The story carried through more than just their town. It went beyond the surrounding counties and well beyond their small part of Ohio. It even went outside of the state itself.

Newspapers in neighboring Pennsylvania, West Virginia, and Indiana carried it. Further west, Nebraska and Wisconsin shared the tragedy of three young boys dying by the hand of the Mahoning. Santa Cruz, California, Brooklyn, New York, and even the District of Columbia told the story of the three lost boys finding their end through the ice of the Mahoning. Then, Ontario Canada carried the story as well.

An ordinary, cold, snowy day in the small town of Alliance, Ohio, had made national news for all the wrong reasons. The tragic lives lost, found by an innocent old barking dog who tried with all its might to get help and ultimately refused to depart the banks of the river and leave his boys behind.

The blurbs usually briefly described the search for the boys found by the barking dog, but one explained it in much greater, sadder detail.

"The three bodies were huddled together lending to the belief that one brother fell into the river and the other two boys leaped into the water to save him and all three were drowned."

As they lived together, they had died together.

It is not known if Russell may have, being the oldest of the three boys, broken through the ice first. Maybe Emil had decided incorrectly that the ice was stronger than it had really been. It is possible Kenneth, age 7, could have inadvertently walked a little too far out into the river to get a longer run at his slide. Whatever did happen that day, the brothers had tried desperately to save one another. None of them left his brothers side and saved himself. They made a quick decision to try with all their might, all their abilities, to ensure they left it all there, no matter what the cost. The cost being far greater than any of those three young boys could have imagined.

All three boys were laid to rest with their mother, and their brother, Keith, who was also Kenneth's twin. For Carl, nothing from that point forward would ever be the same. Making sense of it was ludicrous. He had made as much sense as he could of all that had happened to his family to that point. He would not do so again.

Once again, Carl questioned himself. His moves had seemingly caused so much tragedy, and he continued to blame himself deeply and hurtfully. All he ever wanted was to raise his family, continue with his strong faith, and to believe that one day the things they had yearned for in life would come to fruition. He did not ask for much in life, but what he did, he felt he had earned. It was all entirely gone now.

His brother Charlie had no more words. Nothing he could say to Carl could possibly take away the hurt or change how his brother felt. There would be no lessons of how he had handled losing a wife and child and found happiness once more. Losing a child, his wife, and then three more children was unfathomable. How could one man ever possibly begin to heal from that? Charlie had no good answers and did not try to provide any. He just had nothing to offer and felt horrible for his younger brother.

Aletha was crushed as well. She knew that this meant so much more than what she could see from her eyes. She could feel that everything in life was about to be permanently different from this point on, and sadly, she knew not what that all meant. At only ten years old, she had already grown so quickly. And now? She would need to do so even more. How she was going to help her father through this one, she did not know. How would she help explain to Mary that all the brothers she adored were gone forever? Could she explain it well enough that Mary, this young five-year-old child, would begin to grasp the fact her family was simply vanishing year after year?

Carl became quiet, more so than he had after Phoebe passed. He just closed himself off and those who knew him best were deeply concerned for what would come next. They feared he would harm himself. They feared he would fall into such a crazy mindset that he would need to be committed. No one would blame him.

At first, he did nothing. Nothing. He did not go to work. He could not wake up early enough if he wanted to. Nor did he eat. For the first few weeks, he would not touch food. It was as if he was willing his body to cease without being the one behind it.

Charlie was approached by his mother and asked to check in on Carl with greater frequency. She was terribly concerned for her son and the two little granddaughters he was still in charge of. Although people were coming each day to pitch in and check on things, no one knew for sure what was going on in Carl's mind, and she begged Charlie to see if he could connect with his younger brother and perhaps gain some understanding. Charlie, of course agreed, but wanted to tread lightly. This was new territory, and he did not want to close Carl off to him. He felt he would have one shot to get through to him.

What Charlie did, required such patience and under-standing. He would find an excuse to stop over and instead of talking with his brother, he observed from a distance. Aletha would hug Uncle Charlie tightly on these visits and ask what he was doing there. Charlie, for his part, would explain that he was just in the area checking on some job that was coming up. It was usually something about a carpenter job that he would use as an excuse. Charlie was excellent with his hands and so it would seem logical. Aletha was smart, and probably wanted to believe his excuses, but she more than likely knew what he was there trying to do.

Sadly, Carl never even noticed his brother there. He had trouble coming out of his room. If he was downstairs, it was rare. Eventually Charlie ran out of ideas and excuses, and tried to be a little more forceful.

"Carl, now I know you are dealing with something God-awful. I know it. I'm not here to pretend you need to just get on with things and let this here go, but dammit, Carl. You are scaring us all. Your girls need you. You have two wonderful daughters that are so lost right now Carl. Please. Let us, brother. Let us help."

But Carl would not budge. Week after week and he simply could not get it together. Had he known what he needed to do to get through it, to make the pain bearable, he would have. Feeling the way he did was certainly not part of the plan for him, but what were his options? He could not just put all the hurt away for another time. He had done that with the other deaths and honestly, probably never dealt with those either. He was just not capable of dealing with it and feared he may never be able to. Carl knew he would need to make some tough decisions, ones he never dreamed of making.

One night, Carl walked out of his room and proceeded down the stairs. Rusty was still with him in the house and was startled but happy by the sight of his owner. Carl sat in the same room the men had come to give him the tragic news. He looked at the front door and, in his head, went right back to that terrible night. He heard the door knock but knew there was no one there. He saw himself get up and walk over to the door in a sleepy daze. As he imagined the door opening, he watched himself block the sunlight that was creeping in quickly to meet him. There he was, face-to-face with the men who had come to find him and bring him news. Only this time, they had come to tell him they found his boys alive.

This was the ending he had prayed for, and he just wanted to imagine that this was the ending he had gotten. Even if just for a moment. The men would smile as they saw Carl and usher the boys through the door one by one into their father's waiting arms.

Kenneth would smile wildly as he ran by the shorter man, the one clearly in charge, and embrace his father, telling him how sorry he was and how much he had missed him.

Then Emil would shyly look towards his father and without a word, using just his eyes, apologize.

The tall man with the long face and nose would exclaim "Mr. Bradway, we got one more here for ya!" and Russell would push his way through and tell his father he loved him and "Please don't be upset with my brothers, I am the one who wanted to stay out and had gotten us lost, Pa."

That was the ending Carl had prayed for, no, begged for. He begged for this type of closure that evening, and it was just not what the universe had planned for him. In that brief moment, in his own imagination, it was. So, Carl smiled, feeling as if the dream was real and everything was ok once again. But it wasn't, and that horrible truth would set in soon enough. Just as soon as he was finished with his vision though. He was not ready to let that go. Not yet.

As time went by and the healing Carl yearned for did not come, he knew he needed to meet with some people. First, he paid a visit to Hannah, Phoebe's "bookend sister" who lived back in Beloit.

When she opened the door, she was surprised to see Carl standing there, his weight down considerably. His face was rough and drained looking, and it seemed as if he had not shaven in a month. His hands shook as he raised them to greet Walter, Hannah's husband. Walter could tell instantly that the man before him needed help desperately, and knew without question, that whatever Carl asked for, Walter and Hannah were going to do for him. They had to. He was not the same man he was just a few months back, and they wanted to help in any way they could. They loved Carl for certain and respected him for all he had been suffered and pulled through.

After that visit, Carl headed south, to meet with his sister, Cora, and her husband, Lorenzo, or Duke, as he was better known. Cora had at least known Carl was coming, so she was preparing herself for what her big brother wanted to tell her. She and Duke had simply no idea, but they knew he was coming for a reason, and with him finally being able to leave the house, it was serious.

They talked into the night, and Carl slept there before heading back home. As he left, Cora told him it was all going to be ok, somehow, someway. He just had to keep the faith as hard as that seemed. Duke asked him if there was anything else they could do for him, and Carl just nodded in his direction, signaling a no. They had already agreed to all he needed.

Carl gave all his strength to offer a smile on his way out, but they knew it was forced. He had nothing to smile about in his mind, so anything he did to start one was not going to be genuine. There was no meaning behind it, other than to show his appreciation.

With that he was gone, and on his way back home to Alliance. Home.

Chapter 18

I Must Go Now

* * *

The 1920's were full of change for both the country and for the remaining Bradways. As the war ended, the economy boomed. Many people owned cars, radios, and telephones for the first time. The "Roaring 20's" signaled the end to a lot of people's worries, and a new beginning for families that had once struggled to get ahead.

It should have been the same for Carl, but it was not. Carl was gone. He had left the town of Alliance and moved on, but to where, no one really knew.

Aletha had been shipped down to live with Aunt Cora and Uncle Duke. Mary, she was sent off to Aunt Hannah's place in Beloit, to live with her and Uncle Walter. They were told nothing of where Carl had gone, and honestly neither Aunt knew. He had simply told them that he needed to get away and hoped they would take in his daughters, so that he could go off and collect himself. Of course, both of them agreed knowing that had they not, Carl would surely have a nervous breakdown, and that would be good for no one.

Carl's place in Alliance was packed up and cleaned out. Most things were sold off, and the girls took what little they had with them to their new temporary homes. He explained that even though it was to be temporary, it was just easier for Carl to sell off what he could, hold the money, and later simply repurchase items with what he had made from the sale. That was the plan he had put before everyone, and no one questioned it.

The sisters of Phoebe and Carl had the daunting task of promising the children that all would be all right. Their father just needed to get some things organized and in order, and he could not do so and care for them as well as he wanted. Oh, it was not their fault, they assured them, he just needed time and space to figure himself out and decide what was next for them all. Alliance was simply no longer a place that brought him peace, but rather one that haunted him at every turn. It made complete sense when they thought about, it that he needed to get away, but there was a lingering fear quietly shared by all: what if Carl did not return? No one wanted to dare think of it, but the fear remained below the surface, just deep enough to be pushed aside, so that for a time they could simply take things as they came.

Mary, who saw her sixth birthday come and go in new surroundings, was becoming more aware of all the things going on. Her father was not there. Her sister was living somewhere south of where she was living, and she missed her terribly. Thankfully, Hannah and Walter had Mary's grandmother living there, and that was a treat for her. She was able to feel somewhat at home, because she had been around her grandmother before and felt quite comfortable with her. So, she began to settle in sooner than most expected. While those first few months she still asked about her father and when he was coming back for them, she was not terribly lost. Plus, Hannah had made sure to stay in close touch with Cora, so that when it was good for them both, they would plan to get the sisters together.

At first, the sporadic visits with the girls were difficult. The sisters hated being away from one and other. Aletha and Mary shared an almost mother-daughter bond. After all, Aletha had, for the years after they lost their mother, overseen raising Mary when their father was off working those late days. The separation had them both feeling a great void. It was particularly hard on Aletha, as she had grown accustomed to caring for her brothers and Mary, and was so used to being around children, that living with Cora and Duke was almost unmanageable. Everyone held out hope that things would change with time though, and Aletha would hopefully fall into being a child once more. They were going through so many adjustments; nothing was meant to be easy this early on.

They waited it out. Aletha was painfully lonely and tried to arrange to see Mary more and more. It was not possible and when she asked if she too could move in with Hannah and Walter, she was told it just was not something that could be done at the time. That crushed poor Aletha, and she went quiet, just as her father had done after the boys died. She went completely quiet.

Both Cora and Duke tried to reason with her and told her to give it more time, and things would be okay. They would figure out a way for Aletha to see her sister more, and in fact they had heard that the new neighbors moving in had some children of their own. She could make friends and perhaps begin to feel at home. Only the neighbors that moved in, had no children either. She was utterly alone, and began to sink fast into a state of depression no child should feel, and one both Aletha and those around her feared she may not recover from, not after all the loss she had already had. She needed something vastly different than what Cora and Duke could offer her, but no one quite knew what that was.

It is not clear why she did not go back and live with other relatives at the time. Perhaps she did not want to, or maybe she felt a little out of place. Charlie, as Aletha's uncle, wished he could help, but he had begun to grow his family once again, and money was tight. Adding another mouth to feed in his house would be far too difficult. He did, however, visit the girls as often as time allowed.

Aletha would need to decide between staying with her Aunt Cora with no siblings around, or she would need to look elsewhere for a place to lay her head at night. At just ten years of age.

Charlie grew curious about Carl's whereabouts and asked both Cora and Hannah if they knew which way Carl headed. Had he mentioned anything, anything at all to them about his intentions?

Cora just said that she was told he needed to breathe.

He was heading to find himself and hopefully learn to deal with everything he had not been able to, but that he had no direction in mind. She was concerned but did not push her brother for fear he would snap and grow angry with her. Besides, any man in his position would need a break, surely it would just be a small one. She assured Charlie of that. He would be back for his two girls, find a new place to live, and start over. Maybe find another wife and do what Charlie had done. At least, she wanted to believe that anyway.

On one of Charlie's visits, he looked on as Aletha walked around in the back yard, mindlessly gazing out to the old tall oak trees, and playing with a blade of grass between her fingers. Charlie wanted to go say hi to her, but he thought better of it. It was not that he did not want to tell her how much he loved her. He just could not look her in the eyes and tell her that she could not come back with him. It just was not possible. Not yet. That hurt Charlie, so he just watched from a distance, and put his head down before turning and walking away.

When he stopped to see Hannah, Mary immediately ran to give Uncle Charlie the biggest hug she could find. She was such a loving little child, innocent to all that was going on around her. For her, she did not see it as Uncle Charlie not wanting her. She did not even see it as her father not wanting her. It was almost a sleepover for her. Time did not matter to her as much as it did to Aletha. They were in vastly different spaces in their heads, and Mary was all right with it.

"So, Mary dear, tell your Uncle Charlie all about your day! What have you done?"

Mary would tell him everything. She would talk about chasing a grasshopper in the house that had hopped through the door when she left it open by accident. When her grandmother came down and asked what she was doing, Mary tried to hide it by placing it in her cloche hat that Hannah had picked out for her. The snug hat was moving slightly along the floor as the grasshopper tried frantically to leave, and her grandmother would just roll her eyes and carry on with whatever she was doing. It was cute, Charlie thought to himself. Plus, Mary seemed truly at home and comfortable in Hannah's home.

Walter could tell Charlie was bothered and on one such visit asked Charlie if he could talk with him outside for a moment. When the two men walked out, Walter placed his arm around Charlies shoulders and said,

"Charlie. I know you have a lot going on. We sure do appreciate you stopping on out here and seeing Mary. It's important to that there girl," he began.

"Just as important as it is for you to see Aletha. They need family, and so we promised Carl we would watch over Mary. We wish we could do more, but gosh, for now this is what we can do. I know you question yourself, but you have a big family, and well, we get it. No one is judging you."

Charlie needed to hear that. Inside he was hurting because he wanted to offer more help, but he knew he simply could not do so without causing potential damage. He just was fighting with himself over it all and Walter had seen it.

But he was seeing the girls when he could and felt at least

good about that fact. Had he not, then he would have to question just who he was as a man. That much he knew.

As the men talked, the conversation quickly went to Carl. Where was he? Had he mentioned to anyone something in the way of a plan? Maybe he had dropped off a handwritten note to someone with an update. Had anyone heard from him?

No one. He simply up and vanished and not a trace of him was to be found anywhere. If he had gone back to Alliance, people surely would have noticed. If he were in Beloit, they would have seen him for sure. It was a small town. Maybe he ran back to the Salem area and would get his old job back and settle down there. Wherever he was, he was out of sight from the family. Not a peep was heard of him.

They all agreed that the moment anyone heard from Carl, they would let the others know, no matter what. Even if they could not disclose the whereabouts because Carl had made them promise, they would at least mention that he was all right, and working on things. This was something they would all need to know. Understanding the enormity of the pain that man was carrying around was almost too much for them to think about, and they could not imagine how he was dealing with it all.

Rumors began to surface that someone had seen a man resembling Carl walking through town. A woman had sworn that he was seen out by the Mahoning River one spring morning when she was out on a stroll with her children. "He was sitting by the edge where them boys of his drowned and tossing rocks into the water," she recalled.

No one knew for sure if any of the sightings were actually Carl. What they did know, was that none of them had seen or heard from him. That much, they knew.

Chapter 19

She Must Move On

* * *

As the spring came, and the colder weather gave way to budding flowers and gentle, warm rainstorms, things with the girls began to change with the season.

Aletha was not doing well and had decided that she needed to be closer to her sister, Mary. She discussed her concerns with family, and they began to send out word that anyone who was able to take her in for a short time, or anyone needing an extra set of hands to help around the house, should inquire. She was good with household chores and great with younger children.

Luckily, the search did not take long. Her family was deeply seeded in the Mahoning County area, and this was a blessing for her. There was a relative named Amy Stanley that lived just eight miles west from where Mary was staying with Hannah and Uncle Walter. Amy was married to a farmer by the name of Homer. Amy knew the family very well. In fact, her cousin happened to be Phoebe, and she remembered as children getting together at large family reunions and playing with her dear sweet cousin. She was thrilled to have one of Phoebe's children stay with them.

It was a touchy situation though. Everyone knew about the deaths in the family, however, not everyone agreed with Carl leaving. There were questions and concerns for the children's well-being. How would Aletha be now, almost a year out from when she had last seen her father? Amy and Homer had a ten-year-old boy and surely did not want to put their son or Aletha in an uncomfortable situation.

They prayed on their decision, but in the end, they decided family was family, and they would do what they could for the young child who was Amy's cousin's daughter, and who had lost her entire world in a very short span of time.

Aletha packed her things, and thanked Aunt Cora and Uncle Duke shyly, as if she were concerned that she could be seen as abandoning them. Cora, though, smiled at her niece and kissed her on top of her head, telling her she was so proud of Aletha for all she was doing, and knew for certain her decision would send her on a grand adventure that she would find fascinating. Her understanding and encouragement at least made Aletha's departure a little easier. She had been feeling ill about her decision because she was not sure what she really needed. Clearly, having her father home was not going to happen, and she was homesick for her sister and friends and needed them closer.

The trip to Garfield, Mahoning County Ohio was a time for Aletha to reflect. Cora had packed her some biscuits she had made the night before just for the occasion. Aletha ate them while she searched deep within herself for peace and answers to all her concerns. Why had her mother gone so soon, before Aletha had really had the chance to know and learn from her? How could all four of her brothers be gone? How was it possible her father was unable to care for them? And while she was smart enough to understand how terrible the losses they all suffered were on him, she still wondered, when would he be back? She knew in her heart that he would return one day, but she had thought, that would have happened much sooner. She dreamed about that reunion with her father. She could see it just as Carl had seen the vision of his boys running through the front door on that wintery morning. The story that never happened the way he had hoped it would.

When she arrived at the farm that would be her home for a bit, Aletha felt somehow relieved. Here she was once again moving around, but she was used to that part. What put her at ease was that just a short distance away was her little sister, Mary. The knowledge that she would be able to see her often graced her soul with a comfort she had lost in the previous year.

When she walked into the home of Amy and Homer, there waiting in the main house was her sister, Mary, who smiled and ran right up to give her sister a big hug. Aletha was so happy, that she began to cry tears of joy that poured down the side of her face. Everyone in the room watched as the sisters embraced like they had not seen each other in years. They imagined the reunion was exactly what they both needed.

Time went on and each of them settled in. Aletha enjoyed doing housework with Amy, and she also enjoyed watching Homer working on the farm. Sometimes he would call her over to where he was and talk with her about whatever he was working on. Homer could see the child in his care who had grown far too fast, just needed someone to pay more attention to her, and he tried to be that person for her and share little lessons wherever he could.

For the most part Homer kept his opinion of Carl to himself. He wanted to give the man the benefit of the doubt. Going through what he had, Homer was not sure he would do any different. It was hard for someone to live in another man's shoes. Until you experienced what he had, you would only be guessing. Homer was not the type of man to judge others, and he refused to start with Carl. He was not happy that Aletha and Mary had to be without a father, but he also was aware that without some time to gain an understanding, Carl would be no good to himself, or his girls.

Homer was in the field working his crop with Aletha one early afternoon, when she asked him a question.

"Uncle Homer, would it be possible to go and visit with my mother and brothers?"

The request caught Homer off guard for a moment. He assumed she meant to where they were buried, but he was not equipped to answer those questions. He never looked up from his task, but responded that if Amy were ok with it, he would be happy to take her. He changed the subject quickly and asked her to help with the task at hand.

Later that evening when they were washing up for supper,

Homer pulled Amy aside and whispered to her what their talk had been out in the field earlier. Amy just smiled and assured him she knew they were gone, and probably just needed to visit to feel them. She would speak with Aletha, but agreed, it was not a terrible idea. She kissed Homer on the cheek and told him she would be just fine.

After Supper was finished and Amy and Aletha were cleaning up, Amy asked Aletha if she wanted to go Saturday to see her mom and brothers. She figured why go around the subject. Just ask her directly and let her lead with any questions she may have.

Aletha was pleased and responded with assurance that she would very much like to go see her family. It had been sometime since she had been there to visit, and she just felt the need to be in the same place as her brothers and mother once again. Just being there somehow made her feel somewhat at peace with it all, and it gave her time to slow things down some. Everything was moving so darn fast around her, and she hoped a visit with her lost family would change that for a short while.

When Saturday came, they loaded up and left early that morning. The ride was not long at all, but Aletha had gotten up early and was anxious. Homer and Amy were farmers, so getting up before the sun was second nature to them. They had let Aletha sleep until she was good and ready.

When they arrived, their worry for how the visit would go increased. Amy took Aletha's hand in hers and walked her toward where her family had been laid to rest. Homer got out slowly on purpose, to give them the time they needed to get a head start. He knew Amy was going to have a brief talk with Aletha to assure she was ok and ready to face the emotions that were sure to emerge. It was important to them both that Aletha not feel overwhelmed, and they wanted her to know that if she needed them, they were right there, even if Homer was 10 steps behind.

When they reached the spot, Aletha knelt and gently placed on the ground a bundle of flowers Amy had picked that morning back at the farm. Amy smiled to herself as she watched the small child before her carefully place the flowers, so particularly, as if to ensure they faced just the right way to look their best and to capture the fullest of the sun's rays. Then Aletha saw something that immediately made her think that either her father had been there, or something even stranger was going on.

At the foot of the sign marking the burials, sat a 2-inch by 2-inch gray-tone stone, placed in a perfect way to revel the shape of a heart. There was no mistaking that fact. Someone had certainly intended for that rock to have purpose. Aletha knew that straight away.

"Aunt Amy, look, Pa was here!" she said with excitement she had not shown since before her brothers had passed. "It has to be him."

Amy knelt down as well, and Homer, who had heard the excitement in Aletha's voice, walked over and looked over her shoulder.

"How do you know dear? What is that exactly?", Amy responded confused, but trying to show some type of excitement in response.

Homer was thoroughly confused. Neither he nor his wife had known anything about the heart-shaped stones Phoebe had collected over the years. It was something more intimate for her family, not something she advertised to others around her.

"Father saved the heart-shaped rocks Mother had found and kept them in an old worn tin. I remember seeing them and asking him about them once. He told me she collected these anytime she was out and was able to find them," Aletha started. "He never had much luck finding them on his own and swore he would always look when he could. Only, I don't remember seeing this particular one and I would because it was larger than most she had."

Even she was confused now, poor Aletha. She hoped this was not a cruel trick, and prayed it meant that her father had been close by or had stopped by to see Phoebe and his sons recently. Maybe the fact that he had, would help him realize he had two more children who desperately wanted and needed him back. In her desire for it to be true, Aletha grew confident that her father had been there. He wanted them to find the heart stone, so they would know he still cared. She was sure of it.

She placed the heart rock back down exactly where she had found it, facing the same way it had been placed before she picked it up with her hands, and stood back from it all. Amy stood beside her, and wondered to herself, if it had indeed been Carl who had stopped by one day and left the rock there for his Phoebe? Had he done it to show his children he still cared greatly for them, but needed more time?

It had her thinking more about the entire situation and how bad she felt for the girls, but now she also began to feel sorry for Carl. How had he survived all he had been through?

They left that day wondering how close they had been to seeing Carl, and they knew that Aletha had found a new sense of hope inside her that had faded some over the previous year. Maybe it was good for them all that they had paid a visit. Only time would tell if her new sense of hope would change Aletha for the positive, or if it would simply be another letdown for her that she could not afford.

Chapter 20

A Broken Heart

* * *

Little Mary Elizabeth had settled in quite nicely in her new residence, and although she was only nearly seven, had handled all the change surprisingly well. She particularly enjoyed spending time with her maternal grandmother who lived with them, but then on August 22nd, 1920, Mary, her grandmother, passed. The young girls had to, once again, deal with the loss of a beloved family member after having already lost so much.

Mary died just three years after her daughter Phoebe, but she had lived a full 75 years, and a death at that age was considered to be natural for most.

It seemed Mary and Aletha were numb to death by that point, and while they would surely miss their grandmother, they knew very well that people died and if you were lucky enough to live into your old season, you had lived well. So, they would not allow the loss of their grandmother to pain them as the others had. They were growing stronger and harder like a callus by all the loss, and this was both a blessing and a curse.

Whenever Aletha would come to visit, or ol' Uncle Walter and Aunt Hannah would head over to see the Stanley's, Mary would grow full of tremendous excitement. Those were the days she would be reunited with her "mediate" family as she called it. Sadly, for her, only Aletha was left, until her father returned. If he ever did, that is.

Mary Elizabeth never really talked much about Phoebe, mainly because she had been so young when she died, but she remembered the brothers a lot. She would often ask when she was going to be able to see them next, and Hannah would always try to help her understand the truth and the finality of their absence. Hannah saw little need to sugarcoat things of that nature. Why have them confused, was her mindset on such things.

As the year 1920 faded away, people who knew the girls had to wonder, when things would change for them. They had lived through a decade of immeasurable loss, a war, and a pandemic. They were survivors for certain, the people around them would say. True survivors for having endured such terrible odds that were clearly against them, and yet they remained, living day-to-day, and perhaps beginning to thrive and heal.

As fate would have it though, the girls were not quite done with loss. January 1921 saw another tragic death. It was beginning to look as if nothing was going to slow the constant death down, and people had to wonder if this family was maybe simply cursed.

On January 21, 1921, Walter Toole passed away from

pneumonia after coming down with an illness while he was working in the Mahoning County coal mines. Walter had taken on extra work in the mines several years prior, and usually worked them when the weather was not conducive to crop growing. It had taken his life and Hannah was left alone to raise Mary on her own. Of course, Hannah had decided before her husband had passed, that she would help Mary. She intended to follow through and would raise Mary for certain until her father returned.

Wherever Carl was, people wondered if he was somehow keeping watch on the children. Did he know that Walter passed? Had he heard about Mary, Phoebe's mother passing just a short time before that? No one knew for sure. All they knew was that he had yet to return and was missing much as time ticked by and the children continued to grow.

The Spring of 1921 had allowed for some much-needed rest, as the families figured out how to keep their households and the children in their charge as happy as possible, or at least moving with forward momentum. Hannah found herself solely in charge of the farm and without Walter handling the daily tasks she had some difficult decisions to make. Among her first thoughts when he passed was that she would need to adjust a great deal to balance all her own work with all that Walter had been responsible for. There was much to consider, and she knew swift decision making was in order.

Mary wanted to help as best she could. There was a part of her that worried she would be sent off once again to live with another family. She did not know that when

Hannah decided on something, she stuck by her decision. Her word was strong, and she made no buts about that. Besides, Mary was no trouble. She was a happy child who was simply lost in a world of ruin and Hannah just wanted to help her find her way through it all.

There was a hope that Mary and Aletha would be reunited at some point, but with Walter's death, Hannah was simply not able to take in another mouth to feed and body to clothe. She wanted to reunite the sisters so badly and had even talked with the Stanley's about the possibility, but she just could not find a way to make it work.

Though she longed for her sister, Aletha still enjoyed the Stanley's hospitality. She had never settled into feeling at home with them, though. Something was off, and she needed to find more for herself. She was uncertain what she was looking for, however. Perhaps she needed to be in a larger family setting. Maybe she needed to just get away from the area for a while to find herself without the distraction of tragedy that loomed over her head and that lingered in the minds of those around her. It wasn't as if local people had not heard of all the death that cursed her family. Even those new to the area learned of it quickly, and if they did not ask questions directly, she certainly felt their eyes, heard their hushed whispers, and saw the pity they cast her way with every glance. Aletha did not like all that attention on her and Mary, and began to feel it would be impossible to settle into a semblance of normal unless she could escape all the history.

As 1921 wound down, it became clear that Carl would

not be returning that Christmas, or possibly at all. No one had heard a word. No one. People began to wonder if something terrible had happened to ol' Carl. Maybe he had been injured. Maybe something worse. The curse, as some would call it, of the Bradway clan. People were beginning to think there just may be something to that.

Aletha had met up with some children that had stopped with their family to do business with Homer, and on several occasions, she wondered if this family may need some help with the children that they were raising. She felt this could be an opportunity for her to move out of the area for a little, and to put herself around a larger group of kids that she had desperately missed. It was becoming clear that her idea of having Carl and Mary all under one roof was just not possible. She had been praying hard for this, but so far, there was no sign of this coming to fruition.

So, in early 1922, Aletha once again packed her belongings, and decided to move to Holmes, Ohio, which was southwest of Alliance, and just south of a town called Shreve, Ohio. The move was far enough, that it took her out of the mindset she had been in, and with all the work the couple who owned the farm needed help with, she would be busy most of her days.

As she settled in, Aletha had to wonder if she had made the right decision or not. While feeling good that she was away from all those places that had haunted her for several years, she was also away from Mary and because of the distance, would not be able to visit as often as she had once done.

The distance from Mary further caused Aletha anxiety, but she swore she would stick the move out if she could. Moving again, after all, would not make much sense, and regardless, there was nowhere else for her to go.

When she left, she begged Amy Stanley to let her father Carl know exactly where she was, if he decided to come back for his girls. The thought of missing her father's homecoming hurt her something awful, so she had written a note of her whereabouts in case Amy would forget. Amy assured young Aletha, she would not forget and would certainly save the note for him. How could she not? She tucked it away in an old tin and placed it under her bed for safe keeping.

Mary was heartbroken to have her older sister move so far away, but Hannah told her it was for the better. Aletha needed to find herself and when she did, she would return to the area and be with Mary. After seeing all her family die and knowing her pa Carl had moved to God-knows-where, this felt more like a lie to Mary than a promise.

Hannah had tried to talk Aletha into moving closer to where she and Mary were, but Hannah also knew she may be leaving that farm behind after Walter died. She simply could not take care of all that was needed daily. The workload was massive and time consuming, and with all the other things Hannah had to attend to, she quickly realized it was time for them to move on as well.

Soon after Aletha left the area, Hannah and young Mary packed up, left the farm behind, and moved on back to the outskirts of Alliance. Hannah needed to simplify her life and that of Mary's and it just seemed to make the most sense. There were factory jobs in and around Alliance, and Hannah could find work quickly. It made sense for them to make this move, and Mary by that point trusted Hannah and went along with whatever Hannah decided. She was more afraid to be alone than she was to move again and again.

That was how they would spend the next several years. Aletha moving from family to family, trying desperately to fit in and to forget some of her born identity, and Mary living alone with Hannah, building a bond with each other that would not be broken. It was all they could do to survive what they had seen, been through, and done.

Chapter 21

And One Returned

* * *

As more time went on, talk of where Carl had gone, or rumors of having spotted him in town or by the Mahoning River, dissolved. If he had returned, no one took notice any longer. He had been gone for several years and the children had somehow settled into a new way of life. If Carl knew, perhaps he did not want to disturb them.

All through the roaring 20's people were laughing, dancing, and eating like never before. The country was thriving and the girls, well, they had realized that this was their new way of living.

Aletha continued to work harder and harder, never really sitting still. It was thought that she simply did not want to deal with her past, and instead had an innate desire to push on and build a different life for herself. Hard work was how she intended to do this.

Occasionally she would venture out to see her mother and brothers. Each time she did, she would grab Mary and they would walk the soft, green grass together, over to where their family was buried. Mary would always run ahead to check first to see if a new heart rock had been placed there recently. In the beginning, she would find one here and there, but eventually even those stopped showing up.

When Aletha saw Mary's disappointment each time she did not discover a heart rock on the graves of their family, she would gently remind her sister that all was not lost. Their father had been through so much and probably could not bear the thought of losing anyone else. Aletha had grown from a confused child, into a more understanding young woman. She could not blame her father for leaving, even if she hated it for the deep hole it left deep within her. She felt he did what he had to so that he could survive. Knowing he had blame in his heart for having moved them so often and seeing his wife and sons go with each new move, had surely pained him to no end.

Mary would take a little longer to come to that realization, but she would. It was just a matter of time.

By 1925, Aletha had decided to move back to the Alliance area. She missed Mary tremendously, and at the ripe age of 17, she felt she had done enough healing while being away. It was time to get back to where her only family was and try to enjoy life as she had always wanted.

Mary was excited to have her back, too. She would turn 12 later in the year and was working herself, in a factory close by, when she was not attending school. The days were long but having her sister close by to see when they were both free, meant a great deal to her.

Hannah was happy to see the sisters playing and laughing with one another as they had years before. It was as if they had started life once again, and there seeing them together gave her the hope that possibly all would be okay. Those two young children had turned into beautiful young ladies and had seen so much in their short lives, even for the times. Somehow though, they had refused to allow their pain and tragedy to define them. It made them stronger people, and they had a different respect and appreciation for life than a lot of folks did.

Being close to the Mahoning River certainly brought mixed emotions for the sisters, but they decided that to move on from what had once happened years ago, they needed to learn to accept her waters for what she had claimed, and what she brought to the town. Needing to separate the two made little sense anymore. It had happened and was done. So, that river simply became that. A river that ran through Alliance, along Ohio, and into Western Pennsylvania, spilling its water along the way for all to use as they saw fit and as was best needed at the time.

In Alliance, Aletha had found work keeping house for a family that knew her father many years prior. While they certainly wanted to ask Aletha about all that happened, they respected the situation enough not to. If she had a desire to bring it up, they would tell her about what they knew of Carl and leave the tragedies over the years that her family experienced, out of the discussions.

Eventually she did bring it up.

One evening after putting away the supper dishes,

placing them back in the cupboard, clearing the tables and sweeping the hardwood flooring, she sat down and asked Mr. and Mrs. Lobb about her father. She wanted to know what he was like as a younger man, and what his upbringing had been like.

Mr. Lobb had known him from the time young Carl worked the farm with his father. While Mr. Lobb was a little older than her father, he still had known his mannerisms and quirks.

"Your pa was something special, missy. He ever tell you about that time on the farm where he and his own pa, your grand-dad, fought with that terrible storm?"

Aletha had heard the story more than once, she recalled, but it had been some time since she imagined what her father had gone through on that warm day.

Mr. Lobb placed his pipe in his mouth, took a draw from its base, and sat back in his chair. He paused for a moment, with a slight grin forming on his face.

"Yes. I remember that storm. Came through our family farm as well. We were all inside, so we had little to concern ourselves with. Folks that were outside at the time had a lot to worry about. That there storm came out of the clear blue, and whipped chaos all over Alliance."

He took another long draw, allowing the smoke to billow around his face, almost hiding it completely for a moment.

Aletha watched him closely as he was clearly back in another time, looking out at the incoming storm of long ago, that came from seemingly nowhere. She could see in his eyes that he was looking right into her fury. He was watching the storm grow and Mr. Lobb, for the moment, looked almost nervous.

"Well, anyway, lots of folks lost their livestock. Roofs were torn clear off barns and stables. A few people lost their lives, but your pa? He refused to allow that to happen. If I recall right, they lost some animals as well. You know your pa hurt his leg something bad that day, right? Both of them, now that I think about it. He ever show you his scar?"

Aletha had to think for a moment, but she could not recall in that instance. Maybe she had seen him favor one leg over the other, but it was not noticeable enough for her to question it. To the best of her knowledge, it had healed enough that she honestly did not know.

She tried to envision her father coming home from work that evening when the boys went missing. How he walked in as he had any other day. The look of exhaustion upon his narrow face, and how his soft gray eyes gave way to his desire to simply rest, before he knew that the boys were no longer there. Before he had frantically searched late into the evening through the cold wet snow, until he had nowhere left to search. Before their lives changed forever. She could see his face in her memory's eye, the same face of intense exhaustion he had worn almost every evening she could recall because he worked so tirelessly for their family.

As Mr. Lobb fussed with his tobacco in the pouch next to him, he leaned forward to light his pipe once again. He then continued telling young Aletha what he remembered.

"Missy, I will tell you this. Your pa's father was scared that day. He thought he had lost his boy. I remember him telling me that if he had lost Carl that God-awful day, he wouldn't know what to do. Them two were close. Real close."

He paused, not knowing how far to go with his story, or where he should stop. Aletha was bright, but he did not know if she was catching what he was throwing at her. In his mind, he was trying to explain to her that her father left because he could not handle losing not one son, but four. Not to mention his beloved Phoebe. His story, while exactly how he had remembered it, was in a way, an explanation for what maybe she could not understand well enough now.

But Aletha knew. She knew that Mr. Lobb was trying to let her know in his own way, that her father was not abandoning her and her sister for no reason at all. He was doing what he had to, so that he could survive. As much as she did not want to think about that all, she had to. She was a 17-year-old young woman, trying to navigate the world as best she could, almost entirely alone, and she had often forgotten to understand the why. She felt for sure it was unfair, but she also felt that maybe Mr. Lobb had a point. Maybe it was even more unfair to expect her pa to stay.

Aletha thanked Mr. Lobb and removed herself from his presence. She had chores to do, and wanted to give herself a bit of time to take in all that he had shared. It was a lot for a little story, and she knew there was greater meaning hiding deep within what happened all those years prior when Carl was just a boy not much younger than she. He had grown up working hard and had his fair share of questions and confusion. Just as she had now.

When Mr. Lobb fell asleep in the chair he was perched in, his pipe slid out of his fingers and onto his lap. Heading out to sweep the porch, Aletha retrieved the pipe and laid it on a table next to where he rested. She covered his legs with a small woolen blanket and turned to walk out of the room.

Mrs. Lobb had been watching, and when Aletha turned, she smiled at Aletha. She had thought Aletha viewed her position with the family as just a job, but quickly realized that Aletha took it much more seriously. She wanted to be a good house guest, and the Lobbs' enjoyed her presence. She also wanted to be close to her sister, and back to where their lives had changed, or perhaps where they had started. It was important, and in the moment, she watched as young Aletha gently removed her husband's pipe and covered him with a blanket. Mrs. Lobb recognized that much.

When Aletha met her eyes, she placed her head low and smiled slightly. Her mind had gone back to when she took care of her father after her mother had passed, how she worried about him all the time and tried her best to fill the far too big shoes her mother had left. All she ever wanted was for their family to be whole, even if it was less than that. Why they could not continue to be what they had once been was hard for such a young mind to grasp, but as she grew, so did her understanding.

Thankfully though, she was beginning to heal, and Mary, who was close by and stopped over often, was also beginning her healing. The two sisters began to build a different relationship with each other. No longer were they simply sisters. They were friends, surviving together through anything that came their way.

Aletha had felt horrible for leaving the area while young Mary stayed behind, but Mary never made her older sister feel anything but good. She would tell Aletha all the time that she was merely glad she had her back now. That *now* was all that mattered for her. And she was right. All that mattered, was now.

Chapter 22

To Forgive a River

* * *

On Saturdays, when both girls were free, they made it a plan to walk along the banks of the Mahoning River, just as their mother had once done, and as their father had tried to do. Not since the boys died, did Carl get to the river, as far as they could tell. There hadn't even been reports of anyone spotting him there for some time.

It would be hard to walk the riverbanks, but they figured they could do so and allow it to bond them together, and to heal them some from the pain of the past. Also, they could do this at their own pace. There was certainly no rush or agenda.

On the way to the river for the first such walk, each of them tried to hide any doubts they had, and wondered when they reached the river, what they would feel. As it turned out, once they arrived, they did not even know how they felt initially. Everything inside of them just paused.

Mary walked towards the river's edge first, enjoying walking and wondering if each footstep was in the very same place as the ones her mother had taken. Had she looked out to the rippling waters and had the sight been the same that her mother had viewed? Maybe a tree had grown some more, or a large branch felled by a storm. But still, she had more than likely cast her gaze onto the same row of green trees and tangled grass, perhaps even sat searching for hearts on the very same rocks Mary now sat on.

At first, the sisters did not talk much on their visits to the water. Instead, they would feel the area out and find comfort where they could. For Mary, this task proved easier. She was young when the events that placed her where she was, had happened. She knew about the stories, and had remembered her brothers, but the memories of her mother had faded almost entirely. She could see her mother occasionally, but over time, those thoughts disappeared and made it increasingly hard to envision her round face with those glasses she wore.

Aletha though, remembered them all clearly. For her, there were more memories and emotions she wrestled with. Looking out at the waters running free, was for her, full of wonder of what her brothers had seen. She tried to imagine how the ice had looked to the boys. She contemplated every scenario her subconscious brought to the forefront of her mind. Had Russell misjudged the thickness, or Emil miscalculated what was in front of him? Perhaps it was Kenneth who playfully ran out onto that frozen river, to find it was not so frozen. Whatever transpired, when she gazed out over the river, she felt that pain was sitting right there in front of her. She knew that the brothers loved each other, and no doubt fought with all they had to come out of the river's grasp and return home. It seemed the river had simply set its eyes on them and her strength and will were stronger than theirs.

Mary started to look around for the rocks that she imagined her mother most likely had once held in her very hands. She picked them up, allowed them to gracefully tumble into her cupped hands, and then, gently laid them back down on the ground for someone else to touch. Each time, she peered at the shapes, and colors, and felt their weight and textures, it was soothing for her. The rocks brought a little bit of her mother to a place that was otherwise a painful reminder of loss, and feeling her mother's presence was exciting and peaceful to young Mary.

The girls visited the river several weeks in a row, and with each trip it became easier to be there. It wasn't too long before that they began to drop their guard and talk more freely. At times, it was just about the weather, or what Mr. and Mrs. Lobb had done the week prior. Mary would tell Aletha about Hannah and her nightly readings she enjoyed, or supper and what they planned to make on Sunday.

They would dip their toes into the water's edge, and playfully splash water towards each other. They discovered laughter was the perfect medicine for such a time, and they did that well. Eventually the girls both quietly came to the realization that things were going to be okay somehow.

Mary asked Aletha if she thought about getting married someday. She had heard Hannah tell someone that in time, Aletha would make a wonderful wife, and have children of her own. Mary wondered where that would leave her. Would she not see Aletha as she was now? Would they never live under the same roof again? She had dreamed of the day she would live with Aletha again and had wanted nothing more than that one thing since her pa had left; except possibly for her pa to return and for all of them to call the same house home once more.

Aletha was at that age and had been thinking about boys more and thought that she would make a good wife one day, but she was not ready for that all just yet. But the thought did cross her mind as she grew older. Would she be like her mother and have several children? Or would she instead raise a small, more intimate family? Maybe she would not have children at all, like her Aunt Cora. Truth be told, she did not know what the future held for her regarding a family, but she would find out when she was meant to know and there wasn't much point in ruminating on it.

She couldn't help but wonder though, if the universe intended her to have a family, how she would handle the loss of a child should that happen. Would the curse her family seemed to carry continue, and would she be able to survive the unspeakable loss of a child? Her father had faced that loss and more, and she naturally wondered what she would do if faced with the same.

At any rate, the river was calm most days, and the birds chirped high above in the pine trees that covered the banks like a blanket. There would be no ice, only sun and soft sounds coming from and through the trees. That was the river on her good days, a calming, nurturing scene for anyone who cared to take a break from their day and appreciate what she had to offer. On Saturdays, when the weather was clear, the calm, nurturing Mahoning was exactly what the sisters had needed.

Mary started to ask more questions about what had transpired with their brothers and father. She had been asleep when Carl came home from work the evening the boys were gone. She was too young to understand then, but her curiosity piqued over the years as she grew older. The boys' deaths were a well-remembered part of local history, so being back in Alliance, it was still a much talked-about affair by those who knew them personally. So naturally she would hear bits and pieces of rumor about in town. However, she felt that Aletha would be able to provide the most reliable information about that night. After all, Aletha had been there, and being that she was old enough, her recollection was likely better.

When she asked, Aletha had to think back. She was unsure what she should tell Mary and didn't know how much she wanted to relive that night herself. Of that night, or the next morning for that matter. That morning was painful, and she had tucked much of it away deep, but she was aware that eventually her sister would want to know about that horrible weekend in January of 1919. The time had come. She thought maybe she could give her some details about what she remembered, without bringing it all back to the surface entirely. She also hoped to explain why their father had left abruptly and possibly make some sense of it for Mary.

As she began to tell the story of that night, she drifted off into a daze of sorts, having returned herself back to that home and time. She once again watched her father come in, hungry and ready to see his family on the fateful evening, and it was as though he were right in front of her. She remembered his exact look when he realized the boys were not home, and then how his expression turned when he shifted from anger to fear. The emotions changing along his face as the color ran away from his cheeks. It was not something she had thought about in so long, but she was feeling it all once again as she faced the memories to help fill in the blanks for her sister.

Mary listened intently, trying to find some understanding as to why it had all happened. She did not realize at the time that understanding and the peace that would accompany it, was something she would never truly find. The why was gone with those brothers of theirs. The moment they slid through the surface of the ice to the rushing water below, and their lives were given to the river, whatever the reason was, no longer mattered. It was done.

She remembered their dog, Rusty. As Aletha talked about Rusty at the river, running frantically back to where their father had pulled him from the cold, wet night, she could see his coarse fur, and his long tail wagging in the air all about him. Rusty. He had been a pleasant dog, always playful and chasing the boys wherever they ran. But he was real. She had not imagined him, just had forgotten about him, until Aletha helped her retrieve the memory of him.

When Aletha got to the part where the men knocked

on the door, she made the decision to shorten her version. She did not want Mary to feel any worse about what their father had endured that night, and so she simply said that the men had asked their father to walk outside so they could talk to him and tell him about the boys. She did not have the heart to give her the details of how he was no longer the same man he had been just a day before, how his lust for life drained away in one single night and that she had witnessed that with her own eyes.

It did not go much further. Neither wanted to talk about or remember the river and its unrest more than necessary that night. Once the story was complete, Mary looked out over the river, and asked Aletha if they could go back. Without a word, Aletha put her shoes back on, picked one pebble up that was sitting by the bank, and tossed it underhand into the river. It was not an angry toss, but it was one that said, "you took something dearly from me, and I forgive you now." She needed to find that forgiveness and somehow sharing the story on that day, with her sister, allowed her to find it. The ripples in the water gone, and the surface calm once more, she turned away and reached out for Mary's hand. Mary smiled, took her hand, and they walked away, back towards where they had started their Saturday morning. It was a good day for both girls. One that was absolutely needed.

Chapter 23

A Sister Beckwith

* * *

Lyman Beckwith lived in a town just north of Alliance, and in 1928, he met Aletha while visiting a neighbor of the Lobb's. Shortly after smiling her way that very first time, he asked Aletha to marry him. She was immediately hooked.

Aletha was turning 20 in July of that year and finally, she would have a place to call her very own. Lyman rented a place up North in Akron City and so Aletha told the Lobb's that she was thankful for the years she had spent with them, but would be off onto the next stage in life. They, of course, would miss her hard work ethic and gentle nature, but understood and wished her well, telling her she was always welcome and to not be a stranger.

The hardest part for Aletha was that she had to tell Mary that she was once again leaving Alliance and would be further from her. It broke her heart to know she would not be by her side as she had been for the past few years. There was nothing to be done about it, however. Lyman wasn't willing to move to Alliance, so she just had to promise Mary that she could visit as frequently as she liked.

At first, Mary was confused. She couldn't understand why Aletha didn't simply take her along with them. If Aletha was going to finally have a place of her own, it seemed simple enough to have Mary move in with them.

Aletha realized her sister had a point, and told her younger sister she would indeed propose the idea to Lyman and see what she could come up with. She simply had not even thought of the idea, but it did make a lot of sense. She could think of no reason her sister couldn't move with them and she grew hopeful that her husband-to-be would approve of the plan. She and her sister could finally both be under one roof again in no time.

She approached Lyman excitedly, before the marriage, which was not going to be a ceremony at all but a simple quiet service. Aletha sat down with Lyman and asked him what he thought about them bringing Mary up north with them until she was old enough to find a place of her own, or a family to work for that may take her in, much like Aletha had done time and time again.

Lyman was the type of man to not hold his opinions. His deep dark hair and thick brows, high cheek bones and warm skin tones, along with his strawberry red curled lips, made him stand out. So naturally, he was used to being the center of attention. He brought everyone into his view with his words and how he was able to command a room. It was probably what first drew Aletha to him when he first smiled her way. He also had a way of assuring everyone around him that things would be well, no matter what they asked for or received from him.

When she had set out her proposal in front of him, Lyman sat back and smiled warmly at his soon-to-be wife.

"Dearest Aletha. It's a fine idea for sure. I love your heart and your wonderful intentions most certainly. Just as soon as we get back home and settled in, I will sit and think on this. Just give me time. I have a few affairs to get in order, and we still need to marry first. Then, let us revisit this discussion. Does that sound fair?"

Aletha was strong-willed for sure, and generally could read between the lines, but she also was extremely captivated by this man of hers. When he spoke, she listened with all her heart, sometimes to a fault. It sounded okay, but it was not an answer to her question. She needed to tell Mary something, so she asked Lyman to promise her.

"Yes, of course I promise my love. With all my heart, I promise we will revisit this just as soon as I can. Now, let us start to figure out a date for our wedding, shall we?"

Mary was simply told that Lyman had agreed for the most part, but that he wanted time to see how they managed the house and where they would have room for her. Aletha told her he promised to talk with her just as soon as he could, and then she smiled at Mary.

If Mary had a doubt, she had not shown it to her older sister. She smiled and just nodded in acceptance. Hannah was an amazing person in Mary's life and Mary knew that telling Hannah she was moving away would break her heart, so a little more time saved everyone trouble. Besides, she was easy and hardworking, so why wouldn't Lyman agree to having her move in? It would give him more time to spend with his new bride. She just decided to be patient and wait for the okay from her sister.

In November of 1928, Aletha and Lyman wed. It was a simple ceremony with no guests, other than Mary and Hannah. Lyman felt that making this a big to-do was just silly. They loved each other and everyone would know because they had married. Wasn't that enough for his bride?

Aletha was not one to really worry about those things, so she agreed. But she did insist on her sister and Aunt being there. She needed them to be a part of her special day, a day that she had long imagined. It made Hannah proud to be a part of this, but she, for whatever reasons, did not really trust Lyman. She saw something about him that made her heart heavy every time he spoke. Not wanting to tell Aletha, she decided to keep that to herself. For if she were wrong, it could cause Aletha to resent her or have caution where she did not need it. Lyman knew, though. He could tell Hannah saw something in him. So, he tried to overdo it with her by laying it on thick.

"Hannah, you look lovely today. Thank you so much for attending our day. Aletha and I would not have it any other way. In fact, I begged Aletha to remember to have you and Mary as such an important part of our day. It means the world to me to have you here. Truly," Then he smiled with that wide grin of his, as if he had something on his mind that only he knew.

Hannah kept her guard up around Lyman always. She

was no fool, and she could see right through his dashing words and bright smile. She could tell there was something going on with this man, and Hannah wanted to remind him that she was watching him. But Hannah just smiled back and thanked him. This was Aletha's day, and she nor Lyman would ruin that for her niece.

They moved immediately to Akron to the small single home that Lyman had secured just prior, and settled in. Aletha had thoughts of a family and wondered if their children would be like her brothers and sister were. She tried to make the home as warm and inviting as she could for her husband, so that when he returned home from his job, he would smile at her and know he had found the perfect wife.

She often thought back to how her father loved her mother, and how he would look at her whenever he was around her. She thought about her mother, Phoebe, and how she worked tirelessly with the children and home to give Carl nothing to worry about when his long days were finished. That is what Aletha wanted, to be just as her father and mother were in their marriage. She knew that they had a bond that was unbreakable until death, sadly.

Lyman worked as an appliance salesman and often-times would come home late at night, after Aletha had gone to sleep. She did not have to work because Lyman promised her he would sell enough appliances to take care of them both. He much preferred that she be a housewife. No wife of his was going to have to work, not as long as he had breath in his lungs. That is what he told her. She did not know how she felt about this at first, because she had worked for so many years as a maid and farm hand, and was used to being busy all the time. In a new town with new people around and the faster pace of Akron, she felt as if her head was spinning. She could only clean so much and cook so many meals.

After a few months, Aletha sat down at the supper table with her husband and asked him again about Mary. She now reminded him that she knew so few people, and with him gone so many of the days and nights, Mary would be no trouble at all and in fact, she would keep Aletha great company when she was feeling lonely.

Lyman just smiled and said,

"I understand Aletha. I do. Please don't think I do not. It's a swell idea, but I just need a little more time. You see, I heard a rumor that I am in the running for a promotion that would take us from this little home of ours, and into a grand place. I should know more in a few weeks. Can you give me a few more weeks to get some things lined up?"

Again, she wanted to be supportive of her husband as she promised she would. He worked long hours and while he was bringing home a check, it wasn't as if they were living comfortably just yet. He told her traveling was expensive and by the end of the year, his company would settle with him on all that. Lyman always knew how to make her feel at ease, as if everything was going to be perfect. She just needed to stay patient, was all he asked.

But she was starting to feel as if she would not convince him that having her sister there was a great idea. That was hurting her heart and she was feeling anxious over this.

She wrote Mary daily and promised her she was trying to persuade her husband, but at the same time, not make it appear hopeless. It was a delicate balance for Aletha, and she was feeling desperate for something that would bring this all together. She always ended the letters to Mary the same:

"Stay positive, dearest Mary, for your sister is always and will always be here for you. Until we are under one roof again, take care of Hannah. I will write to you soon."

The late nights for Lyman grew even later, and his trips were no longer overnight. Some had lasted two or even three days at a time. Aletha told him that if he was going to head out for days at a time, she was going to ask Mary to visit for a few days. It was only fair, she told him. Lyman finally agreed to this, but only for the time he would be away. He wanted to have his young wife all to himself when he returned. So, she agreed and mailed a letter to her sister right away.

On the trips Mary took to see her sister, Hannah would remind her to keep a close eye on Aletha. She told her to make sure she was doing well and was genuinely happy.

"Aunt Hannah, but how will I tell? Will it be obvious?" Mary asked.

"You know your sister better than anyone, Mary. You will surely be able to tell. Then, you tell Aunt Hannah, okay dear?"

Mary smiled and dropped her head some, both understanding but nervous she would miss something and disappoint Hannah. But she would do her best and make sure

166

she reported back to Hannah anything she discovered.

So off she went, ready to spend some much-needed time with her sister, and to be back under one roof, if only for a short while. But it was all she cared for at that time.

Chapter 24

A Shocking Truth

* * *

In the fall of 1929, everything changed for the country. That October 25th, the day after the largest sell-off of shares in United States history, the stock market crashed. Forever known as Black Friday, the country embraced for the worse to come, but they would not be ready at all. Entire savings were wiped clean out. People lost seemingly secure jobs, and families were forced from their very homes. It was a terrible time for just about everyone, and Lyman and Aletha were no exception.

As Lyman struggled with sales during the start of the depression, he began to grow temperamental and spend nights away even when he was not working. Aletha felt she needed to speak to him with more force to get him to understand just how she was feeling, but he simply would not listen.

While he tried to remain his calm self, assuring her and everyone around him that things were good, he was losing his ability to do so. Now, he was saying no, more than explaining why. When Aletha offered to get a job, he no longer prefaced it with, "No wife of mine shall ever need to work". He simply told her that was not possible, and he would have no more talk of it. At times, he would not listen to his wife at all, and walk out the front door storming off down the street to wherever he was heading.

Aletha decided to write a letter to Aunt Hannah and asked her for advice. Maybe she would be able to assure Aletha all was going to be okay. After all, Hannah had been the most calming voice Aletha and Mary had up until now, and with her so far away, Aletha stopped asking for such advice until she needed it without a doubt. This was such a time.

Hannah did not respond, but instead showed up on Aletha's doorstep a short time later. With a wide smile, and comforting touch, she assured Aletha she was there to help her in any way she could. Behind Hannah was Mary, who too, was there to give her sister some much-needed support and love. This made Aletha instantly happy, and she knew, they would help figure this all out. Family was there for such situations as this, and she knew she could count on them.

When Lyman did not return that evening, Hannah grew angry. She held her tongue, but one could see in her face what she really wanted to say. Aletha tried to make an excuse that Tuesdays were long days for him and perhaps he was held up at the train station, but she could tell Aunt Hannah was not buying into this. Not even a little.

Hannah knew no one in town, but quickly made conversation with neighbors and passersby. Her intent was to find out what anyone knew of Lyman, and she was able to gather a little here and there. Hannah was smart, but she also had an ability to pull folks into conversations and quickly make them feel warm enough that they were willing to speak freely. She never explained why she was questioning what people knew, but instead figured out ways to draw it from them, almost without asking. It was ingenious how she operated.

Aletha did not want her to pry, partially for fear Lyman would find out and place blame on her for inviting Hannah and Mary in the first place, but really, she had not. All she did was to write her dear old aunt and ask for help, but she knew he would blame her, nonetheless. She was not going to win either way, but a part of Aletha was abundantly proud that her aunt was so inquisitive. She had no ability to do what Hannah did, and so she just allowed what was going on to continue naturally.

When Hannah finally found a nugget of information that seemed important, she sat Aletha down and told her they needed to talk.

Lyman had a girlfriend prior to Aletha named Mae and promised Mae the world. They were engaged for short time when Mae had caught Lyman with another woman. He begged her for forgiveness and promised her it was a one-time affair that would not be repeated ever. So, Mae reluctantly agreed to forgive Lyman, and once again they had planned to marry.

When he left one day for work, he told Mae that he would be away on business for a few days, but not to worry. He would be back just as soon as he made his quota. This happened to be the same week he had met Aletha in Alliance. He told Aletha on that trip he was simply visiting friends because he was taking a small break from sales. He had sold so many units that his company gave him paid time off. She had not questioned this, and why would she? She hardly knew this man.

Now, Hannah was wondering if his frequent trips overnight were for work, or for pleasure. So, she decided to go down to where he worked and inquire there. Aletha was absolutely against this, maybe for fear of what he would say, or for fear of what they would possibly learn. Either way, she did not want Hannah to do so. But Hannah had her mind set.

The following morning, she woke early, had some farm fresh eggs and ham, and walked out the door and down the road. On her way she told herself to just remain calm and to be a lady about this. But when she arrived at the front door where men were laughing and patting each other on the back hoping for a turnaround in sales, she pushed her way through forcefully. The men stopped and just stared as this woman held her head high with intent and seemed to know precisely what she was after.

As she approached a room to the right of the main hall, she knocked with almost a fury on the door, and saw a short balding man sitting on a desk, speaking with another man who seemed startled.

"Yes, can I help you lady?" The short man asked confused.

"You most certainly can. I'm looking for the man in charge of Lyman Beckwith. Are you that man?" She replied, once again, with force behind her voice.

The other man looked back at what seemed to be the one in charge of this entire operation and told him he would just wait outside.

"I am that man, yes. What can I do for you miss?"

Hannah pulled herself together so that she did not come across like some crazy woman. She wanted to be fair to this man because she did not even know him. But she also wanted him to answer her questions and honestly. It would require her to settle her emotions down some, and to just ask as politely, but sternly as she could.

"My name is Hannah Toole, and my niece is married to Lyman Beckwith. He works here and seems to be traveling an awful lot, leaving my poor niece alone in a place where she hardly knows a soul. I'm just wondering, why does this man need to travel so much?"

When she first said it, she wondered if maybe she was asking something she ought to. Was she really questioning this man's work about how much he had to work, during a time where men were losing their shirts, and jumping off bridges? She suddenly felt foolish for this, but she had asked it, so she had to act as if she was still very much interested.

"Miss, it's Hannah, you said, correct?"

"I did." She replied.

"Miss Hannah, please. Sit. Here," as he pulled out a chair that the other man who left the room had one foot on just moments ago and wiped it with his hand.

"Thank you, Mr.?" She asked, remembering she had not asked his name.

"Mr. Willow ma'am." The man replied.

As Hannah sat, Mr. Willow walked over to the opposite side of his desk, pulled out his own chair, and began to sit. He had a look on his face like he was about to give her news she was not hoping for. His eyes dropped to his desk, and he took a deep breath in, and then began to speak.

"Miss Hannah, Miss Toole, sorry." He started. It was clear this man was from the south, as he had that southern twang with a warmth in his voice, and a certain respect about him she had not seen so often in this area.

"Lyman hasn't worked her for some time. We let him go prior to the market crash, ma'am. He was coming in late, taking days off all the time, claiming he had a sickly wife at home he was helping, but the guys around here knew better. I knew better, ma'am. I'm sorry. I wish I had something better for you. I really do."

Hannah looked stone-shocked. You could have hit her with a maple board and probably not shocked her as much. How could a man do this to his young, loving wife, whom he was married to less than a year? It made no sense at all, and they had not even started a proper family yet. So, it was not as if she was busy with a child and neglecting her husband's needs. She was a good wife and loved him, or so she said anyway. Maybe young love was blind, and she just had wanted to feel a part of something like she had once done when she was with her mother and father and siblings, all under one roof several years back now.

She rose up, still holding her head high and looked over to where Mr. Willow was now also rising to his feet. Her eyes met his and she could see he was sincerely sorry for what she would now need to tell her young niece. He knew this was wrong and he could do nothing to change it.

"Well, thank you for your time, Mr. Willow. I appreciate your honestly. It's much appreciated," as she reached her hand out to shake his, and he returned the gesture, still with his eyes lowered.

Hannah walked out of the office, past the man waiting to finish his meeting with Mr. Willow, and out the front door that she arrived.

As she hit the street, she looked left and then right, forgetting which way she had come to this place. For a moment she wanted to cry. But Hannah was not going to allow this to do what she knew it was going to do to poor Aletha.

Aletha had been such a strong young woman who had to deal with many things no child should ever need to, and now once again she would face something that she would need to pull herself out of. At what point would this stop for Aletha? Had she not experienced enough in her life? Where was her father when she needed him once again? So much ran through Hannah's mind, but she honestly had no answers for this all. Not now anyway.

Chapter 25

Revisiting the Past

* * *

In 1930, Aletha found work at a residence not too far from where she and her now ex-husband lived. It was work as a maid once again, but this time she was in a different position. Her marriage had failed after such a short time, and she felt that life was unfortunately meant to be this way for her. Yet, she pressed on despite feeling this way.

She had wanted to return to her hometown of Alliance, but she had affairs to sort out, and honestly, she needed to work as quickly as she could and concluded she could not be picky looking for a place of employment.

Earl and Ann Knorr were a well-to-do family living in Akron. Despite the Depression, Earl was one of the few people doing well enough to have a maid. His job was Assistant Superintendent for a rubber manufacturer. Of half German descent, Mr. Knorr was hard-working and fair, but expected work to be done correctly and promptly. Aletha was well-versed in working hard, so she figured this would be what she needed to do to get past the issues she was dealing with.

She continued to write letters to Mary as often as possible and continued to pray that eventually she would find a way to bring the two back together. But time was not slowing down any, and maybe, she reckoned, it was more of a dream than a plan. Plus, Mary was turning 17 this year and would eventually find a man of her own and start a family as well, leaving Aletha alone.

Aletha settled in well to her new employment and although Mr. Knorr did not converse much, Mrs. Knorr did. She would ask Aletha about her upbringing and appeared genuinely interested in what she had endured prior to arriving in this town of Akron, how she had struggled so much and yet still pressed forward. That amazed her. She reminded Aletha to not pay much mind to Earl, because he was simply someone born for what it is he did. Mrs. Knorr understood things about her husband others did not, and this made her love him in a way most could not.

When Mrs. Knorr asked about Aletha's father, it was initially hard for Aletha to open up. Eventually though, she decided to. Carl had left some 10 years prior, and so she reckoned it may be time to open that wound up some and ensure she had healed properly. Besides, she realized that she may never see her father again. There were no reports of him anywhere, and she had not heard from him at all. She didn't even know if he would know how to find her if he wanted, but she thought if he did, he would contact either Cora or Hannah for her whereabouts. Aletha had long since stopped asking Hannah if she had heard any news.

Mrs. Knorr listened as she and Aletha sat and drank tea on the front porch. Occasionally, she would place her tea down, and look at Aletha with amazement, but she tried to not tear. As she got to the part about her brothers and what had happened in the winter of 1919 along the cold banks of the Mahoning, Mrs. Knorr reached out and grabbed her arms to stop her from continuing.

"Dear, do you mean to tell me you are the sister of those three children that lost their lives that January? You poor child."

Aletha was amazed for a moment, thinking to herself, how had this woman in Akron known about what she was referring to.

Mrs. Knorr took a sip of her tea that she held firmly in her hand, and then placed it down as if she were finished. She rose for a moment, wanting to reach over and hug Aletha, but not wanting to cross the boundaries they had set considering her duties and what was expected.

She knew, however, that she had to say something.

"That event was in all the papers throughout Ohio. I even heard that other states carried the same story from relatives of mine. Aletha, dear, that was a big tragedy and people all over felt that pain your father had been dealt. That your entire family had to suffer through."

She had to catch herself, trying to balance saying what she felt came naturally, with what needed to be said to keep things from turning depressing. Her intent was not to open old, closed wounds, but to let Aletha know that she knew who her family was, and she appreciated how far she had come despite all the things she had been forced to accept. It was amazing to Mrs. Knorr that this girl, now a woman, was still able to smile at all.

Aletha felt strange talking about her brothers because it had been several years since anyone had asked. Maybe partially because they didn't want to make her upset, or perhaps because it had happened, and was now hidden away in the past. Whatever the reason, she now was talking openly about that night with her employer. She tried to walk a fine line and not act too emotional, but it was hard. Thinking about Russell, Emil and Kenneth was not easy. She had tucked that away for another time and felt that another time had simply not come about. Other than the instance she spoke about them with her sister Mary along the banks of the river, she had not spoken of this at all.

They sat on that porch for longer than they had previously. At times, they talked and Aletha answered questions. There were also stretches of silence, where both wondered what to say or how to feel. The moments were not so much awkward, as they were more one trying to not say or ask the wrong thing.

When the brothers were found, Aletha had to tuck her feelings quickly and forcefully away. She had barely gotten past her own mother dying just over a year prior, and here she was trying to comfort her father, while raising her young sister Mary. There had not really been much time to understand that all for herself. But here she was, with basically a stranger, miles away from where so much had happened in her life, and she was openly talking about all of that for the first time.

When they finished, Aletha realized that they had been out talking longer than expected and excused herself hurriedly so that she could start supper. Mr. Knorr would be arriving soon, and she wanted to continue to do her job well, even though it was now evident who she was and what she had pulled through.

When Mr. Knorr came home that evening, he was his normal self, trying to differentiate his work from his home life. Sometimes it took him longer that Mrs. Knorr would have liked, but he eventually settled in and came around.

Mrs. Knorr kissed her husband as she did every evening he walked through the door, but this time she asked him to step out into the rear yard to help with something.

Aletha felt she knew what was going on. She knew that Mrs. Knorr was going to inform her husband of who was working for them, and probably had to remind him of the story. Maybe he too remembered that time all those years back. Maybe he would just look confused as if he had no idea what his wife was referring to. He was a hard man, but a fair one. Maybe he simply would not care much at all, as he seemed to have few emotions most days.

As she prepared the supper of peeled potatoes and cooked carrots with a side of a roasted beef and onions, she was a little worried, not knowing what to expect, or if they would want to discuss this over the meal she was about to serve.

When they returned, she tried not to look at them, and

instead focused on her task. She placed the round plates onto the table and called the children down to eat. Laying the food at the center, she continued to look down and busy herself. Never once did she notice that both Mr. and Mrs. Knorr were watching her, slightly different than they had before.

Mr. Knorr told her that the food looked fine, and that she was doing a wonderful job. He had not said words like this at all for any previous meals. He was never rude, but he just saw people doing their jobs as that. Doing their jobs. It had never occurred to him that he could see someone for something different, until now.

Their two daughters, Elizabeth and Sarah, were young. Elizabeth was five, and little Sarah just over one year of age. They enjoyed having Aletha around, especially Elizabeth, who preferred to be called Eliza. For little Eliza, she had someone to look up to, and to ask questions of, especially when her mother was consumed with Sarah.

Aletha enjoyed the kids, because they reminded her of her own family that she was now without. So many times, she simply wanted to play with her brothers and sister but could not. Even before that night her brothers passed. After her mother Phoebe died, things changed. To have these little children around her brought Aletha great joy and a chance to enjoy some of what she had taken away from her.

She had almost forgotten all about her husband, thanking God that she had not had children with this selfish man. Knowing how that would have complicated things further, she counted her blessings. She had left, and that was that.

The Knorr's felt a different closeness after that night.

Not only did they know more about her, but they started to open their eyes more to how Aletha was. She cooked, cleaned, played with the children, and brought a certain positive aura to their home that had been lacking. She was an employee for sure, but they also were seeing her as much more, and this made things more comfortable for all.

Chapter 26

He Was Here

* * *

The 1930's were interesting times for the two Bradway sisters. As they grew older, they became more independent and were able to get together more easily and more frequently than they had previously. Mary was doing well, working and helping Aunt Hannah around the home they still shared, but she was looking for more substance in her life. She felt that it was time to find out just who she was and what she was destined for.

Knowing what her sister had been through in her extremely short marriage, Mary wanted to avoid that fate if possible. She would not jump into something blindly without knowing more about an individual. She was bright and generally heeded lessons well.

During the Spring of 1933, Mary asked Aletha if she felt like traveling back to Beloit. She had intended to visit with their mother and four brothers and did not know when Aletha had last been there herself.

Aletha had realized it had been quite some time since she

had ventured over to Beloit, and felt it was a splendid idea for the sisters to do so, and to spend some time together catching up.

Mary had met a man named Mervin. She had mentioned him to Aletha but hadn't said all that much. It seemed as if things were starting to grow serious, and Mary felt that Mervin was going to propose to her any day now. This was exciting and welcome news to Aletha, even though she had suffered a short lived, failed marriage. Her excitement for her sister was all she could think about.

On the way there, Aletha could see Mary was beaming. Her soft smile was playful, and her words meshed, almost as a child who desperately wants to get everything out in a single sentence does. It was clear that she knew that Mervin was the guy for her, and she was thrilled to let everyone around her know.

When they arrived at the spot where their mother and brothers were laid to rest, Mary, as she had always done, ran ahead, expecting to mostly find nothing, but hoping to find at least something in the way of a previous visitor.

To her surprise, she had. She called out to Aletha, who was trailing not far behind, but walking at her own pace.

"Sister come here! He's been here!" Mary exclaimed.

At first, Aletha did not know what she meant by "He's been here." Who, she thought to herself, but then quicky realized who she was referring to.

"Are you certain? How do you know, Mary?"

As she approached, Mary held her small once soft hands out, opened them up, and revealed what she had seen that gave it away. It was a simple heart-shaped rock, different from the others that had been left there all those years. Most of the other rocks had either been moved by someone, or the weather had hidden them beneath the thick grass growing around the markers denoting where Phoebe was placed.

"It was right here, placed just so." As she motioned to mimic how the stone was laid out.

The heart-shaped, flat stone had a reddish tone to it, with some grays mixed in. There was no mistaking that it was a heart-shape, and intentionally laid there. There was certainly purpose to how this peculiar rock was placed. It was not there by chance, but rather by intent.

As the sisters knelt, they began to wonder if their father, Carl, had been the one to place the rock, and if so, was it for Phoebe, or perhaps to let the sisters know that he was alive? Or maybe a combination of the two? Either way, they felt something they had not in many years. They felt the love of a father who had left because he knew not how to live the way he did. Had they had any anger or resentment, it was not there this afternoon. They felt love, sadness, and hope all at the same time.

Aletha took the rock from her sister's hands and carefully examined it. She turned it in different directions to see just how well shaped this one was. It was almost a perfectly shaped heart for sure, even much more so than the others he had laid there over the years. Sadly, there had not been any others placed there for many years, but here one was now.

Why had he not tried to contact them? It was the 1930's, after all, and finding them should not be a difficult task. Cora knew where they were. Hannah certainly did because Mary still resided with her. Did he simply not want to encourage them? Maybe he just wasn't willing to face the decision he had made back in 1919, where he felt as if he had no choice but to abandon them. It could have been a decision he made in haste, and one he felt he could not reverse.

It did not matter in that moment though, because they felt they had confirmation, finally, that their father Carl, was alive. Or at least that he had been recently.

They spent over an hour sitting there on the grass, talking about Mervin, about Aunt Hannah and what she was up to, and about what Aletha saw coming in her immediate future. Everything they said was from their hearts, and the bonding they were doing was building some sense of wonder at how they had arrived where they had.

When they were preparing to leave, Mary took the stone she had found resting there, made a mental note of its color and size and shape, and placed it back exactly as she had found it. It was not her rock to keep. It was meant for her mother, Phoebe, and she would have that.

She felt a little pained that she had not searched for a rock of her own to place there. Wanting to let her father know that they had seen it and were both still alive as well, Mary dug into the grass and dirt just on the outside of the marker. She searched until she found two stones that her father seemingly placed there years prior. As she rubbed away the years of dirt that had encapsulated the stones, she gently placed them next to the new one. There lay three heart-shaped rocks, representing the three family members who were still alive, and Aletha simply smiled.

"Well done, Mary. Well done."

As they walked out, the two sisters held hands with one and other and almost walked with a skip to their steps. They had not expected this visit to go as it did, but the day had been a surprise and a much needed one at that. Finally, they felt as if they had some better news, and it was welcome.

When Mary returned later that evening to where she was staying with Hannah, she mentioned what they had seen. Hannah looked confused, but tried to be encouraging. Once again, she wondered if it was indeed Carl, and why he had not reached out to the girls. They were older now, but maybe that made it even harder. Perhaps he felt that if he came back now, they would push him away and he could simply not bear that. He lost so much time with the girls, and probably felt incredibly guilty for that fact.

Maybe it was just a coincidence, she muttered to herself. After all, if he were still alive, and if he traveled back to see his wife and boys where he had left them behind, he surely would have spoken to someone to let them know, or to at least get the latest news on how everyone was doing. It had been 13 years since he left the area, and not a soul had heard from him. It made little sense to Hannah, but she knew Mary had desperately wanted to believe he was back. At least for a moment, in her mind, he had been.

Hannah decided to ring Aunt Cora, who sounded just as taken aback by the news that Mary and Aletha had felt Carl was back at some point but had not spoken to anyone.

Cora assured Hannah that she not heard from nor seen her brother. She mentioned that Lorenzo was out working, but that she would certainly speak with him and see if they could stop out to pay a visit.

When they reached Hannah's home, Mary was out with her boyfriend, Mervin, so it was the perfect chance to catch up with one and other, and to discuss all that had been going on. Hannah was all too pleased to fill in both Cora and Lorenzo on how Mary had grown, and what Aletha had been doing recently.

Cora had talked with her niece Aletha but had lost time recently and wondered how she was making out. She heard that Aletha had a failed marriage and was saddened by that. Lorenzo just nodded in agreement whenever either woman would look his way. He was easy-going and trying to be supportive where needed.

When Mary finally walked in from her date, she was pleasantly surprised to see Aunt Cora and Uncle Lorenzo, or Duke, sitting there in the main room.

"Aunt Cora, Uncle Duke, what on earth are you doing here? I mean to say, what a wonderful surprise!" Mary said, confused.

They understood Mary's confusion and knew she did not mean to sound upset or ungrateful. She just did not know they were coming to visit, and Hannah had not told her for her own reasons.

"Dear," Cora started. "tell me. Tell me about the visit you made to your mothers and to where your brothers are. What did you see?"

Mary knew exactly what she was asking her. She wanted to know why she felt her father had been there, and what made her believe he had done so more recently than not. It was probably confusing to Cora that he had been back and not said at least a hello to his own sister, but this provided proof that he had not. Otherwise, Cora would not have been here seemingly so confused and interested.

Mary sat down, placed her hands onto her lap, and looked over to where Cora and Duke were sitting. She began,

"Aunt Cora. You know how mom loved her heart rocks, how dad had kept the ones she had collected and saved them in a box," she paused for just a moment, looking at her hands fidgeting in front of her.

"When Aletha and I arrived, I ran ahead as I always do. Honestly, I did not expect to stumble upon anything really, but when I got close enough, I could see plain as day that rock. That heart rock that had simply not been there the previous visit. It was most certainly a heart, and in fact I left it there. It wasn't mine to take. It wasn't Aletha's either. It was Mother's. So, we left it right there where we found it," she finished.

Cora sat up straight in her chair, looked over to her husband, Lorenzo, who was just sitting there listening and agreeing, and then over to Hannah. She was searching for something, although she did not know what exactly. She just could not quite understand why Carl had been back and had not said a single syllable to anyone. It just did not make any sense to her, or anyone in that room for that matter.

Chapter 27

A Sister Risden

* * *

Chatter began to die down once again as often happens. While Aletha and Mary kept wondering if their father had stopped by, it was apparent to them he had stopped doing so again. There were no more new rocks left at their mother's marker. It did not appear as if anyone had groomed the grass around the stones on the site of their brother's graves either. It was all so undisturbed. Even the red and gray toned rock that Mary had laid back down just so, as well as the two she had dug up and brushed off, were still sitting there in their exact spots as she had intended for them to be.

Mary had other things she was concentrating on as well, and in the Summer of 1934, she would marry her love, Mervin Risden, in Brooke, West Virginia. She was now referred to as Mrs. Mary Risden, and she felt entirely excited for this new chapter in her life.

With all she had seen and gone through, it appeared she was catching some peace at last. Mary had loved growing up with Aunt Hannah, but this was just some independence she sought after and now held firmly.

Aletha was genuinely happy for her younger sister. She felt that no one deserved happiness more than her Mary. Even if Aletha had not been able to make her marriage work the way she had envisioned, Mary could. She knew she could. Mervin seemed like a steady man who only had eyes for Mary, and that was so important to a strong, loving marriage.

Hannah was sad at the thought of losing Mary, but she knew it was inevitable. Mary was a beautiful young woman and had such an energy about her, that people naturally wanted to be in her presence. When she met Mervin, Hannah knew immediately that he was not going to let her go, and thus she had prepared for this day as best she could.

As Mary and Mervin married, Mary could not help but wonder about her family. How very different this day would be if her mother and father were standing side by side, holding each other's hands, proud and smiling. If her brothers had all been there with their wives and children, looking over at their youngest sister on the day of her wedding, looking pretty, nervous, but excited. She wondered. How would this day have changed? So far it was a wonderful occasion, but she felt an emptiness knowing it should have been something it was not. Her family should all be there smiling, laughing, and celebrating this day.

When the ceremony was complete, Aletha went over to her sister Mary and smiled at her intently. She placed her arms around her neck, pulled her in towards her, and whispered into her ear how happy and proud she was, happy that her sister had the day she deserved, and proud for the woman she was becoming right before her very eyes, from the struggle of life she had been living for years now.

Mary was crying, knowing her sister spoke words she felt fully and deeply. Aletha had no trouble saying what was on her mind, and little trouble conveying her happiness when she was.

Mervin and Mary rented a small place in Alliance, right across from where Hannah was currently living, so they were still close enough to each other and could certainly get together whenever they chose to. It was not far from the Mahoning River, where so much had changed for Mary over the years.

Aletha was still living with the Knorr family, and things were going well for her. She became close with the neighborhood and especially a family that lived just to the right of them, the Thomas family.

The Thomas' had four children consisting of two daughters and two sons. One of the daughters, Lucille, was married and had a young baby boy at home. She lived with her husband, Joseph, in the house her father and mother owned, along with her other siblings.

Aletha and Lucille became quite close and could often be found sitting on the rear porch steps of one of the homes, talking after supper time or early in the morning enjoying their first cup of coffee before going their separate ways. They both enjoyed the simple conversations they had, and neither said much about their past life's trials, but rather concentrated on what was going on in the present. It had made Aletha feel more at ease knowing she did not have to go over the same questions and stories she had every time people heard a bit of her past and felt the need to learn more.

Lucille was happy in life and could often be found smiling away at her son Joseph Jr., who was just four at the time. Joseph would run as fast as he could right by Aletha, often giggling to himself as if he had heard the greatest, funniest line ever told. As he tumbled along in the back yard grass, his life seemed so pure and innocent, that Aletha remembered a time long ago that hers was very much the same.

It certainly also made Aletha reminisce about her own life and how she yearned for a child of her own, but how that had not happened yet. She knew her mother, Phoebe, had wanted to have children right away, but that it had not happened that way. So, she felt she just needed to continue to be patient and things would eventually fall into place for her. For now, though, she loved watching Joseph as he tumbled in the high grass as the two women spoke about nothing too important.

One of the many things that Aletha admired about Lucille's husband was the fact he arrived home from work and would immediately walk over to his young bride, kiss her, and then would run over to grab his boy and lift him high over his head while smiling. It was something Aletha had not had the chance to experience, and she wondered just how that made Lucille feel. She did not have to wonder much though, as she could clearly see that love in both their eyes, the same love she saw in her sister Mary's eyes when she married her Mervin. A love she would feel at some point in her life. She just felt she needed to believe that.

When the year was closing in on its end, and the weather was growing cold and increasingly miserable, the women would take things inside to chat and enjoy a cup of tea together. Over their hot drinks, Aletha started to open more about her past. At first, she said that her mother had passed when she was young, but not much else. She began to talk more openly about her brothers and the tragedy that had changed her life. Aletha found it easy to tell her friend just about anything by this point.

What became especially hard was when she would get to the part about what happened with her father. She knew so little, and hardly remembered the last time they spoke. Maybe she had tucked that away someplace deep down where even she could not find it, or perhaps she had just not paid much attention with the pain she was also feeling at the time.

Either way, this was a tough spot for her to be in. Lucille could tell and started to back off, but Aletha just smiled and pushed on.

"Well, he went through a lot," Aletha began.

"I knew he missed Mother dearly, and then after losing his three remaining sons after his other died, I knew it was just too much for him to handle. Truly, I had hate in my heart, but as I matured, I began to understand the why."

Lucille was focusing on her friend's expression, how

her eyes drifted off, her hand clutching the other tightly.

"Mary was so confused for so long, but I figure by now, she understands too. How one man had to endure so much makes no sense at all, but it is not for us to decide how our path is carved out," Aletha finished.

Lucille had to admire Aletha for her strength if nothing else. She had lost just as much as her father, yet she saw what he lost as too much to bear. That he had all the weight on his shoulders and had felt it too heavy to continue as a man should, and Aletha grabbed that weight and struggled with it herself.

Lucille sat back in her chair and looked out of the room to where Joseph, her husband, had been standing in the shadow looking on and listening to this young woman talk about her loss with such a strength he had never seen before. As he caught his wife's eyes, he walked into the room slowly, over to where the two women were. He placed a hand on Aletha's shoulder, startling her for a moment, and gave her the warmest smile she had seen in a long time. He needed no words, for she understood he was letting her know it was okay.

She shook her head as if trying to remove the fog and smiled gently back.

"Anyway, we have not heard from him since the moment he left. I often wonder where he went, or if he is even alive anymore. I suppose one day I will have that answer. I suppose it would be nice to know, just what happened, to tell him I love him and that I understand why he had to go. I suppose that is what I would like."

The mood shifted, but they all felt as if something had been lifted off Aletha, and the air was clear. Not that it was their business, but they cared for their friend and knowing this about her made them understand better what they had not known. It had opened a place in her heart she had closed long ago but was able to let go for just a little while. Sometimes, they figured, we needed to do that.

Those winter nights were what Aletha needed and enjoyed most. Her life was becoming calm once again, as it had after each draining issue she faced. She had too much tossed her way, and calm was what she desired more than just about anything.

Christmas approached, and the neighbors had all gotten together for a feast. Each brought what they could, and no one felt as if they had to. It was a nice evening, and everyone seemed to get along well. At one point in the night, there was a man who caught the eye of Aletha, and she tried her darndest not to make it noticeable. She failed miserably.

His name was Charles, and he happened to be the cousin of Lucille, just visiting with his parents for the evening.

Charles took notice of Aletha just the same as she had him, and walked over shyly to introduce himself. She was hoping he would, and when he did, she could only tuck her head down embarrassed perhaps.

Now here he stood in front of Aletha, smiling at her and expecting one in return. She was caught off guard and did not at first. She turned away as if to prepare to walk in another direction, but then she quickly caught herself, turned back around to face him, and smiled shyly back at him. She thought, why not? I am a grown woman and free, and it seems everyone else around me is happily in love. Maybe, I deserve that as well. Maybe this man will be the gentle, loving type of man I deserve in my life.

Chapter 28

The Man in Shreve

* * *

In a year, a lot of things can happen. As time passes with each fading season and new ones are once again born, people tend to understand that what they may not have expected to transpire over the previous twelve months, did anyway. You start off with thoughts of a trip, or perhaps finding love, or maybe a job promotion you were promised.

It doesn't always happen like that, though. You get laid off when the market crashes. The one you fall head-over-heels for, doesn't feel quite the same way towards you. The family trip you planned to take gets cancelled because you come down with something. It's just part of the surprise with the coming seasons ahead. You trust it will go better, and sometimes it does, and sometimes it does not.

For Aletha, January 2nd of 1936 made a change in her life once again. Only this time, it was a good thing for her. She wed Charles Thomas on that cold, winter day. Just a week after her parents' anniversary. Charles had asked her if she wanted to marry on Christmas day, but she wanted that to be her parent's special day. He completely understood.

This was her second time at this, but she felt so different about Charles. He was caring and honest, hard-working, genuine and understanding. Nothing like Lyman had been. These were two entirely different men and everyone around Aletha saw that. Even Mary told her that this was the man intended for her. Who was she to argue with her little sister, who had found her true love first?

Aunt Hannah had also met a man and remarried. She still lived across the road from Mervin and Mary, but had a new husband after all these years. Her husband's name was George Edward Fahey, and he was 17 years younger than Hannah was. No one questioned Hannah's decision, but they all thought she had gone off the deep end for marrying someone so young. However, Hannah was happy and content and that was all the nieces could hope for. Their aunt, who had sacrificed so much for them over the years, had every right to be just as happy as the next person.

Aletha was going to be leaving her job and moving once again, but of course by now she was used to this. She was moving to be with her husband, Charles, and for once, she felt just completely right about this decision in her life.

All that first year, Aletha had felt like never before in her life. It was as if she was changing to an entirely different version of herself. One that was waking up with excitement and hope for the day, versus just another day filled with despair and loneliness. She was feeling alive and good about herself. Aletha needed this. She deserved this.

Mary had made her sister a promise that they would get

out to Beloit at least once a season, and to visit each other at least once a month to keep in touch. While they could phone each other, and they still hand-wrote long letters to keep things intimate and personal, it was being in front of each other where the sisters felt best. They knew no matter what, they were not just sisters, but best friends.

Charles enjoyed talking with his new bride after working. In fact, he had focused on coming home and asking her each day, how her day was. It was simple, but it showed his bride that he was genuinely interested in knowing all the details. He would sit there, looking at her while she went over what she did, and who she had talked with. Even details about something she remembered from a past day, or year, or what seemed like a lifetime ago.

He was also aware of her failed marriage. Aletha was almost embarrassed about this, but her husband assured her she was so strong for having come out of that as she did, and for walking away when she knew he would not change. That was something he really tried to drive home, how proud he was for the incredible strength she had inside of her, despite the odds facing her at each turn.

Lucille still talked with Aletha as well. They would get together at family gatherings and often when both were in need of a good woman-to-woman conversation. Aletha felt she could confide in Lucille about certain things she could not with others. She always had Mary, but sometimes having an outsider who did not have the same upbringing as you, gave you advice from a much different perspective.

In the fall of 1936, Lucille had decided to visit with

some friends in a town called Shreve, Ohio. Shreve was Southwest of Akron, roughly 50 miles away. It would be a long weekend away, and she promised Aletha upon her return she would phone her and tell her all about it.

Aletha wished her well and went back to her daily chores while figuring maybe she had ought to plan to see Mary at some point for their trip to Beloit. It had been a few months, and with the colder weather approaching, it would just be easier to stop out sooner rather than later. Mary tried to avoid the cemetery when snow was piled high on the ground below them. She was worried that she may miss a sign of a visitor, even though she had seen none in many years.

Aletha told her they should probably accept the fact that their father Carl may have passed. For sure, if he had not, he would have contacted his family by now. He had not.

Mary, though, continued to feel positive that at some point, he would just walk back into town, knock on her door, and grab her with his strong arms. He would pick her up and twirl her around and around, as if he had not missed a day and she would still be his little child. She was more of a romantic than Aletha was in that sense, but it made her happy to picture this, so she continued to whenever her heart thought of him.

They planned to stop out at the end of October, hopefully before the snow would cascade down on the Ohio landscape. It made sense. The weather would still not be overly cold, and it would give them time to walk around and look at the changing leaves. Before that though, she had other things she wished to do.

Lucille had been gone for the long weekend and was set to return on Monday afternoon. Aletha had said she would phone her that afternoon, but instead decided to surprise her friend by showing up in person. It would give her an opportunity to visit with Mr. and Mrs. Knorr and the children as well. She would leave early Monday morning, spend the day with the Knorr's, and then walk on over to see her dear friend. Charles thought it was a splendid idea and would give her some time away from her daily chores. He was always very understanding of that.

When she arrived, the Knorr's were excited to see their friend and former maid. Mr. Knorr was so happy to see her in fact, that he pulled her in and wrapped his arms around her. He had never done that to her before. Mrs. Knorr just smiled at her husband. She knew he enjoyed Aletha and had always had a hard time showing her that. He was not very good at separating work from pleasure, and so he had never been able to see young Aletha as much more than a woman doing her duties. Now? He saw her as a friend. Aletha treasured that moment.

She told them all about her Charles, and how hard he had worked for them both. Her eyes lit up when she mentioned her life with that man. It was so different from her first marriage, and she felt having that failed marriage prepared her for what she considered the perfect of unions.

Mrs. Knorr poured some hot tea that she had steaming, and the two women sat and sipped tea, while Mr. Knorr excused himself. His wife would fill him in on how everything was going, and besides, he was not one for small talk. He preferred to busy himself around the house whenever he was home.

The women chatted and talked about the economy, the ever-changing weather, how Mrs. Knorr was handling the new maid, who was the third since Aletha left, and shared some new recipes they had both learned. It was as if two old friends had found each other after years apart. Both women talked and talked, until the moment they could see a car approaching down the road.

Aletha leaned over the porch just enough and saw the black and green colored car slowing down next door, to where her friend Lucille had been staying.

"It must be her," she said to Mrs. Knorr.

Lucille was home, and as the door opened, Aletha initially waited. She wanted to allow her friend a few moments to grab her belongings and get into her door before barging over. This way she would be relaxed when she saw Aletha had come down to see her, and to surprise her in person.

She noticed that her friend looked to be in a slight daze of sorts. As if she was not truly content that she was home. Maybe the trip was just a little longer than she expected, or maybe it was that she was tired from the drive and needed some rest.

Lucille grabbed Joey from the car along with two bags she had brought with her. She placed them over her shoulder and walked slowly towards the door.

As she reached the door, Mrs. Knorr also saw the look on Lucille's face and of her friend Aletha.

"Dear, she had a long weekend. That's all. That Joey is so full of energy, and she just needs to put her feet up and relax. As soon as she sees you are here, well, dear, she is going to be tickled pink. You just watch."

She smiled at Aletha and patted her hand. Mrs. Knorr told her to finish her second cup of tea, and by that time, Lucille would be ready for her visitor. It made sense to give her a few more moments to unpack and unwind, so she continued with her tea and small talk, and then got up and thanked Mrs. Knorr. She told her to please thank her husband as well, and that she would be back when she could to visit once again.

Mrs. Knorr smiled and told her, "Anytime deary. Anytime."

Aletha grabbed the bag she had, and a small gift she picked out for her friend and walked over to the other yard. She approached the front door and was just slightly apprehensive, wondering what had happened that made her friend Lucille look so befuddled.

She walked up the concrete steps onto the porch, and towards the front door that was slightly cracked open. Lucille had not pulled it all the way shut behind her when she had gone in apparently.

She knocked lightly on the door, which made it creak open enough that she could see her friend, Lucille, sitting in a chair, with her hands on her lap. Lucille looked over to the now partially opened door, and through the light shining behind Aletha, she could make out the silhouette of her friend. She knew instantly who it was but was shocked to see her standing there in her doorway.

"Aletha?" she exclaimed with both excitement and confusion.

"What on earth are you doing here? Come in!"

She sprang from her chair and walked quickly over to meet Aletha, who was walking in her direction as well.

"I wished to surprise you, and saw you get out of the car looking out of sorts. Is everything all right?" Aletha questioned.

She could see Lucille smiling but straining to say whatever she needed to. Little Joey was out in the yard now playing, and Lucille peaked out to check on him.

"Aletha, sit down. I just tried to phone you and did not get you. I now understand why. Sit. I want to tell you something."

Aletha was confused but did as Lucille had requested. Lucille sat right beside her friend on that chair and placed her hands on Aletha's lap. She looked into Lucille's eyes and could see she wanted to tell her something that was clearly at the forefront of her mind. Whatever it was, it was causing her friend to feel confused and was not easy for her to let go.

"Aletha, I was in Shreve as you know. We were eating at a diner and just catching up with each other. There was a waitress at the table next to ours talking with a fella about a farmer that had stopped in last week."

She paused, carefully trying to find the next words.

"This waitress, she was telling the fella sitting there on the other side of us that this man had lost his three sons years back," pausing yet again to think for a moment about exactly what this waitress had said and how. She wanted to get the story right.

"That waitress told the man she felt so bad for this farmer, because he had lost a wife right before that. His wife had passed and then, shortly after that, his three boys. Aletha, I couldn't believe my ears. I just stared at her and wondered, was she talking about my Aletha's father? Could it be?"

The room was dead quiet. Not a sound could be heard other than Joey singing a tune out in the rear yard. Aletha was stone still, as if she had seen a ghost. She was searching for words to put together but could not seem to find any at the moment. She was never at a loss for words, until this moment. Was her father alive? Was he living in Shreve, a town in Ohio, far enough that she would never hear about him, but close enough that it made sense? Could there be more than one man who had lost three sons and a wife in such a short period of time?

"Lucille, tell me, this waitress. Did she say anything else? I mean, did she mention him by name or where he was from, or where his boys had died and how?"

Aletha had so many questions and was trying to understand what all her friend had heard. She wanted Lucille to patiently walk her through, step by step, all she had heard and seen. This was not news Aletha was expecting today, or any day in fact. She could see why her friend has asked her to sit. Had she not, Aletha may had fallen flat on her face to the hardwood flooring below her feet.

Chapter 29

A Difficult Decision

* * *

On Tuesday morning, Aletha awoke as she had always done, but this time she did not immediately rise from the bed she was laying in. Instead, she laid there, trying to figure out what she needed to do that day. There were so many thoughts running through her head, and she still needed to get things ready for Charles as he dressed for work.

She had not yet told her husband what Lucille had mentioned to her. Honestly, she first wanted to be sure she had not dreamt it. She also needed to tell him, and her sister, Mary, and Aunt Cora and Hannah, somehow. Her head was spinning once again at the thought of it all. What if this was just a strange coincidence? It could have been, but it did seem unlikely.

Plus, all they knew was that a man entered a diner, sat down, ate some food, and talked with the waitress who served him. He was a farmer, which made sense to her, and that this particular man had said he lost his three sons years back, and a wife. He had closely cut hair, a strong face, and sad, marvelous grey eyes. He was from Ohio, but the waitress told Lucille she did not know exactly from where he was talking about. She had just started working there not long ago and had never seen the man before. But she said she remembered those mesmerizing eyes and that they were filled with regret the likes of which she had never seen. She could see that plain as day.

When Charles arrived home that evening, she had decided to let him know what she had been told, and to seek his advice. Should she get her sisters hopes up, or should she let it go? It had been sixteen years. They had not seen their father in sixteen years. Her emotions were high, and her curiosity was taking over. She began to build an anxiety about her right then and there.

Charles sat down at the table and held Aletha's out-stretched hands in his. He looked intently at his wife and told her what he felt. He asked her how she would feel if she did not at least check? Would she have regrets for knowing it could potentially be her father? Would she feel pain for not letting Mary know what she had heard? How would she feel? His words were calming, and he had a genuine concern for her. All he wanted was for Aletha to know, whatever she felt was right, that he would stick by her side through that decision.

Aletha told him she was going to pray on it for a few days, and then she would come to a decision on what she felt was the right way to proceed.

Her husband nodded in approval. He knew the power

of prayer and that Aletha would come to a decision and be good with it. When she set her mind to something, she did that. This was nothing new to his bride. She was resilient like no other person he had ever come across.

So, she just went about her day. She worked on the house, preparing her supper plans, and had some errands to run around town. All day, though, it was there. The what if. The thought of not knowing if this man that was in Shreve was her father, or just some other unlucky man who had felt that same pain her father had.

By the end of the week, she had her answer. She would not go off and chase some story she had heard second-hand, or third-hand even. This did not mean she was not going to tell Mary. She may, but she was still not certain. Should she tell her that some waitress in a town over an hour away had heard a tale from some man she did not know? Mary may head out to find him herself and be let down if she learned it was not him. What good would that be? It would only open up an old wound that had long since closed, and the bleeding stopped. Why do this to Mary?

Aletha did not like the fact she had to make a decision for several people, including Aunt Hannah and Aunt Cora. What right did she have to make such a decision for them?

As Charlie told her, he would respect her decision and back it without question, and that is precisely what he did. He did not ask her further questions, and he did not try and change her mind. This was her journey and she needed to figure out what it was she needed. Her decision was made, and that was that.

Another Christmas was coming and going, and the sisters had paid their visit to Beloit twice since the story of the man in Shreve. Aletha had said nothing to Mary about what she had heard, but had brought up Carl a few times, which certainly caught Mary's attention.

"Why now sister? Why are you bringing up father after all this time? Is there a reason, or perhaps something bothering you? You can tell me," Mary said to her.

Aletha did not have the heart to tell her and felt guilty for not having the courage to mention this earlier. Mary had every right to know, but she had tried to protect her. In doing so, she now felt pained.

"No, Mary I just wonder after all these years have passed, and after all the times we have been to Beloit and have seen those heart-shaped rocks, and then nothing. What happened to us? How did our family end up as it did? Why are you and I the lucky ones to have survived such turmoil?"

Mary had no answer. She had wondered that herself many times but knew she could not find the answer. They had made it this far, and to question that made little sense in her mind. They were alive, married, and life was heading in a direction both could not have imagined, but surely prayed for. Happiness was there, but she sensed still, something was bothering Aletha. But what?

Just after the new year in 1937, Aletha was having terrible trouble sleeping. She would try to rest early to catch up on the night before where she could not keep her eyes closed, but that did not work. She tried staying up later to wear herself out, in the hopes her body would fall into a deep sleep. That too did not happen. She just could not get the rest her body and mind so desperately needed, and she knew why she struggled so badly.

"Charles. Can I talk with you?" She asked after finally realizing, she needed a better direction.

"Please, be honest with me. Do you think I did the right thing? Not telling Mary about that man in Shreve. Or do you think I should have mentioned it, and allowed her to make her own mind up? Be honest with me, please."

Charles was seated across from Aletha, drinking his morning coffee, black as he preferred it. A newspaper was in his right hand, covering his face from where she was seated. Slowly he lowered the paper, took one more sip of his coffee, and placed it on the table in front of him.

"Dear, I see you struggling with this. I always want to support your decisions and will, but if you are genuinely asking me for my advice, I will give you that."

Aletha smiled nervously, because although she wanted his advice, she was not certain what he would have to say to her. She knew in her heart what she had wanted to do now, but she still needed her husband to reassure her. She felt that she had made a mistake in not telling Mary, and to hear that she should not once again, would only confuse her further.

He looked at her deeply, almost as he had when they exchanged vows on the day of their wedding. Then he began to speak once again,

"What harm could come from it? If you find out it was

just some other poor fella who lost his boys and wife, then at least you would know it was not him, and possibly put this out of your mind for good. Maybe even making this the last time you need to wonder. But, if you travel to Shreve, find this man that entered the diner that day and discover that he is in fact your father, well, can you imagine how you will feel? What questions you will have and what emotions will travel with you? Aletha. I think you owe it to Mary, and to yourself as well. I think you ought to try. That is my advice to you."

Aletha felt a massive sense of relief just fall from her shoulders. She had been carrying this around for a while now, and truth be told, she was feeling the burden of that.

That was that. She was going to tell Mary, Hannah, and Cora what she had heard from her friend, and if they were upset with her, she would deal with that. Then, with them or without, she was going to travel to Shreve, and figure out if she could locate this mysterious man and find out who he was for sure. She needed to know for certain, who the man from Shreve with the sadness in his eyes really was.

Her plan was to call Cora first and let her know. She knew Cora would not tell the others but would offer some insight into what to maybe look for and ask when she arrived in town. Then, she would phone Hannah and let her know she was going to tell Mary, so that in case Mary needed someone to talk with other than Aletha, she would not be surprised.

Of course, Mary would know as well, but not until after she spoke with the other two.

She began to feel a nervous energy about this all. Just the thought of traveling to this town scared her. Not because she did not know the town. She had moved all over Ohio already, so this was nothing new. Adapting to areas was what she did best. It was more the fear of seeing this fella face-to-face. Would she know it was him for certain without asking or would she need to have a series of questions to know it was her father?

What if he had created this story from the facts and was pretending to be her father? It was a possibility she had to face. He could have read old newspapers and carried them with him to remind him of the facts. People pretended to be other people all the time. If he was doing this, it was a sick thing to do.

What if her father had decided long ago that he no longer wanted to see his only remaining children? Maybe he would be upset that they traveled to find him, when all he wanted was to live out the rest of his life alone in peace.

"Aunt Cora, it's Aletha. I have some news for you. Are you sitting down?"

Chapter 30

Ida Mae

* * *

As the weather started to turn yet again, and the cold gave way to a warmer season filled with pleasant rains and colorful flower blooms, two sisters were packing a bag for a long weekend away together. They were in search of answers and perhaps satisfying a curiosity that had gotten the best of them.

They talked along the way, sifting through memories they had long since forgotten, but somehow were able to reach once again. A story about how their father had once faced a vicious storm and walked away to tell the tale. How he had brought a dog home for them all, after their mother passed, to show them that he knew they were pained from loss as well. Each story they pulled to the surface brought either a crying laugh or a sad smile. They were all welcome stories.

The trip was not that long, but they felt as if it were taking forever. Both were anxious, but not fully prepared for any answers they found. How could they be? This man was either their father they had not seen in many years, or another heartbroken man that they would possibly sadden further by asking him about his eerily similar story. A few times Aletha asked if they should turn and go back, but she was more trying to sort things out in her own mind, and not really being serious with her sister. She knew Mary had no intentions of going back until she knew the truth in Shreve.

Another issue they talked about before arriving was what plan would they use? They had little to go on. A waitress who may not even work at the diner any longer. A man who worked on a farm somewhere in the area, but they did not know the direction in which he came from. Just a secondhand story about him. That was it. Were they insane for doing this? Maybe, they thought, but they were bonding like they had not done in some time.

They always talked on their trips to visit their mother and brothers. They bonded on the back-and-forth visits they made to each other's homes. This was a bonding in a most different way. Talking about mostly their youth was something they had not done in forever. Mary was only five when her brothers had passed. She remembered so little, but as Aletha spoke, she quickly realized she knew more than she had thought. She saw their faces for the first time and remembered how Russell would lead the way. She saw Emil cocking his head sideways as he tried to figure out how to make a better fishing pole from the one he had. Kenneth was giggling away at chasing that old dog Rusty around the street out front of their home. It was all

IDA MAE

so crystal clear to her as if she could simply reach out and touch each one of them.

When they arrived in Shreve, the first thing they wanted to do was to get something to eat. They knew the diner that the woman had worked at, but they wanted to relax before diving into this just now. So, they chose a different place to sit and relax over coffee and some danish.

Aletha had a pad and pen at the ready with some notes she jotted down prior to leaving. She had the name of the waitress, Ida Mae, at the top left corner, just under the phrase "Finding the man in Shreve".

Further down she had scribbled a few short notes about her father that she had remembered. She planned to ask the waitress if this man had said anything else and her notes may jog the waitress's mind. She felt that if she recalled something after hearing what her and Mary had to say, it may give them guidance as to what they should do. If the man had been heavyset and did not speak well, perhaps it wasn't Carl. If he had piercing eyes and was kind and thin, it could very well be dad. The girls figured he would not change entirely from the man he was when they last set eyes on him.

They finished their danish and asked for a refill on their cup of coffee, knowing that once they were finished there, they were embarking on a journey both wanted, but both feared. It was exciting but nerve-wracking at the same time. They could be just hours or days away from finding their father or finding disappointment.

Each man that walked in through the front door, and

215

rang the bell affixed to the top of the door caused them both to turn quickly. They looked every one of them up and down and listened for a familiar voice. He could be sitting at the counter behind them or working on the farm that day. Neither knew and that made them jumpy. What would they do if he walked by them or bumped into them on the way out? Would they be able to mutter a word, or would they stand still, shocked in tears of confusion? Aletha wondered if anger would come out, or if she would just forgive as she had prayed to do.

When they were finished and could drink no more of the coffee being poured, they asked for the check and knew, it was time. Mary paid the bill and gave her sister a smile, saying to her,

"Well sister, it's time to get this show on the road. We are ready for this. It's going to be fine either way, I know that."

Aletha wasn't so sure, but she did not want Mary to worry. She smiled slightly and nodded in agreement before grabbing her things, ready to get her answers as well.

As they walked out to the front of the restaurant, both sisters looked left first, then right. From here, they were on their own and had to decide what to do first. The obvious answer was to head over to the diner, but both felt if they waited until the evening when the supper crowd was in, it would make the most sense. Perhaps she would be there, and other folks from town. They could get better answers and do so in one trip without looking suspicious.

For now, they decided to walk around the quaint town. It was Saturday, so people would be out in the warmer sun and enjoying their families. Again, each man that passed by, they watched intently. Mary was beginning to feel that people were wondering about these two women looking over every man in town, but she did not care. This was the journey she had waited two decades to complete, so they would just need to mind their own business.

After a few hours, they were beginning to feel overwhelmed and lost, so they decided to head over to the diner for an early supper. They had nothing else to do, so they would simply just take their time eating and people watching and feeling even more nervous.

When they arrived, the sign on top of the diner read "Rosie's". This was the place, and this was where they had desired to be, even if they were a little uneasy about it now that they were standing right outside.

Mary did not wait for Aletha to decide. She was already heading in to find a seat, just as she would in Beloit when visiting her mother and brothers. Aletha just smiled to herself, and shook her head as if to say, "There is no denying that one of what she is after." Mary was not going to waste any more time and was already seated before her older sister had even breached the door.

When Aletha walked in, she glanced nonchalantly around at the other tables set out as families ate and spoke to each other, and along the rail where men were seated alone. Nothing immediately jumped out at her, so she looked over to where Mary had seated herself, walked over and sat across from her sister, placing her purse down along side of her hip. She then placed her hands in front of her in a nervous fashion. They were here.

"Now what?", Mary asked with a slight smirk on her face.

"I don't know. Just be patient for now and let us see what is going on here. Maybe if we listen to the conversations around us, we will hear what we need to hear without having to pry." Aletha responded.

Truthfully, she had no idea of what they were hoping to hear, or what they wished to see. They were in a town they had never visited and knew not one person here. Aletha just wanted to sit and be patient, while Mary was ready to ask every soul in the joint if they knew this man from Shreve with the sad eyes and lost boys.

"What was that waitresses name again, sister?", Mary asked.

"Ida. Ida Mae," Aletha said without needing to look at her notes.

Just then, a waitress came over and asked the two women if they would like something to drink to start them off. Both sisters said they would start with a water for now and would like to see a menu.

Mary asked her sister if she caught the name of their waitress and she said that she had.

"It's not her," she responded.

As they looked over the menu, each could be seen stretching their necks to see if they heard a sign of anything. They were stone-quiet at times, listening for anything that would lead them to inquire more. Nothing though came about. People were simply talking about the warm weather, or how the kids were doing in class, or when Uncle Bert was coming to visit next. Nothing that made them think of their father at all.

As they were eating their supper of ham and string beans, the waitress came back over to see how they were doing. She may have sensed something was going on with these two ladies who seemed to be paying a lot of attention to everyone in the diner.

"You two all right? Something I can help you with?" She asked as she poured water into the half-emptied ones the girls had in front of them.

"Ma'am, is Ida Mae working tonight? We were looking to speak with her perhaps," Mary shot back quickly.

"Well, no. She ain't. She has been out all week sick as a dog. Poor child. I don't know when to expect her back to be honest with you two. Is there anything I can do to help?"

Aletha looked slightly dejected. They were planning on no more than three or four days here and already the first day was a total bust. They had not even secured a hotel yet, so there was a lot to do. Money was tight, but Charles had worked a little extra prior to them leaving so that she could take this trip and not need to worry much. That at least made Aletha a little more relaxed.

"To be frank, we are looking to speak with her about a man that came in here last year. We were told that Ida Mae may know something about him and can possibly point us in the right direction," Aletha said.

"Well, there are a lot of folks that come and go in through here. A lot of men, too. I don't know how she will remember this one particular gentleman, but stranger things have happened. Tell you what. Let me ring her here on my break. Maybe she will remember something. Maybe not. Who exactly is this man you are seeking?"

The sisters were pleased and thanked their waitress and waited. It's all they could do.

There was a place renting rooms out by the night across the way, so Aletha told Mary she was going to head on over and secure a room for them before it got too late. Mary nodded and just sat there, waiting for this waitress to return with hopefully something of substance. If she knew nothing, this entire trip may be for naught. They needed Ida Mae to point them in a direction, or they would be lost in this town for sure.

When Aletha returned she told Mary that all was good. The room had been rented and was theirs for the next few nights. It was a relief to know that was behind them, but she noticed Mary was sitting there with a peculiar look on her face. One of shock, and almost as if she were frightened.

"What is it?", Aletha asked confused.

Mary did not say a word at first. She just looked at her sister as if in a trance, and then she began to open her mouth as Aletha waited patiently.

"She reached Ida Mae. The waitress phoned her and was able to get her. Aletha, she told Ida what we were doing here and why, and Ida is on her way in now to speak with us. She said for us not to leave. She will be here just as quickly as she can," Mary told her.

Aletha was a bit shocked that this waitress who was off work sick, was coming in to see the sisters. Why? What could possibly make her want to come down here and now? She was confused but curious and so they would do just that. Sit and wait for Ida Mae to come in, and then they would see what this woman had to say about a man.

Chapter 31

A Sadness in the Eyes of Shreve

* * *

It was now just past seven in the evening, and the diner was winding down as people began to shuffle out. The girls had consumed more water today than possibly at any other time in their lives. There wasn't much to do but sit there and drink water refills and nibble on bread until Ida Mae showed up. They began to wonder if she were really coming, or if perhaps she decided against it. Maybe she had no news that would help and felt bad, thus changing her mind about coming in.

Aletha was feeling a bit tired and thought that the sisters should consider calling it a night, but Mary refused. She was here to find out who this man was, and that is exactly what she intended to do. With or without anyone's help.

So, they waited some more. At almost eight in the evening, the sisters heard the bell as the door opened, leading into the dining area. Figuring it was just a late-night couple coming in to order some food after a long afternoon, they barely took notice.

As Mary lifted her head towards the entrance of the diner, she tapped Aletha's hand and pointed in the direction of the noise.

Aletha slowly lifted her head, turning it in the direction her sister Mary was pointing, and saw a small black woman standing there looking around. She had short dark hair that appeared to be forced up in place. Her face showed signs of being worn down, and her posture was slightly forward as if she had just walked out of bed.

The waitress that had been attending to the sisters saw this woman, and said to her,

"Hey Ida Mae. You look god-awful. You okay sweety?"

The woman tried to force a smile and just nodded, then raised her eyes as if to ask a question without saying a word.

"Right over there, dear. Those two sitting right over there," as she motioned Ida Mae into the direction of Aletha and Mary.

The woman looked over, placed her hands through her hair trying to ensure it was presentable and started in the direction of the sisters, as both Aletha and Mary looked her way. They were trying to get a read on this lady, even though by now they clearly knew who she was. They could tell she was still not feeling well at all, but had worked herself up enough to get dressed and head on out to meet them.

As she arrived at the edge of the red and white trimmed table, she looked at them both as if trying to find a resemblance to someone she had met, and Aletha knew it. She knew that Ida Mae was trying to see a little of them in the man she met that day the year before, before saying anything.

So many questions were coming to Aletha's mind, but she waited. She waited for this woman to speak before she too said a single word.

"I'm awfully sorry it took me so long. I'm...I'm just starting to feel myself some. Whatever I had sure took me out. That's for certain. But I am here. Is it all right that I sit down here?", as she motioned with her tiny hands to where Mary was seated.

Mary took a second before realizing the question asked of her.

"Oh yes! Yes, of course, I'm sorry. Please, sit. Can I get you anything?", Mary asked her.

"Just a coffee, maybe." Ida Mae responded back.

The waitress who had seated them and brought their food over had known Ida Mae would want some coffee before she even had the time to ask, because she had already poured a fresh cup and was walking it in our direction. She placed the cup in front of Ida Mae and smiled as she walked back to finish whatever she was doing before.

"So, tell me. Tell me about you all and what brings you to Shreve, other than the fine cooking here," Ida Mae said trying to relax the mood with a little humor.

It worked, because Aletha put her guard down some and smiled gently. She needed to feel relaxed and this woman whom they had never met, sensed that. She had in one sentence allowed the table to clear of any nervousness towards each other, although clearly the nerves were still high over the "what-if" part no one really knew yet.

"Well, Ida Mae? I'm Aletha, and that seated next to you is my sister, Mary. We came here because a dear friend of mine overheard a conversation you had last year, and we needed to know a little more."

Mary was fidgeting in her seat, trying to not ask a million questions all at the same time, but she was keeping herself as relaxed as she possibly could. It was not easy. So many thoughts were at the front of her mind and on the very tip of her tongue, but she knew to be patient. She knew to be patient long enough until it was the proper time to ask, and then that she would need to do so without throwing them all at this woman at one time.

Ida Mae nodded as if she knew this part already but wanted to be polite and allow her to continue.

Aletha went on, telling this woman they had never met before about where they had grown up, the moves they had made over the years, and about her brother, Keith. She then told Ida Mae about her mother and how she had died suddenly, or at least how she was told she had died, and then…then she went on to the story of her three brothers and that fateful night they disappeared. How exhausted men came knocking on the door early the next morning with horrible news. That her father simply could not handle any more loss and found a place for each girl to live until he could figure out his own life.

Ida Mae never took her eyes off Aletha as she spoke. At one point, she held her hand out for Mary, who was seating right next to her, and Mary took it without hesitation. Ida

Mae knew these sisters had been through such great loss and had struggled to find their way in this world without the family they once knew, and had by chance ended up here, in this diner on a road they would have never traveled otherwise.

As Aletha finished, she realized that she told this stranger more about her family than almost anyone else in her entire life. The Knorr's knew a great deal, but even they did not know some of the intimate details she had just shared with a stranger. Her friend, Lucille, knew probably more about her life than anyone outside of her family, and she was the one who had overheard the conversation in the first place, so she was glad she told her dearest friend so much.

Mary had been holding her thoughts in while her older sister shared away, but now she had to ask.

"Miss, was it our father you saw?"

Aletha looked at Mary, and then at Ida Mae. She too, wanted to know if there was a chance.

Ida had said little until this point. She sat back in her chair, and again placed her hands on the top of her head to fix her hair, and finally spoke.

"Do you perhaps have a photo of your father? I wonder if I would be able to see who you are talking about. It would help."

Aletha had forgotten that she indeed had a photo and brought it with her. She took her flower print purse and placed it directly in front of her, opened the top and reached in. Out of it she pulled a small black and white, slightly faded photo that had tattered edges and looked at it for moment before reaching out to Ida Mae and handing it over.

Ida thanked her, put on her glasses, and studied the photo closely. She saw a young man with a strong jaw and dark hair. He had wonderful, soothing eyes and a smile that showed true happiness. She smiled at the photo, saying to the sisters,

"This man is proud in this photo. Truly happy and content. It's a wonderful picture."

Mary wondered if she meant that the man was not the same one Ida Mae had seen, and a sinking feeling filled her stomach instantly. She was hoping for a quite different response but had not seen that from this woman next to her.

Ida Mae handed the photo back and took off her glasses. She began,

"The man I saw had wonderful sad, pained eyes, and no smile. His hair was turning gray to match his eyes, and his features were hard to see, for he hid them behind his pain. I saw him a few more times after that day but did not talk to him much at all. He seemed as if he preferred to be alone, so I did just that. I did ask him his name on one occasion though. Forget what it is now. Carmen? No. Something like that. Wait, Carl. The man's name was Carl. I remember now."

Mary squeezed the woman's hand tightly and then quickly let go and apologized.

"Child, you okay?", Ida Mae asked.

She could not believe her ears. Neither could Aletha. While it was no guarantee this man was their father, what were the odds of two men living in the same state, having the same name and story of loss? They could not be exceedingly high. Even if his hair had grayed and his features changed some. They both had gray eyes, too. It had to be their father. For the first time in many years, the girls thought that it just may be possible to find him. To find their father who had left with not much more than a goodbye years before, and a vague promise to return. He may still actually be alive.

The women talked for a while longer, and Ida Mae seemed to forget that she had been sick for a week. They laughed some, cried a little, and felt as if they were old friends. Each of them took turns talking about what they had remembered as children, or in Ida's case, what she had learned from that man.

While she did not know for certain where this man was from, or where he lived now, she knew that he was somewhere on the north side of town, working a farm that she swore had cows. She vaguely remembered another man asking him about the dairy business, but she could not be certain.

The sisters were asking questions about the town itself, and who knew who best. They asked when she had seen this Carl fella last, to which Ida Mae could not recall for sure. It had been several months though.

That caused a little concern for the sisters, as they wondered why. Had he moved once again? Maybe something happened to him on the farm while he was working. Any number of reasons were there for why he had not returned to the diner. It was not certain that something indeed happened, so they had that, but there had to be a reason he just stopped returning. Ida Mae tried to keep the girls' spirits alive and told them that it could have been the food.

They all laughed, well, except for the owner of the diner. He just glared at Ida Mae and shook his head. She smiled and waived him off as if to let him know, she was only kidding.

When they had finished, Ida Mae wrote down on a piece of paper her contact information. She asked the girls to reach out if they had any further questions, although she thought that she had given them all she had. She also asked that once they figured out who this man was, that they contact her. In her mind, she had to know how this story ended and if this was the father of these two young women. It would make her feel blessed to know she had been able to bring a family lost in despair, back together once again.

Both Aletha and Mary promised her they surely would let her know, and then they decided it was time to walk on over to their room and get a good night's rest. Tomorrow was coming, and they wanted to get an early start navigating this area and to put a plan in motion. They now had more information than they had when they first arrived here, which was extremely good news for the sisters. Now, they just needed to find this Carl.

Chapter 32

Sheer Luck of Cyrus

* * *

The next morning, both girls woke up early to the sun peeking its warm rays through the window shades. It was welcoming them to wake up and enjoy this fine day. Aletha was the first to rise and looked out the window to the small town below. She saw only a few folks walking the street, and a few more seated at the diner across the street, the same diner they had met Ida Mae in, and the same diner they had learned the man's name from Shreve. Carl. Aletha knew in her heart it was him, but she felt a sense of concern for Mary if it were not, or if they could not find this man. What then? She had no idea. After all these years they wondered and heard stories of someone seeing a man resembling him, to only find out they had nothing. It could have been him those people saw, or just some man minding his business before returning home to his intact family. They never knew, and nor did it matter much.

Mary woke up as Aletha was still peering through the

window opening and asked her what time it was.

"It's just after seven", was her reply.

Mary had always gotten up early, but because of all the excitement and emotions of last night, must have needed the extra sleep. Her body was begging her to rest, while her mind was telling her to rise up to greet the day. Her mind would win this battle.

As they both now stood facing the street from the second-floor room they were in, Mary asked her sister,

"What are the chances we find this man, here, with the few days we have? How are you feeling about this?"

Aletha paused for a moment as she often did. She wanted to be sure she answered the question well enough that she sounded at least hopeful, but left room for doubt so as not to disappoint her younger sister, or perhaps herself. It was a balance she tried to give each situation, no matter what she was doing. Here was no different, and her sister's feelings were extremely important to Aletha.

"Well sister, I think we have as good a chance as anyone would. We have some clues, and if he is out there, I think we can find him. If we do not, well, maybe we just understand that it may not have been him to begin with. Maybe, but let's not get ahead of ourselves just yet. For now, let us enjoy this day and start our search. It is marvelous out and the air smells clean. That for us is a good start, already."

Mary agreed, and the two sisters decided to get some breakfast, and then head on out for the day. They would eat at the diner, then figure out the bus schedule. Not knowing where they were going, this seemed to be the easiest way to get around.

Once they finished their eggs and breakfast sausage, the two women paid the bill, and left the diner in search of direction, each wondering which way to go, but neither clear. So, they decided to just go north on the bus, and were not so worried about east or west. All they decided on was the north. The bus was empty that day, so the women were able to speak with the driver openly. He asked them what they were doing on this fine morning, and where they were headed. When they told him about the dairy farm, and trying to locate a man named Carl, the driver said that he knew where some dairy farms were but did not know a Carl. He would be sure they got off where he felt they had the best chance.

Along the short drive, the women looked out the window to the fields and farms all stretched out. For each, they wondered, had this Carl delivered milk there? Their minds were full of wonderous stories he had not yet told them, about the past almost twenty years he had lived, and what he had done during those years. Had he found a second love of his life and remarried? Had any more children? It had never occurred to them that it could be a real possibility. Maybe they had half siblings they knew nothing about. It began to give them a strange feeling once again in their stomachs. The thought of that all. If he had giving up his two girls and started another family, how exactly would they feel about that?

The bus came to a stop, and the driver reminded them

of the schedule for the pickups back to town. He reminded them that once the last bus left, that would be it until the following morning. The sisters thanked him and went on their way off the bus. As he left, the driver waved and wished them good luck on their search for Carl.

There was not a soul around, but farms stretched out in all directions for miles. What were they to do now? They wondered if they had not thought this out well enough. Mary, though, was intent on finding what they could. Without much hesitation, she started off in one direction and did not turn around to see if her sister was following. Aletha stared at her sister in wonder but knew how she was. Mary was ready and there would be no slowing her sister down. She quickly followed her, and off they went.

When they came to the first farm that had any sign of life, and old farmer saw the two and wondered what in the heck these two women were doing out here on his farm. He quickly dropped what he was doing, and wiped his brow with his hat, looked curiously at them, then headed over to where they were.

"Ya's lost, ladies?", he asked puzzled.

"No, well, sort of. We are looking for a dairy farm," Mary politely answered back.

"A dairy farm, huh? Well, now let's see. There are a lot of dairy farms around, little lady. Are you just looking for any old one or did you have one in mind you was looking for?", he shot back.

Aletha was sensing this was confusing the two of them some, so she spoke up,

"Sir, we are looking for a dairy farm with a man named Carl who runs it. He has graying hair and eyes to match, a strong jaw, and," she stopped, wondering if she should get into the story of the lost boys, but then thought better of it. What if this farmer did not want those around him knowing? What if he had told the waitress on an off day and really did not want that story to get out to those he knew well?

She just did not continue. Instead, she looked at the farmer, who was wearing blue overalls and a white long-sleeved shirt that had the cuffs undone, and dark brown boots with a baseball cap on top of his head.

He removed his hat once again, showing the lack of hair on top of his head. You could see the sun glare and his sweat from working hard all morning.

"Let's see. Carl. There is a fella named Carl who works a dairy farm, but he don't own it. It's owned by the under-taker in town. They grow crops and have dairy cows for sure. Not sure if that is your man fella you ladies are look-ing for, but I can point you in the direction. Matter of fact, I can do you one better. Wait here," and then he walked back to his house, walked in, and allowed the door to slam behind him.

Aletha and Mary looked at each other, not knowing what this man was doing, or if he was coming back. They waited as instructed though. This was more news that could help them on their search, and so they decided it was best to simply wait. It was this or wander off in all directions knowing nothing more than they had now. With

234

the seemingly miles of farms around, they knew they could not visit many.

After a few moments, the sisters began to wonder what he was doing and if they should knock on his door. Mary was ready to walk to his front door, when they saw him exiting. He walked over to an old red barn that was adjacent to the main house and disappeared once again.

When he emerged, he was sitting atop a red tractor, loud and smelling of oil. He drove up to where the two women were standing still and told them to hop on.

At first, they hesitated. Not because they had not known what it was, but because they still did not know who he was.

Mary climbed on first, and Aletha, still uneasy about this, decided to climb on next. As they got to where there was room to sit next to the farmer, he told them he had some business he could tend to on the farm next to the one this Carl worked on. He would be glad to give them a lift there and then back, if they chose to.

They did of course.

The ride was bumpy, but the women did not mind. There was no talk on the way there, except for a greeting.

"Ladies excuse my ignorance. My name is Cyrus. I'm pleased to meet your acquaintance."

"Cyrus, it's a pleasure. This here is Mary, and I am Aletha. And we can't thank you enough for this ride. It's truly appreciated."

Cyrus did not respond, but not to be rude. He probably could not hear well over the engine. He was already a little hard-of-hearing as it was, so he just smiled and focused on the road. On occasion he would point out to a field, or an animal eating by a fence. He did not say anything, but would simply point.

The women felt relaxed at this all and had little trouble calming their nerves. Cyrus seemed harmless and just there to help them. They were grateful for this. At least to this point, everyone had been welcoming and hopeful for the sisters. They needed this more than they knew, and were getting just that. Calm, with a lot of hope.

As Cyrus turned one bend and then another, he drove off the road down a long dusty stretch of what seemed like a road long since not traveled. This was the first time the girls were nervous, and Cyrus could tell.

"It's a shortcut. Old Cyrus knows this town like the back of my hand. Ladies, we are almost there."

When the road ended, Cyrus stopped the tractor, turned off its loud obnoxious engine, and got down first. He reached his hand up to help both sisters off the tractor, and then looked off to the left.

"There. That's the dairy farm the man named Carl works on right there. Just down that road, you will find a white stone house with a rather large barn to the right. He lives in that there house with his wife, May."

Wait, what did he say? His wife? This Carl was married?

"I'm heading over this direction a few farms down. I will be maybe an hour or so but will wait as long as I can. Just meet me back here to let me know if you'll be needing a ride back. Ladies, I hope you find the man you are looking for. I do," he said before he climbed back up on the tractor, started her diesel engine back up, and was on his way.

Aletha and Mary watched as he drove off, and then looked at each other.

"Well, here we are. What now?", chuckled Aletha.

Mary laughed back, as they tried to hide their nerves. They were facing the long road leading to the house at the bottom. Here, they would shortly know who this Carl man was, and, in fact, would know if that man was their long-lost father who had left them long ago.

As they walked down the road, each could be seen looking off into the grassy fields, hoping to catch an early glimpse of the man working the farm. They saw animals grazing in the fields, and spare farm equipment parts lying against the barns on the property. But they saw no one, not a soul in sight. Why? They wondered. Where was this man at? Shouldn't he be out in the field working the farm as farmers did?

When they got to the main house, they looked discouraged. There was not a sound, other than the animals out in the fields. Mary knocked on the door, and then did so again, a little louder now. She took a step back and looked up to the second floor, wondering if she could at least see some motion. There was nothing still.

Aletha eventually told her sister it was time to go. They would just find their way back here another day, perhaps tomorrow even. For now, they had located the farm, and this was good news. They should not see this as a loss, but as a victory. They knew now where this place was.

When they walked back down the path, they took their

time. Aletha reached over and touched a cow on top of its head, that was naturally grazing by the fence. She wondered if that cow knew Carl. If it had been touched in the same place by him, or if this was all a silly chase for nothing.

Mary was looking down, kicking rocks as she walked. She was dejected, and just had no idea of what she should be doing.

"Aletha, will you pray with me?"

Mary and Aletha were both praying women, but this took Aletha still by surprise.

"Of course, we can, Mary. Yes, let's pray," Aletha responded as she pulled her hand away from the cow she was talking with.

"Dear Lord, please send us a sign. We have come so far, and have waited so long, for just a sign that our father is alive and well. If it is your will, please, point us to our father, so that we may be with him once again. Please bless us, we pray. Amen," and Aletha finished.

She hugged Mary and told her it was all going to be okay. It would be the way it was intended to be, no matter what. Besides, Cyrus was still at the other farm, and that still gave them time to catch Carl coming back home from wherever he may be.

After an hour of talking, with a mix of emotional crying, they heard the loud obnoxious engine of Cyrus's tractor coming down the path, and they prepared themselves to tell him that they had not found anything to give them further information on their Carl. Hope was put on hold.

Chapter 33

A Chance Meeting

* * *

Back at the home of Cyrus, they each stepped down from the tractor, ready to walk back to the bus stop to fetch one back into town. But Cyrus had a better idea. He invited the sisters into his home to meet his wife, Mabel.

Mabel was a short round lady, with pleasant cheeks and short graying hair covering her eyes. She was energetic for an older woman, but you could also tell she was strong. Her forearms showed years of working the farm life and she was proud of that.

Instantly Mabel sat the girls down and started to cook for them. She did not even ask. It was almost funny how she was tripping over her words talking with the two sisters. She had so much to say, and more to ask. It appeared they had not had guests for some time now.

Mary asked about their children and how long they had been on that farm. She was looking for conversation as well to pass the time, but also to get a feel for who these two people really were.

"Well, we have three children, Cyrus and me, two daughters and one boy. Our kids are all grown now and moved off with their own families. We see them from time to time, but not often enough," Mabel began.

"Now how long have we been here on this farm? Well since I was born. This was my father's farm and before him, it was my grand pappy's farm. When papa died, Cyrus and I sold our home and moved here to take care of mother and the farm. That was, let's see, almost forty years ago now. My, how time has passed by. I suppose that happens in life. It just passes by, and we end up where we are, which is fine by me."

Mary struggled to keep up with Mabel as she kept talking, until Cyrus interrupted with,

"Mabel, now settle down there. Let the girls talk some. You ain't giving them no room to speak."

Mabel's face grew red, and she apologized.

"Oh no, I'm sorry. You see, I get going and well, it's hard to stop me once I get a-going!" she said.

The sisters smiled and then laughed, although they tried not to. But this also made Cyrus and Mabel laugh as well, and the mood was now easy in the kitchen.

Mabel insisted that the two girls stay the day, and even the night if they wished. They had plenty of extra rooms and well, Cyrus could always take them back to town in the morning. It made sense too, because Mary knew this meant another chance perhaps to catch Carl. If they sat outside, maybe they would see him drive by and ask Cyrus for a second ride back to the farm. It was worth a shot.

Mabel reminded Cyrus about the carnival just on the outside of town. She had wanted to go last year but was not feeling well enough, so she was certainly not going to miss out on it two years in a row. Cyrus did not answer her. Again, either he had not heard her, or was simply in agreement and did not feel the need to say it.

She asked the sisters if they would like to join them, and with nothing else to do, they agreed and thanked Mabel for the offer.

Cyrus told Mabel he wanted to do a few more things, and then he would wash up and they could head out. He just needed to button up a few tasks he had started earlier when he was sidetracked by the sisters. Aletha asked if she could give him a hand, which caught Cyrus off guard some. But, he agreed, not wanting to offend her and happy that she had even offered.

Mary stayed behind with Mabel and gave her a hand cleaning up after the food they had just consumed. Once Mabel got started again with her talking, she wondered though if she should have gone out with Aletha and Cyrus, but she was still glad for the company.

After a short time, both Cyrus and Aletha walked back in and headed to the kitchen for a glass of water. Aletha looked proud, and that made Mary happy. It was as if she was back on a farm with the grandparents helping them, or perhaps side-by-side with their father, helping him tend to the farm he managed.

When they had finished, they walked outside to the

pickup Cyrus had. It was a black flatbed, and without hesitation, Aletha and Mary jumped in the back of the bed and sat down, ready to enjoy some time away from life for a short while. It had been a long time since either had been to a circus or fair, so this would be a welcome event for sure.

Once again, the road was a bumpy ride, but they noticed very little. The sisters looked out over the edge of the bed and watched as farms drifted before their eyes and then faded away over the rolling hills.

When they heard noise over the roar of the truck and the stones on the road, they both turned over their shoulders to see in the near distance all different colors and shapes, and they knew they were there.

As the truck came to a stop, Cyrus helped each of the sisters out of the bed, and down onto the grass. They walked together into the carnival and saw food, games, and rides in all directions. Mabel was so excited that she gave herself the hiccups from talking so much. Cyrus just shook his head saying, "I told ya you would give yourself them blasted hiccups again if you didn't stop yapping so much".

She just laughed and continued to talk through them. It was all so comical, but you could tell Cyrus loved Mabel dearly. He just had trouble expressing it.

Mary and Aletha wanted to go and walk the grounds, so they agreed to meet back up at the entrance in two hours. This way they could hear their thoughts without trying to follow what Mabel was saying. Poor Mabel, they thought, but then Aletha said, "Poor Cyrus!", and they laughed as they ran to the other side of the grounds.

There were rides of all types, and games with men calling the women over, enticing them with prizes high and low. Mary thought they should play a game or two, but Aletha was concerned they would get conned into spending money they just could not. She knew they could ill afford to spend on things they did not need. Charles had wanted for her to get away, but they did not have extra money like some folks did. They had wanted to save and plan for a family, so she was just being extra cautious.

When they got past the games with balls and darts and colorful balloons, they came to a group of rides to the far right of the fair. Some of the rides looked inviting, while others were clearly for younger children. Mary darted off again, and Aletha, rolling her eyes but finding this all amusing once again, gave chase.

The ride Mary wanted to go on was called "The Whip". It's a ride that consists of two circular wheel platforms on the opposite side of a rectangular base. Cars are attached and turn around the track by cables, and as the car approaches a turn, it whips around the bend, hence the name, "The Whip".

Mary stood in line, and when Aletha finally caught up, she stood beside her. They reached into their purses to take out the change needed for the ride. As they dug deep, Aletha saw the picture of Carl down at the bottom of her purse. She pulled it up but did not show Mary. She did not want to upset her sister once again, because she was now happy with this afternoon they were having.

At the front of the line, they were watching to see what color car they would be getting on and started to hand their money to the man with the dark gray felt cap on his head. As he went to thank them and open the gate for the two women to enter, Aletha collapsed. She apparently fell all at once and Mary had no time to catch her. The man in the cap had barely a second to react, but he did, grabbing Aletha on her way down to the hard surface below.

As Mary asked Aletha if she was all right, she simultaneously went to thank the man as well for his efforts and was stopped dead in her thought.

The man standing before her had sad, gray eyes, graying hair under his flat cap, and a strong jaw line that fit his face perfectly. He looked at Mary to ask if her friend was okay, and almost dropped Aletha in the process.

"Mary?", the man said. He then looked at the woman who was coming to in his strong arms, and asked, "Aletha?".

Carl had left the farm that morning to help with the local carnival in town. He was handy with mechanics and so it made him a valuable guy to have around the rides. Carl often took on side jobs when local events were in town and enjoyed getting out of the house whenever he could.

Today, here he stood, for the first time in close to twenty years, face-to-face with two little girls, who were not so little any longer. His eyes felt as if they were deceiving him. How could this be that in Shreve of all places, these two remaining children of his had found their way to him, at a carnival in the middle of nowhere, at this very moment.

Mary couldn't speak a word, and Aletha was now

standing next to her, looking as if they had seen a ghost. Was this their father? Had they actually found him?

Carl called over to another man working not too far off and told him that he needed to take over. The man turned directions and walked over, asking Carl if he were okay.

"I'm not sure, but I need some time. Can you cover here for me, Joe?"

As the daylight started to fade off, and the noise grew increasingly louder as more people arrived at the carnival, there stood a man and two young women, awkwardly shuffling back and forth, looking for words and perhaps a strength that had left them all just moments ago, or perhaps even a few decades ago. In the seconds that had just transpired, they had gone from giddy, to confused, to curious all at once.

At first, they all wanted to speak up but could not. But then, Carl decided to break the ice.

"Girls, I...I want to say so much right now. How, where, I mean, what are you both doing here?", he managed to get out.

It was exactly what was needed. A breaking of the ice that left a door wide open for the two young women to speak up without them having to start this intrusive conversation. They were not prepared at that very moment, having given their journey a break to enjoy this evening. Had this happened as they expected it to at Carl's home that late morning, maybe things would be different. They had questions jotted down on a piece of paper, and both were ready, as ready as one could be in this situation, to ask.

Not here though. Not now. It had caught them completely by surprise and still, they were standing here with this man, knowing exactly who he was, without a single doubt in their hearts.

It was Aletha that spoke up first. Mary would have been the one if both women had to guess, but she was still in a shock and had lost all her words.

"We have so much to tell you, so much to ask of you. Can we find a place to sit, maybe that isn't so loud?" She started.

Realizing that this reunion deserved a better atmosphere, Carl quickly nodded and looked over to the man who had relieved him just moments ago, and without hesitation, the man waved him off to let him know he had him covered.

Carl smiled at the man and nodded back in appreciation. The man knew this was something important, even if he did not know what or why. It was clear as day on the faces of his coworker and the two ladies standing before him.

The three walked gradually through the area of carnival rides, past all the men trying to grab the girls' attention for one quick game of chance that would almost surely win them a prize, and back towards the entrance they had arrived in. They continued through the people marching in and walked over to an area that had a single table resting on the grass just out of the way of all the hustle and bustle.

As they sat, Carl motioning with his outstretched arm for his girls to sit first, they felt a sense of relief. One, because they had found the man named Carl, who turned out to be exactly who they had hoped it would, and two, because they felt oddly relaxed in his presence now, having had time on the walk here to collect themselves just enough and to also collect some of their emotions that were astray.

Then, it began.

Chapter 34

Meeting May

* * *

By the end of 1919, the world was a much different place than it would be in 1937. All the years between had ups and downs. The Spanish flu had ripped chaos through the world and after taking what it had come after, seemingly became tamable. The roaring 20s were full of excitement and money and fame, then that too, was decimated by the Great Crash. People were born, and people died. Good people. The young continued to grow and age, even if they had never wanted to.

For now, life was vastly different and would remain that way. The girls knew they could not regain what had been sadly lost over the past two decades, but they had hopes that going forward, they would have some peace from this all and they would not need to carry this burden with them any further than here.

They could see that Carl was trying to read them. He probably never expected this day to come, and if he did, he would not have expected it today, here, this way.

Aletha could sense that her father was feeling concerned, and she felt bad for him, even if she had felt some anger over the years, stemming from his decision to move away to deal with all that happened. She had truly always tried to give him grace for that decision and what it meant for her and her sister, but truthfully, she still felt cheated in many ways. Her life had been hard, and she needed a father to tell her it was all going to be okay, but he had not been there to do so.

Before she could speak though, Carl spoke.

"Girls. Aletha. Mary. You are both beautiful. I...I'm sorry. I know no words I am going to speak today, or perhaps ever, will make up for all those years behind us. I know that, and I am not claiming you should forgive me, but there was so much I needed to do for myself and you girls, that you never knew."

As he spoke, both sisters hung on every word as if they may never get this chance again. They had no clue what would come later, after this day, and were unwilling to miss something they had yearned for. So, they sat and listened as he continued.

"When Phoebe, I mean your mother, passed, I was lost girls. That woman," and he trailed off into a memory that he probably kept hidden for so long, finding some comfort in that now though. "She was something special. Aletha, you and the boys had made her a gift, do you remember? You made her a gift I was to bring her to the hospital that morning, and I left, forgetting to grab it on my way. I forgot, and when I arrived, I felt bad for leaving it. But what

I did not know on my way there, was that she was already gone. I had no idea that when I arrived to see her, that I no longer would see her the same. That was hard on your pa, but I forgot to see that it would be hard on you all too."

Mary started to tear up, and Carl pulled out an off-white-colored hanky and unfolded it for his youngest daughter. He handed it over to her so easily, comfortably, as if he had done this many times with her already over the past 20 years.

He caught what just happened and realized how easily he had done that, with no expectation or pause at all. That act made Carl question just who he was in that moment. He knew, of course, that he was their father, but what *was* he to these women? Was he still their pa? Could all those years away be erased and could time be forgiving to him, or was this going to be just a simple hello and goodbye for perhaps another twenty years?

"I don't know how you felt at that time, but I know how I felt," Aletha started. "I was afraid, scared and hurt. My mother had left us, and here I was, trying my hardest to fill her shoes for you and our brothers and Mary. I tried so hard to push that pain far away so that I could be what we needed, what you needed. I struggled with that, even if I never said so."

Carl could sense some tension, and he wanted to quickly change that. The last thing he wanted was for the girls to be angry. Not now. He knew they may have anger that he could do nothing about, but not here. He needed them to know he understood.

"Aletha, I now know what you had to endure, and I never meant for that to happen. Mary, you as well. I know you both had to deal with what I was. I was weak. You were both so much stronger. Much stronger than I. Not a day goes by where I do not think about the decisions I made, and wonder, what could I have done differently? I question myself all the time and there are days I hate myself for what I have done. But I knew I was no good the way I was back then. I simply could not handle... losing your brothers like that was hard. I don't even know what to say. The words simply don't exist."

Mary had been sitting by listening as both father and older sister went around and around, trying to determine how they should feel. She knew though, how she felt. She was simply happy to be here and knew the importance of this occasion that she had waited so long to share.

"Can I say something?", interrupting the two of them, and causing both to shift their focus towards her.

"I waited a long time for this, to be here with just the two of you, and I waited to share what I had in my heart all this time. So, I am going to do just that," she continued.

Carl sat up, ready for whatever she was going to send his way. He was prepared now, having a little time behind him to accept what was happening in this monumental moment which he never expected to take place.

Mary went on,

"I missed you, with all my heart, I missed you, and today I feel sadness for what we lost, but happiness because I know we are whole in this very moment. As whole as we could be today. I am happy. From here I just want to never lose this feeling ever again."

Carl without hesitation, broke down right there in that moment, and both Mary and Aletha stood and walked around to where their father was seated and now hunched over, sat next to him, and hugged him. They felt their father under their arms, and so much felt right. The last time he had hugged them was that morning he left Aunt Cora's home and Aunt Hannah's place, and not since.

The questions they wanted answered could wait a bit longer. For in this moment, they did not matter. All that did was that they were all together now, and they knew in their hearts that this was not going to be the last time. None of the three would allow that to happen ever again. They did not need to tell each other this, they just felt it deep within. It was how things would just be.

During all of this, the two sisters forgot that they had arrived there with two other people who were most likely walking around the carnival enjoying the curious sounds and wonderous sights, and they were to meet them at any moment. They had lost track of time, and now sat here wondering how the rest of this night would go, as the sun had fully set on them now.

Carl helped them by asking that very question. He wanted to know just how they arrived there. Not necessarily at the carnival they were on the outside of now, but in general. How had they come to find him here, in Shreve of all places.

It dawned on both Aletha and Mary that they had left

Cyrus and Mabel somewhere on the grounds of the carnival that was still going strong, and they looked at each other wondering what to do.

Both girls explained quickly just the part of arriving here, now, and said they should at least make their way back over to those bright lights and screaming children, to let them know so they did not worry.

Carl, afraid that this was it for the evening, insisted that he walk them there. This man, a father finally once again, was feeling nervous that the night would end before he was ready. He wanted the chance to ask the girls to come back to his place to continue with what they had finally started, so they could learn so much more.

The sisters had not even considered this in the short time that had passed, but it made them feel good to know that their father, their pa, had wanted to talk so much further into the evening. They, too, had so many things to say and learn as well.

When they connected back with Cyrus and Mabel, Carl quickly walked over and thanked them both. Cyrus had seen Carl before and knew his name, but not much else. The farm Carl worked on was owned by the town's undertaker, so the farm was familiar to him, but Carl had kept to himself as best he could over the years.

The two men spoke only briefly, but it was how they both were, hard-working men who kept their heads down and focused on the task at hand. They were not the talkative type to mingle more than they needed to, although they were pleasant enough to each other.

When Mabel heard what was going on, she turned rose red in the face and started to get excited, causing her hiccups to return once again. Cyrus threw his hands into the air as if to say, "not this again," but he too, was genuinely happy for the sisters and Carl. Had he known more, perhaps he would have checked around with other farmers to see if they knew where he had gone, but at this point it did not matter much. What they had come to find, they indeed found.

Carl did not tell anyone he was leaving for the evening. He simply left. His truck was parked close to the entrance as he had been one of the first people there, setting up earlier that morning. The girls had walked by his black truck on the way into the carnival and had never known it was their father's. How could they have known?

On the ride home, there was a lot of silence as it was hard to tell what was okay to talk about, and what was maybe off limits. But as they got to the farm Carl managed, driving down the long, dusty drive the sisters had walked curiously that late morning, and approached the main house, they could see a light from inside. A silhouette stood there in the main doorway, and the girls looked over to Carl to see what he would say. He parked the truck and saw who was awaiting his return, smiled and dipped his head, knowing he had a lot more explaining to do than he remembered.

"That there," without being asked, "Is Mary. She goes by May. Girls, she's my wife."

Both sisters, jaws wide open, looked at each other and

could not find the words to express what they were initially feeling. It was as if the cat caught their tongue, and they were just going to have to wait until something came out on its own.

They began to open the truck door and walked towards the front door, waiting for Carl to lead the way. It was his home and Aletha and Mary were feeling slightly uneasy, as they had no idea of what to expect through that slightly opened door, and how this woman, this May, was going to receive them.

May was at the counter, not looking in their direction and when Carl swung open the door and held it for his two older daughters, she had not noticed them walk in behind him. It wasn't until she greeted her husband, and he did not respond initially, that she looked up from her task to see what he was doing. When she saw what was going on, she slowly placed the towel that she had been wiping the counter with down with and had a bewildered look on her face.

"Carl, who are these two?" she asked with a concerned look.

Carl was grinning and trying to hide his excitement because he still was not aware of how the girls had received him and there was so much to go over and understand. They may not be as receptive as he was about this all, so he was trying to tread lightly.

"May, these two girls are Aletha and Mary. Dear, these are my girls," he responded with great pride.

Chapter 35

The Apology

* * *

W hen 1919 closed out, Carl had headed north first to see what he could find. His job as a union oil man delivering for Standard Oil allowed him some flexibility when it came to where he could work. It was probably the one thing that saved his sanity, if not his very life. Although he worked almost unending, he appreciated that it allowed him to mask all the sorrow he was dealing with, as well as the dark thoughts that he was fighting nightly as he tried to lay his head down to sleep each evening.

At first, he traveled to a few different parts of Ohio, never really finding his way. A new town did not bring change or acceptance for him as he hoped. They simply were stopping points along the way to whatever was to come next in his journey.

He worked odd jobs on the rare days he was not driving, and used his hands to fix things for others, although he was truly broken himself. He did not talk much with folks in those new towns, and rarely talked about the past he was trying to leave behind. Whenever anyone would inquire as to where he had come from, he would either change the subject quickly, or respond that he had been from a town that no longer existed. In his mind, Alliance was merely a memory of a place that had once been his only hope for a better life, and then when she took that from him, along with that river he once loved, it was nothing more than a town that had since died.

May was standing there in a state of shock, as she had heard only stories of these two sisters over the years. Carl's daughters were not only in the wild tales Carl told, but they were real women, and standing in their home, fresh as day. She wondered just what to say, and how to greet these girls but it was not coming to her normally as one would expect when guest arrived.

Mary broke the silence. She sensed that it was an opportunity to clear the tension from the air, and she did not waste that.

"Hello, May. My name is Mary Elizabeth, and this here is my sister Aletha. We are pleased to make your acquaintance. It's a little awkward I know, but still the same, we are pleased to be here."

May dropped the cloth she had in her hand and smiled at Mary. She walked over to her and opened her arms to invite her in for a warm hug. It was as natural as she could make it, but still had a hint of wonder, a curiosity as to what the rest of their lives would look like from this moment on. May knew that nothing would be the same; nor could it. Something had been opened and she was hesitant to see what it would be like, but excited at the same time.

Carl just looked on and his face showed something it had not in many years. A genuine smile of relief that he had yearned to find but knew not how.

Aletha, still standing next to Mary, watched as Mary Elizabeth held May tightly. The moment was truly surreal and Aletha knew that even though they did not expect their father to be married, they had also not expected him not to be. This was a part of this all that they had given little thought to, and maybe that was for the best. Having that to further complicate their expectations would have only drowned out more of what they hoped to find.

"Aletha, my dear. It is lovely to meet you. I have heard so much about you. So much. I feel as if I have known you my entire life. It's wonderful to meet you finally," was how May decided to break the silence with the elder sister.

"Yes, May, yes. It is my pleasure," Aletha managed to reply back, still uneasy for the moment.

"I'm sorry, I am a bit in a shock still. I just need some time to let this all sink in, but I am happy to meet you as well," Aletha continued.

May did not open her arms as she had done for Mary. Instead, she just leaned in towards Aletha and kissed her on the cheek. Her arm naturally found Aletha's neck and the two, while slightly awkwardly, managed to hug. It was not that neither wanted it. It was that they both wondered where they stood. May was Carl's wife. Aletha the eldest of the surviving children, who had sworn to make her father's life as easy as she could after all the death that ravished the family. They both had come from different beginnings and had different hopes for Carl. May hoping that her husband would find happiness with her, and Aletha that her father would know he was not responsible for all the death around him. And perhaps be able to connect with his daughters without the fear he would bring the same to them.

Carl continued to look on but remained silent. He was not willing to disturb this gathering at all. His figuring was that if he let it naturally play out, it would allow them to all find the words needed when they were ready. It would make it that much easier to understand what to say without fear of rejection or pain. Although he certainly was aware that some pain was going to visit them all, nonetheless. There were going to be some hard questions and a fear of answers for certain.

"Well, please. Please, sit. Can I get you both something to drink?" May asked the sisters.

"Water, please. That would be just fine ma'am," Aletha responding kindly.

"Dear, call me May."

As May got the two sisters a glass of cold water, she tried to find the perfect question to start this off. It was hard because although she knew the stories Carl had told her over their years together, she did not know just how much the girls had known or experienced over the last twenty years. She wanted to be cautious, but also seem genuinely interested in their journey to Shreve.

"I guess there is no easy way to start this off, is there

really," May started as she handed both sisters the tall glasses.

"No, I guess not," Aletha replied in firm agreement.

Mary was looking around curiously at the inside of the farmhouse, as Aletha and May went back and forth stiffly. She noticed an old photo of her father hanging on the wall, which was probably taken at the time of his marriage to their mother. Carl was looking straight in the photo and had well-kept hair, a soft gentle smile, and his eyes were piercing as she had remembered her aunts telling her about. There was a small table to the left with what appeared to be a photo of Carl and May, and then a few photos of two older boys on a shelf. In between the photos, there was a small, wooden box that appeared to be made from Ash and had carved into the front, "The heart knows no loss like the loss of the heart."

Carl noticed Mary looking around and decided to sit next to her.

"Mary, you are free to roam around and have a look if you like," he told her.

"I'm all right, thank you," she replied and put her head down.

She had envisioned finding her father for the first time in years and just running up to him and jumping in his arms like a young child would, and that all the pain and anger and fears would simply melt from her heart in that very moment. It had not happened, and it confused her. Here she was with the man she had looked for almost all her life, and she was not sure what she was feeling. It was not as she pictured this day going for sure.

Carl was also not sure of what he was supposed to say, or how close he was able to sit with the girls. The last thing he wanted was for anyone to feel as if he thought this would all be okay just because, and that they could simply forget what they all lost over the last two decades. He knew better and knew this was going to take time.

Aletha sensed the room was growing uncomfortable and decided she had waited all this time and was perfectly fine saying what was on her mind. She felt she had earned that.

"Why? I mean, I know why, but why for so long? Did you not wonder how we were doing, or what we were doing? Did you not want to come back and find us and to let us know you still loved us? Maybe you did not love us, but we loved you and needed you. We needed you," she said, as a tear formed on the edge of her eye.

Carl now had his head held low, and he ran his long fingers through his thinning graying hair as he tried to find the response she was after and most certainly deserved.

"Aletha, I know what you are thinking of me right now. I do. And I don't blame you none for that. I would feel the same if I were in your shoes. It's not that simple, however. It just ain't. I had to make a hard decision. One I never imagined having to ever make, and I did. Not a day went by that I did not regret that decision. Not a one. But I made it anyhow and figured I had to get along and leave what I had done be. I know that doesn't make it right. I know that. I'm...," he trailed off, afraid that his emotions were about to get the best of him.

Mary saw his face, pained and stiff. She saw the

disappointment he had in himself and the regret he had still to this day. It was apparent to her that this man, her father, had struggled just as much, if not more, with his decision as they had. The life he lived was not the life he expected at all, but he had to live it just the same. Maybe he did not. Maybe he had thoughts of not carrying on as he had, but he felt that would cause more pain than to simply vanish. It could not have been an easy decision for him, and she knew that now.

"Dad, I mean, yes. Dad. Did you know about grandma? Mom's mom died soon after you left. And Uncle Walter. He died too. Right after grandma. Pneumonia caught him. We just kept seeing loss after loss. It was hard to watch that, but harder wondering if you had died. We just never knew," Mary said, trying to seem grateful for the moment, but wanting to see just how much he truly knew.

Carl nodded slightly, still not looking at the girls. The night was going on and getting later, but none of them seemed to notice the time. As a farmer, Carl's mornings were early, and May would get up with her husband to ensure he had what he needed for the day. They worked well together through this phase of life and seemed to know what each needed.

"I knew. I knew about them both. They were kind and caring people, and when they died, I knew," he responded.

Knowing the next question that was going to come, he decided to answer it before they needed to ask and wonder.

"Girls, I stopped back from time to time to check on things. I did not have the heart, nor the nerve to show my face, but I knew. I watched you grow, walk with your friends whenever I had the chance to get that way. I had deliveries in and around the area, so when I could, I stopped and tried to find you. I would sit in my truck and watch from a distance at how you were growing. Mary, how did you think I knew it was you at the carnival? You were but a little child when I left, but I never truly left in the sense you think. I watched. I had to, but I could not bring myself to make it known. I knew people questioned what I did."

Aletha and Mary looked at each other, as if they had never suspected that. Each quickly thought about all those desperate years, wondering what he knew, and what he had seen of them. Had he known Aletha had married and divorced and married once again? What about Mary. Did he know she married? Did he know when Aletha moved from place to place, trying to find somewhere she felt could represent anything close to a home for her?

At that very moment, Mary interrupted the stare and turned quickly to her father, asking at once,

"It was you! I knew it was you. The heart rocks. They were you. On Mother's marker. They were you, weren't they?"

Carl managed a small smile, and for this question he was happy to answer. Only, he did not at first. He stood up and walked by the two girls, over to the shelf with the photos of the boys. He grabbed the ash box off the shelf and dusted the top off, blowing a quick two blows of air across its top. He held it in his hands for a few moments, looked at its beautiful features, and walked it back to where he had been seated.

"This box I've had since, well, it's been a while now," he started.

As he opened the box, he looked at its contents and smiled. For the moment he seemed lost in a memory that only he knew. Then, he looked at Mary and Aletha, and lowered the box for them both to see. Inside this ash wood box with the neatly carved wording, were dozens of tiny rocks. At first, the girls did not know what to think, until Carl told each of them to take one out.

The sisters did as he requested and held them in their hands, although unsure of why. Carl asked them to look at them closely, and they did as they were instructed. Suddenly, it had all become clear.

Each sister twisted the rock about, turning it over again and again, looking at the angles and feeling the smooth surfaces. They held, each of them, a heart-shaped stone in their palms.

When they looked at Carl, he just nodded as if to tell them he understood that they now understood. Then he laid the box out on the table in front of the girls, tipped it over, and allowed the remaining contents to flow out onto the wood surface. Each one they picked up and examined had the same unique quality about them. It was unmistakable. Each of them was in the shape of a heart.

Carl then reached into his front pocket of the worn dusty blue pants he had on, and pulled out a larger stone, that was gray in color with a line of red running through its center. The shape was almost a perfectly formed heart and fit well in his palm. He tossed it gently from one hand to the other, and then after examining it, he handed it to Mary.

"That there rock, I've had in my pocket for, let's see now, must be twenty plus years. Your mom slipped that rock to me when I was heading to work one day. She didn't think I knew, but I always did. She would place a different one for who knows what reason, but it didn't matter none. This one? This one here was the first one she placed in my pocket. I never forgot that one, and when she passed...," he paused trying to once again contain his emotions.

May walked over and put her arm around Carl. It was clear she knew that this man still had a fondness for his first wife. It was not his fault, nor her fault that Phoebe had died. May never took that personally when Carl felt saddened. She was a good woman and understood completely.

Carl needed just a moment, and by this point, both Aletha and Mary had found their way over to where he was seated, and were kneeling in front of their father, who was sitting with his head in his hands, massaging his temples as if to fend off an impending headache. They wrapped their arms around their father, and whispered in his ears,

"It's all right dad. It's going to be all right."

Chapter 36

A Needed Rest

* * *

Charles had not heard from Aletha. The plan was for the women to call their spouses when they arrived, which they had done, and when the evening was completed. They wanted to know the girls were all right, and to see what if anything they had learned on their trip. The first night, they had done both.

When the hours went by on the next evening, neither sister had given it a second thought. The fact they had found their father on the second day they arrived amazed them. No one knew the time of night it was, or if they had gone well into the morning for that matter. All they knew was that for the first time in their lives, it felt as if time had gone back and stood still for a short moment. Their father, much older now, was a young man, handsome and married to his beloved Phoebe. The girls were just that. Young girls, chasing their brothers around the yard as they pulled on their sister's long hair and laughed.

It was a memory they had all stored away but were able

to relive somewhat in this room they had walked into. The house was warm and inviting, but not at all how they had remembered their father living. May had done some wonderful decorating, even though they did not have a lot of money still. Carl continued to work incredibly hard, but he never quite figured out what it was he had always dreamt of. That dream had long since gone away, and here stood a man who had simply survived through tragedy. Life had not been fair, but it had spared him for one reason or another.

May had made coffee for what was probably the fourth time, as she understood a lot was left to be said. She was right.

Aletha talked about her horribly short marriage that ended almost as soon as it started, and then how she had met her Charles. She told her dad how vastly different this was, and that she was genuinely happy with her marriage.

Mary Elizabeth talked a lot about growing up with Hannah and how things went after Uncle Walter had died and they had to move. She mentioned that she had gone to the cemetery many times over the years and had always looked for a sign that he had walked the grassy fields to visit with their mother and brothers.

Carl was surprised that she had caught that and was proud that she knew he had in fact been there. While he suspected they may, he never really knew. He had been there more in the beginning than he had recently, so it was possible they forgot all about those stones, but clearly, they had not.

At one point, Aletha decided to ask May if she was okay with this all. She wanted to ask her father all she had kept in her heart for years, but also wanted to be respectful of May, who was now her father's wife. So, she decided to ask May outright if this was all okay with her, and if she preferred, they not get into all these details just now.

"Dear, you waited a long, long time for this moment. You ask whatever your heart desires. Your mother Phoebe was, I'm sure, a wonderful woman and I am fine hearing about her. Carl loved her and I understand that. He loves me and I understand that. It's just how life has been for us," May responded.

It made Aletha and Mary feel more at ease, but they had felt bad for not asking sooner. At least now they knew it was all right to continue freely asking what they needed to. It was, after all, May's house and her husband now as well.

At some point they all realized it was after midnight, and they all had a long, grueling day of emotions running deep through their veins.

Carl told them they had a spare room off the back of the home and that the girls would be comfortable there for the night. May grabbed some blankets and a few pillows off the couch and placed them neatly in a pile just inside the threshold.

As the two sisters got up from where they were sitting that evening, they each gave their father a kiss on the cheek and told him they would like to continue speaking the next morning when they would all arise. Carl told them he would like that very much, and if they wanted to, they could even give him a hand doing some work around the farm in the early morning. He was half joking, knowing they would most likely still be asleep, but the offer stood just the same.

That late night, which was basically an early morning by this point, was finally ending. As Aletha and Mary Elizabeth laid there, they talked quietly about what had just happened. It was still a shock to the girls that they were laying in the home their father was living in with his new wife. This was not at all how they expected this to happen, but it had anyway.

Eventually Aletha closed her eyes and could no longer form a sentence. She was drained and her body was letting her know she had enough for one day. She fell into a deep sleep and Mary was left looking up to the ceiling with its cracks and stains, wondering if this was really happening. What if she passed out and when she awoke, they were back home in their own beds next to their husbands? Could she handle that? Not that her life was bad. They were both happily married and excited about their future and children, but this was something she did not want to lose. Not now. She wanted this to all be the same come morning when the sun was waking them.

Then, Mary closed her eyes to dream, and quickly, the night was over. Just that fast.

The morning came as it always did, and Aletha was the first to open her eyes. She stretched and yawned, looking around the room to see what all was in there. When she came to this room the night before, she had not taken inventory of anything. She simply came to close her eyes and rest.

There were hangings on the walls of different people

and places. A bureau was at the far right of the room, just underneath the only window that was seeping sunlight into their space. On that was a single photo. As Aletha cleared her eyes with the outside of her hands, she sat up to get a closer look. She knew the faces and decided to give it a closer look still.

Walking past the sleeping Mary Elizabeth, she carefully walked over and grabbed the photo in her left hand. She then walked over her sister again, who was on the floor still seemingly in an unconscious slumber and sat back down.

As she studied the photo, she knew she had seen it before, but not for many years. There were five children in the black and white photo, all close together and smiling slightly. She knew these children. Rather well she knew these children.

In the middle of the back row, she recognized herself as a young girl, with pretty, uneven bows and her hair neatly parted right down the center. To the left of her stood her older brother, Russell. He was looking down at his younger sister and smirking as if he was loving on that child. He wore a suit and tie and looked extremely handsome.

Aletha wiped a tear away and smiled as she continued to look over this small photo in a nice dark wood frame.

To her right in the photo was Emil. He was just a year younger than she was and had a wool jacket that seemed a little too long on him. His wide collars were overshadowed only by his even wider smile. She laughed to herself remembering how he was so adamant about wearing gloves for the photo. Carl had told Phoebe, "What the hell. Let the boy wear them."

Seated underneath Russell was the youngest of the boys, Kenneth. He was the twin of Keith, who had died years before this photo was taken. She studied his face and saw so much future and curiosity in it and was saddened that she did not get to see what he was capable of.

Last, seated at the very middle of the photo, just under where she was standing, was Mary Elizabeth. She was a tiny girl, looking at the camera in a most bewildered way, and probably knowing not what was going on. She lifted her head and focused on where her sister was still sound asleep and smiled because she saw the amazing woman that little child had grown into. It was a surreal moment for her now. Seeing this photo brought her back to that very day, but knowing they were decades later now was reality and she could see both so clearly at the same exact time. That day, she remembered well, even though she had forgotten for decades that it had ever been taken.

She placed the photo back down, and then decided to walk out and let her sister sleep a little longer. They had time today so there was no rush, although she knew there was a lot to still talk over. She thought about all the questions they asked last night late into the early morning, and she hoped today could be a little easier. Maybe today, they could all just be a family, under that one roof, as they had so many times begged for.

She walked into the kitchen and noticed no one there. As she poured herself some coffee clearly made earlier in the morning, she looked out through the front door that had once again been left cracked open and gazed over the long path leading up to where they had first entered. She watched as the sun blanketed the animals in the field and warmed them up.

Aletha saw two figures in the distance and fixed her eyes to adjust to the morning light. She began to see the shapes and colors of those figures, and knew it was Carl and May. They were a short distance away, but she could still see them clearly.

Carl was helping a cow that appeared to be stuck in the fence. May was keeping the animal's attention as he lifted its leg free and helped it back to where it had been grazing in the field.

As they finished, Carl placed his arm around May, and they sat back admiring what they had done. It showed Aletha that this woman made her father happy. While he had lost so much, he did find love once again. Although he had left an entire life behind, he was given another chance at it and took that opportunity to live again. She was happy he did.

Aletha smiled and continued to watch, feeling much different than she had the evening before. Her father had made some extremely tough decisions and only he was able to understand the why. Maybe he knew if he stayed, his life would have ended. Maybe he feared for what would come for the two remaining children he had. It could have simply been he thought it was the only way to save them.

As she wondered, she heard Mary Elizabeth coming towards her.

"What are you looking at?" Mary asked.

"Look, there," Aletha responded in a whisper.

Mary opened the door wider to see and saw what Aletha was watching. Her father and May were walking, hand in hand, over to the remainder of the animals grazing. Carl was inspecting the area and looking for holes to fill in so that the animals would not break a leg when running. May was looking at the fencing and ensuring no holes had been created recently, other than the one the cow was caught in earlier. They were a team, and it made Mary smile as well.

"Well, shall we?" Aletha asked, knowing her sister knew what she was referring to.

"Yes, we shall," was her immediate reply.

They both put their shoes on, took the warm coffee mugs they had in their hands, and walked out the front door, off the porch, over to where Carl and May were.

Carl looked up as the women got closer, tapped May on the shoulder, and smiled. They stood there and waited for them to reach them, and then handed the sisters some old gloves the two had on. Aletha and Mary put on the worn gloves and got right to it. Very few words were needed. This was not about words. It was not about the work at hand. This was simply about being in the exact moment, at the exact time they were. It was meant to be simple. Meant to feel exactly right.

Chapter 37

Three Stone to Lay

*   *   *

In just a three-day period, so much had happened. More than anyone would have expected really, but it was a high they all felt. Nothing could take that away from them and they knew this.

The girls eventually called their husbands and told them the news. They had been so concerned for the women, and Mervin insisted that he was about to head out to try and find them. Mary laughed and said she understood, but that they were all fine. The girls would call Mervin and Charles prior to heading back home. They promised to for certain this time.

When they were ready to head back, Carl told them he would drive them all the way back home. He mentioned that he wanted to meet their husbands if the girls were all right with that. They were. He also told them he would need to see Hannah and of course Cora, but he thought they would maybe need some more time. Not wanting to overwhelm anyone with the situation, he decided to leave that to both Aletha and Mary.

May was going to stay behind and manage things while Carl did this. It was not her place and her journey she felt, so she wanted Carl to do this his way, without any interference to cause issues.

Both Aletha and Mary offered and said it would be fine, but she still politely declined, saying "Perhaps another time. Let this be about you all."

On the ride back, Mary wondered what things would be like from this point forward. Clearly, they had established an interest in a future together, but how would that look? No one really knew for certain and that was simply fine for now. There was no need to rush this.

As they got closer, Carl asked the girls if it would be all right to stop and visit with mom and the boys. He had not stopped by for some time, and what would be better than to do this as a family? Nothing he could imagine.

When they arrived, they at first sat in the truck and just looked over the landscape. The weather was mild, and the sun was peeking through the clouds, attempting to warm up the day. The grass was a lush green from the heavy rains that they had a week or so ago, and it made things look serene. Again, words were not needed, but Mary finally opened up.

"Any chance you brought a heart rock for mom, dad?", she asked.

Carl reached into his shirt pocket, pulled out three stones, and placed them in his hand. He then opened his palm and handed each daughter a rock. He kept one for himself, and said,

"Let's go see mom and your brothers. They've been

waiting for us to visit together for long enough, don't ya think?"

When they arrived at the spot where they all were buried, Carl spoke first.

"Hey Phoebe. I know, it's been a while, and I deeply apologize. Sometimes I just don't have the words to give you, and I feel pained about that. I want to tell you I miss you, and then I feel bad for leaving as I did. Today, though, I have something to tell you. We are all here. Me, the girls, we are here. I never imagined this happening, but your girls, those girls of ours are resilient. They never gave up and because of them, we are all here in one spot again. You, me, the girls, and the boys. All here. I wish, though, it were very different."

The sisters watched as their father spoke words they had not heard, nor a voice that had graced their ears in what seemed like forever. It was beautiful watching him as he treasured this moment. He needed this possibly more than they had, and they could see that now.

Carl had a difficult time keeping his emotions hidden, and Mary told him it was ok to just let it out. He earned that.

"Girls, your mom was special. More than anyone else in the world. She loved you all with every ounce of her soul, she did. Those boys, too. When she left, a part of me left with her, more so than you understand."

He looked at both of his girls and told them he had something to tell them.

They could only imagine what he needed to tell them that he had not already. They had spent day and night talking about so much. What could be troubling him now?

"I lost more than your mom that morning. With her she took another child. She was pregnant when she passed."

Aletha looked at Mary in shock. They had known their mother did not feel well, but they never really knew what happened to her, other than that her stomach was hurting her, and she did not come home from that. Other than that, they knew nothing else and never questioned it.

"Dad, how, I mean what, how far along was she? Why did no one ever tell us this?" Aletha interjected.

He looked at both his grown girls, standing there in disbelief and surprise. He knew they had never known. No one did. Just he and his Phoebe.

"She didn't want anyone to know. She felt that when she came home, she would tell you all herself. She had what the doctor's called appendicitis. They had to abort the baby, and this hurt your mother. She did not want that. She would do anything for her baby. She was so beautiful. The last time I spoke with her, she felt better and thought she would be home in a few days. She just never did come back home."

It was hard for the sisters to hear that after losing a son, then a wife and a child no one knew about, and then once again the loss of their three remaining sons, all at the same time and instance, that Carl had to carry that secret with him. He said that he had never even told May. It was something he planned to take to his grave, and he was prepared to do that. For some reason or another, today felt like the time to finally let that go. It had been eating at

Carl for years, and now, it was finally out of his heart. For that, he felt a great relief. Sadness, but relief.

When they were ready to leave, and the time was approaching for Carl to meet his sons-in-law for the very first time, each of them knelt down and placed the heart-shaped rocks they held in their hands onto the marker. They placed each one facing a different direction. Mary placed hers facing towards the town where she went after Carl left. Aletha positioned hers to face towards Aunt Cora's home, the place she had been placed. And Carl, he placed his facing Alliance. This was where he had hoped to retire with his bride, and where he had desired to raise his family that he loved so dearly.

They left but promised this would not be the last time they came here as a family. It was long overdue but would not be for long. Things were different, yet better.

Charles was excited to see his Aletha home at last. He was worried for so many reasons and concerned for how she would feel once she found this Carl fella. She had indeed found him, and he was more than happy to meet this man. He held no judgement of him, because Aletha would never allow that. He was respectful anyway, and felt that to judge a man, you needed to walk in his shoes. He would never be able to do that and was happy that he would not. Charles knew he could never handle the pain and anguish that Carl had been forced to deal with.

When Carl saw him, he walked over to him, put his hand out to shake it, and told Charles,

"Thank you for keeping my Aletha happy. She has told

me so much about you, and I am honored to meet you son."

He did the same for Mervin. Just as Charles had respected this man for his decisions he was forced to make, so did Mervin. Again, he understood that he would never want to be put in that position. He could not imagine what this man Carl had to deal with in his heart on a daily basis, but here he was now, face-to-face with Mervin, and Carl was smiling as if he had not a care in the world.

It seemed to both sons-in-law that this man had come back from the depths of hell and found himself again. He had crawled through a raging fire they could never imagine, burned, and smoldered, and somehow survived to tell the story.

Although he had been gone for so many years, he was here now and the daughters he brought into this world had found peace in that somehow. They forgave their father almost before they had even found him. It was not necessarily the act of forgiveness they needed, but more the act of allowing him to know they had wanted him back in their lives. They loved their dad, and he was always going to be their dad, no matter where he lived. That distance was not as far as they anticipated, and not as far as at the end of the 1930's as it had been in 1919. Cars moved faster. Buses and trains as well. He was simply in another place, healing in a way only he could and needed.

Both Hannah and Cora had heard he was back, but only after Mary Elizabeth had phoned them. She wanted to wait until he met their spouses first, so that it would not be so overwhelming for him.

Cora headed to Hannah's home, and they waited for Carl to arrive. As they waited, they sat back and talked about what they remembered of him when they last saw him. He had dark hair and those beautiful eyes. His body was strong, and his mind sharp. That is up until his boys left this place. They saw a rapid decline in that man, and they wondered what two decades had done to heal or destroy him further. They had no idea of what to expect.

When his truck pulled up, Cora heard the engine stop and ran to the front door. She swung it open, and the second Carl exited, she was on him, hugging him like one would expect after such a reunion. She did not let go, and he whispered in her ear, "I'm sorry. Cora, forgive me."

Hannah waited on the porch, watching this display of brother and sister reuniting.

It was important for Cora to let her brother know she missed him, forgave him, and most importantly, understood him. She was not willing to let him go in that embrace she gave. It would be a long moment before she would, and even then, she would be by his side. Almost as if she were afraid to let him go again, but Carl assured her, he was not going to walk away again. Not this time.

When they finally made it to the porch and Hannah had a moment to talk with her brother-in-law, she told him as well, she did not hold any ill will towards him. She knew Carl loved her "bookend sister" more than any other man could have. That meant a lot to Hannah. For Carl, it meant he no longer needed to fear what others thought of him. He had only worried about those that were the closest to him.

But still, someone was missing. Carl had not even thought about his mother, but he noticed he had not seen her. The girls told him she had remarried a man named John Brock, and that he lived with Cora down in West Virginia, but he knew nothing more. Perhaps she still needed time to see her son that she had not seen in forever and thought she had lost. He was okay with this and understood.

As Hannah opened the door of her home to let Carl in to sit and catch up, he saw in the very first room a woman who was crying but smiling at the same time. Carl was face-to-face with his mother, and dropped to his knees, because this completed his journey home and included all of those who had mattered to this man from Shreve.

Chapter 38
Back Home

***

In May of 1938, Charles and Aletha would welcome a child into this world. Charolet Eileen was born to the couple, and a change was coming. This would be the first of the new generation of children, and after having fathered six children of his own and losing one before birth, Carl was finally going to be a grandfather.

It had been a year of catching up for father and daughters, and sisters and son. Now having a new addition to the family, Carl, was excited in a way he had not felt before. He knew just how blessed he had become after losing hope year after year. Now though? He had a baby grandchild that he could watch grow from the time she was born, until he would breathe his final breath. That he knew was not going to be taken from him, and he would refuse to allow anything to step in the way as he had before.

Aletha swore to bring the baby by when she could and told her father that anytime he would like to visit, he was most certainly welcome.

Then, as it had so many times to the family already, tragedy struck once again.

Just weeks after little Charolet was born, on June 9, 1938, at the young age of twenty-nine, Charles T. Thomas died. He had been taken to the hospital a few days prior, complaining of intestinal pain, and would never return home.

Heartbroken once again, Aletha wondered why her life continued to test her, and she just needed that to stop. She was angry, lost, and alone.

As they buried Charles, Carl knew he had to do something. His daughter was struggling in the weeks after he died and having a newborn baby to raise alone with all she had going on was going to be no easy task.

So, Carl approached May and asked what she would think of Aletha and Charolet coming to stay with them for a while. Just until she could get herself straight again. It made sense, he explained. They could continue to learn about each other, which was something they worked on over the past year anyway and give Charolet something Carl had not been able to give his Aletha. A chance to make a difficult start to life a little more manageable. One where when someone left you, it did not mean everyone would. He had learned a lesson about pushing through the greatest of tragedies, and how while hard to navigate sometimes, in the end you would find a way. You just had to stick it through, no matter what the obstacles in your path may be.

May, of course being by her husband's side always and watching the re-bonding that had transpired within the last twelve months, was all too happy to have them there. She told Carl,

"This is your family. Your child. Your grandchild. They are welcome in our house today, tomorrow, and for as long as they need. We are family, Carl. There is not a question of if, but only of when we can get them here."

Shortly after that conversation they had, Carl left for Akron and headed to Aletha's place. She was holding her new baby as Carl knocked on her door.

When he entered, he sat down and asked if he could hold his grandbaby for a few moments. Aletha welcomed the small pause in her day, and sat down, exhausted from the whirlwind she had just been through, and was still not out of.

"Dad, why does this continue to happen to us? I mean, we are good people, right?"

Carl sat there for a moment and looked into the half-opened eyes of Charolet as she fussed lightly in his arms. It was a question he had asked himself over and over and had truly never come any closer to an answer now, no matter how hard or long he pondered.

"Aletha, I do not know. Truthfully, I do not," he said with a soft tone.

He tickled his grandbaby's belly, and looked at her tiny feet that were peeking out from under the blanket she was wrapped in. She was simply gorgeous, and he thought back in that moment about all the children he had raised, at least until that cold January morning that is. Had he stayed, what would have become of him? How would the lives of Aletha and Mary Elizabeth gone? One thing Carl could not shake from his mind was that feeling of loss that seemed to follow him like a black cloud. It was as if that great storm he fought through intended to take him and could not. So instead, she followed him throughout his life, taking all that he loved, because he would not submit to her call that day.

Seeing Charles pass just a year after reuniting with his children gave Carl concern. It seemed as if it may be all happening once again, but he would not allow this to change his course any longer than it had already. If she wanted him, she could come back for him. He was not going to abandon his family ever again.

Certainly, Aletha had to wonder too, but she never said a word. At this point in her life, she had lost all she had, but she was a strong-willed woman, and she was not willing to change her course either, just because the universe had something to say. It could take her if it liked, but she was not going to alter anymore of her life either, for she had done that for several decades now. It would simply need to find someone else to move on to.

After she and Charolet moved in with Carl and May that year, things came into better view. Loss was still in the air as that December of 1938 saw Lorenzo "Uncle Duke" Dray pass, but no one wanted to talk about the "Bradway curse" anymore. There had been such a large gap between the children dying and him coming back, that they would simply dismiss this as just misfortune.

Plus, most of the folks that remembered the boys falling

through the ice, Phoebe passing, and Carl leaving, had moved on to other areas, or passed away themselves, or simply forgotten after twenty years. Time went on and erased some of the memories of those broken years, but not for the ones who lived them. They could not just let them go or dismiss them as something that just happened.

Charolet loved her grandfather, and being able to grow up on a farm, watching as he plowed fields and milked cows, was more than a child could hope for. He would grab her up in his arms, pull her onto the tractor that he was working with that morning, and scream in to Aletha,

"The squirt and I are heading to do some work for the day! Be back soon!"

Aletha would run out and scream from the porch,

"You better be careful with her! And stop calling her squirt!"

Sometimes in life, skipping a beat means finding a new you. One that finds a path not walked through, both cold and lonely. Sometimes we do this to find a better future. Carl went through that cold. He experienced the pain of loss and defeat. He nearly lost his life when all he knew was departing from his world, and he gave up the only thing he had left. His little girls.

He was blessed to have these days back. He enjoyed having Aletha and Charolet by his side each morning and every night. Watching his grandbaby crawl, speak, and eventually walk, was more about starting over, than it was about getting back. He lost all those years and knew he could never regain the memories he had not been able to create, but here he had a chance to at least live that through the eyes of Aletha. He could see just how she enjoyed each thing her daughter accomplished. He could watch as she encouraged her little girl to "try again for momma." He could watch as she struggled and failed as a parent as we all do at times, and how she pushed through and continued on despite the odds. That was something he needed to see.

It pained him to know he could have done things differently, but in his heart, he knew he did what he needed to do. It had not been a decision he took lightly. He agonized over the thought of leaving those girls behind and found that to give them a chance at life, it was the best he could do. Carl was not able to see a chance at a better future with him trying to survive the heartache he was reminded of daily each time he saw his daughters. He felt he had failed them by staying and failed them by leaving. He could not win in his eyes.

Here and now though, he was going to give it all he had. With May by his side, they changed how they saw life and created a legacy for their children and grandchildren to share for generations to come. That with loss comes defeat, but only for a moment. With determination comes victory, and another day to battle.

The girls had battled the elements of time, and although time had seemingly pushed them further away from the truth, they found a way back with the help of some important people. A simple conversation one night at a diner in Shreve had proven to be all they needed to find their father, but it was still up to them to find that will. They did.

May Bradway passed away in February of 1947. She was 72 years old. She left behind her husband, Carl, a son, two stepdaughters in Aletha and Mary Elizabeth, and five grandchildren.

The same year May passed, Aletha found love once again. This time she married a man named Paul Sprang. She would stay married to her husband, Paul, for the remainder of her life. They had just one child together, Mary Ellen, along with raising Charolet of course.

Aunt Hannah remained in Alliance for the rest of her days as well. She would depart from this life in September of 1953, and her second husband George Edward, died just one year later. She was the other end of the "bookend sisters" and was now back with her sister, Phoebe.

Aunt Cora lived in West Virginia until 1966, dying just a day after the anniversary of her nephews' drowning, having never remarried.

One night, Charolet went to her mother Aletha and asked her for something. She desperately wanted a pair of ice skates. She had seen other children using them so gracefully and thought it looked like a fun time. Aletha told her that she would never purchase a pair of ice skates for her children. She could not bring herself to, after what had happened on that deceptive, frozen Mahoning River that cold, miserable January 18th, in 1919.

The End

Epilogue

This story happened to a family that simply wanted to live. They worked incredibly hard and were good church going folks. Somehow, along the way, they went from living to surviving.

For Carl, meeting Phoebe was more than he could have hoped for. He fell deeply in love and suffered greatly for that. When she departed his side in 1917, he was lost and confused. Trying to get a handle on things was hard enough as it was, but after the tragic loss of his sons, he just could not find his way again. Giving his two young daughters to family was a decision he would not take lightly, but he had to find a way to survive. He knew in his heart he would be no good for his girls in the state of hopelessness he was in. That was just the sad reality.

Leaving those children behind as he had, was simply an act of altruistic love, not of selfishness. He loved them enough to give them a chance at a life he no longer could provide. While people may have questioned his decisions, including himself over those years away, he knew in the end that he made the correct call. His girls grew to be wonderful people and were strong enough through times most may not have been.

Through that sacrifice, Aletha and Mary Elizabeth formed a bond that took them both high and low. When they heard that a man over in Shreve had lost his three boys, they could have just ignored it, and no one would have thought anything of it. But they did not. They could not. It was something they had always wondered deep within their souls. Where had their father gone? What happened to him after he made that difficult decision to leave? Why had he left and never returned?

Carl loved having grandchildren around. It finally gave him a sense of pride that he had once lost. It showed him that even though life can be inevitably difficult and painful, beauty can arise from those ashes like a phoenix.

He also learned that true forgiveness could come, even if you do not expect it or feel deserving of it. In those nearly twenty years he had gone off, his girls grew to forgive him, before they ever stumbled onto him at the Whip. Their life was filled with twists and turns that allowed them to better understand the man they had known as their dad. With each ghastly heartache they faced, they could see why he needed to make such a terribly difficult decision. By the time they were face-to-face with him, it was more about rekindling than it was about revisiting the loss they felt. It was just time to move on together, and they were willing to do so as a final means of healing.

On January 31 of 1962, Carl went to be with his beloved Phoebe, his boys, and May. He was 79 years old. It was almost 43 years to the day he lost those three boys of his, and saw his world changed forever.

He spent the last twenty-five years of his life making up for the twenty years he lost in between. Had his daughters not heard of the man in Shreve, he may never have seen them again, and his life would have looked different at the end. But they had found him, and he allowed those final years to be a blessing to him, and no longer a curse. No longer concerned with why things had happened as they did, he only enjoyed what true life had left for him to enjoy. It was a lesson that took almost his entire life to understand, and an ability to let go of great loss while not forgetting, but he did eventually figure that out.

Aletha remained in the Shreve area until July of 1972, when her heart gave out and she passed away at the age of 63. Her life was full of enough reasons to give up, but she never allowed herself to. She was a strong-willed woman who accepted what she needed to, and never gave up hope.

Mary Elizabeth though, lived on. She had outlived her entire family. Not until early October in 1995, with the cool air of fall making its appearance, did she finally give in. She had always wanted to be under one roof again, and she finally had her wish granted. They were all together for the first time since the early part of the century.

Life is about chances and paths and what we do with those opportunities. We sometimes lose hope but find it again as we grow older and more accepting. It's not meant to be perfect, but what fun would that be? Carl and Phoebe set out to create a family they could raise and love and admire. They did just that. The length of that life was certainly not what they had expected, but the people in it made the best of it regardless.

It all started with a vicious storm from nowhere and ended with a calmness no one saw coming. For life took a man to the brink of ruin, and he somehow fought back enough to survive her savage wrath.

A man learned that what he thought was lost, had always been there. He just needed to see through the terror of the storm, stare her down, and open his eyes that much more to show her he was not going anywhere until he was good and ready.

This book is a work of historical fiction. Although many of the names are real, a few characters were added to fill in the blanks. I tried to stay as true as I could to what we knew, but since some was unknown, I had to create some scenarios to tie things together to better tell the story.

The idea of this story came by chance. An old newspaper clipping explaining a tragic loss, happened to come across my computer screen when I was searching my genealogy records one evening. I had discovered that a sorrowful time found its way to the small town of Alliance, Ohio, as well as to a line in my family tree, and thus was drawn to the how and why.

As I dug deeper, I realized there was an entire story that was long-lost and all but forgotten, and I wanted to bring that back to life. Not because of the tragic loss a humble family endured, but because of the sheer strength of the people involved to carve a path through that loss.

Many people quit fighting due to loss, and some never regain the ability to push on through, but not in this case. Not with this brave family. Somehow, forgiveness was so much stronger than hatred. A will to live and a need to find the truth were greater than anything thrown at these people, and they pressed on.

I had the chance to speak with Charolet, Aletha's daughter and Carl and Phoebe Bradway's granddaughter. She is a wonderful, kind person who knew more about the family than I could have hoped for. The stories she shared with me were both interesting and heartwarming. I felt like I understood the story so much more before I began to write. She was invaluable to this publication, and I am humbled to have had the chance to speak with her.

I was also able to get wonderful photos through the generosity of Charolet, and both Mary Ellen and Jara, who happens to be the Aletha's granddaughter. This gave me faces to the names and allowed me to create personalities that had been lost for many years. I hope I was able to do them all justice.

When I completed this book, I realized just how much that family went through, and often wondered if I could have been as strong as Carl Bradway was. What he must have felt with each devastating loss, each monumental setback that he was dealt, had to be nothing short of powerless. The same could be said for Aletha, who had lost more in her life than anyone I know.

We often have these incredible stories in our family line, but we seldom hear about them, or rarely care to. Sometimes people choose to forget the sadness they know, and often the younger generation doesn't ask, and so they are never told, and those marvelous, sometimes romantic, and sometimes tragic tales are lost with time. I encourage each of you to ask questions. Pass these stories down to the next generation and remind them that our past can teach us a great deal about where we are going and encourage us to never give up.

We all experience loss in our time here, but we all can learn to gain from that loss if we just take the time to understand that life is going to happen, with or without our approval. We should never stop living, and never stop searching for what it is we are after, because in the end, it may prove to be the best years we have. I believe Carl, Aletha and Mary would agree.

Top: Carl working as a delivery driver.
Middle: Carl and his second wife, May.
Bottom: Aletha and Mary smiling for the camera.

Carl when he was a young man.

Carl working on the ride, the Whip,
where the sisters would find him.

The only known picture of Phoebe.

Aletha and her 2nd husband, Charles Thomas
who passed away on June 9, 1938.

Aletha, Carl, and Mary, after they found
their father almost 20 years later.

Made in the USA
Las Vegas, NV
01 March 2022

44767006R00184